T0162451

Published by *feather*proo*f* Books

First edition
10 9 8 7 6 5 4 3 2 1

Library of Congress Control Number: 2015911757
ISBN: 978-0-9831863-7-3

Edited by Sammi Skolmoski
Cover image by Brian DeGraw
Design by Zach Dodson
Research and assembly assistance by Joseph Demes, Ellie Diaz, Cameron Moore, and Jonathon Humphrey
Proofread by Sam Axelrod

Written thanks to the support of The Millay Colony for The Arts and The Ragdale Foundation.

Set in Georgia

Printed in the United States of America

SUNSHINE ON AN OPEN TOMB

Tim Kinsella

Sunshine on an Open Tomb

Tim Kinsella

featherproof BOOKS

*Dedicated to Virginia,
Mark Lombardi, Richard Brautigan,
and DMC*

Our heart survives between
hammers, just as the tongue between
the teeth is still able to praise.
   Rilke, "The Ninth Duino Elegy"

Oh, I gotta get rid of my goddam Halliburton stock.
   L-BJ, overheard at 1:00 pm, 11/22/63

A NOTE FROM THE AUTHOR

Trusted Reader,

It seems meaningful to me given the current and ever-accelerating circumstances of *Life on Earth* that I make something clear: I wrote the first draft of this book immediately after the 2012 U.S. presidential election, hoping for it to be out in time for the 2016 election season. *Hahaha!*

When I missed that goal—the book at that time was more than 2.5 times its current length—I wasn't sure exactly how it would resonate in the shifting cultural context.

Turns out, still don't know.

But here it is.

Best Wishes—

Part 1

10/22/88

CHAPTER 1 I Did Not Want This Mission

Games! Games! Games! Games! *Games! Games! Games! Games!* Games!

Who even *knows* who taught you what, you know?

Arriving back at my condo, knuckle sprainy from that meek Barbarian's nose, I unwrapped a second Polish but never lifted it from its paper.

I pondered my reflection on the surface of ze Tube, other and vertiginous.

The distraction of *other people* does indeed prevent me from collapsing inwards.

So I grabbed a tape from my stack and clicked it on.

But it really is *impossible* to block out that the ball will roll between Buckner's legs, so I flipped to Le 24-Hour-News Channel.

The Personality lamented a salty-eyed orphan's looming blindness.

Footage showed the child burying a feather at the beach.

I considered masturbating, masturbating and fantasizing that I was masturbating in a hotel room.

But I hated doing it in front of Aaron, standing there silent as furniture, when I wasn't sure I'd be an alligator.

A bomb at the Iranian embassy in Beirut.

A car bomb kills seven and injures 11 near the Lebanon border.

A man strapped with explosives blows himself up in a Gotham subway station.

The room reeked of fabric softener and vinegar from a week-old side salad left untouched.

The paper on the coffee table had become translucent with Polish grease, and the girl dozed off sitting up on the far end of the couch.

On a hastily built tarmac stage, Junior waved that weird wave he'd developed ever since his stigmata.

They'd cut his hair, shaved his beard, and peeled him out

15

of those dingy tunics.

Test marketing proved that Junior triggered generalized despair in The Barbarians, so he never lingered near a mic longer than to blurt single words like *Freedom* or *Hope.*

Sprawled substantially on my sticky couch, Jell-o streaks across my jersey, I dug under a crumby cushion to find the remote.

And Le 24-Hour-News Channel cut from Junior waving on the tarmac to Junior lit hot in a studio sitting with The Personality.

Freshly spiffed up from his *State of Grace,* they let him talk.

The Personality's show was an austere circus.

He expounded ideologies so *extreme* they made *Political Realism* appear reasonable in comparison.

An old Family chum, only his unrestrained, *boundless* shamelessness qualified him for his position.

Of course, he was also blessed with pre-existing conditions for soapboxing and bloviation.

I found the remote, oily chip crumbs lodged between rubber buttons.

I couldn't turn away, but instinctively I muted ze Tube.

And well aware of how self-defeating my instincts can swing, I hit record.

Junior and The Personality stared into each other's smiley gazes, longingly.

I swear they kept winking at each other.

It was hard to believe that after the studio's hot lights browned down, they wouldn't slowly kiss.

And though I did fear death by gagging on puke, I dared up the volume to its lowest audible level.

And there sat Junior, happy and flattered for his *pen-*

etrating insights.

His cultivated drawl: "The Objective Biography is a very interesting read, very interesting. Of course, it's been a unique experience to grow up in our family, and I've never before seen, or heard, or read such a fair'nbalanced, informative account of our family's long history of service to The Homelan. It's not without its criticisms, but it's fair. Everything that I know has been recounted accurately, and it even filled in a few blank spots I've had. Some things make sense to me now in a way that they never have."

That moment *right before* someone goes bananas in which they *know* they're about to go bananas, like in Edgar Allan Poe movies, that was me.

Under my own repugnant reflection dim on the surface of ze Tube, Junior, my own *flesh and blood*, said in summary: "I endorse this book entirely as, finally, the *ultimate* biography of my family's long history of service to our great nation."

The Personality, in closing, asked Junior—the army reserves deserter, the *State of Grace* survivor, the high chandelier smasher—pleasant and small-talky: "And what's up with your youngest brother? Haven't heard much from him lately."

Junior smirked pleasantly, as if defecating.

And then, The Personality clarified: "Your brother I'm asking about is not The Future-Gov we all know, nor the famous businessman banker with The Kingdom that occasionally pops up in the news. I'm asking about your *youngest* brother."

"That's right."

"Who many of our viewers may not even realize is part of The Family."

"Yes."

"And how is he?"

"My youngest brother?" Junior jostled and cleared his throat.

"Yes, what's he up to these days?"

"Well actually, you know my youngest brother died."

"Yes, yes. Of course. *The Tragedy.*"

"Yes."

"But there is *another* brother who is now the youngest."

"Oh, he's good," Junior said, keeping in line with The Family's official comment re: me. "He's good. Happy and healthy."

"OK, well good then," The Personality said, pleased with himself for having asked the *tough question.*

"Well," The Personality followed as an afterthought, "we have to have our producers contact him. It'll be interesting to get his thoughts on the issues this *eleccion* season."

Le 24-Hour-News Channel had so much time to fill that suddenly even *I* became worth interviewing.

I did very much consider it finally time to bite down on my cyanide capsule.

CHAPTER 2 Bringing Barbarians to Box Seats

At first, the big variable that night was that my ChapStick had melted in the dryer, and I spun its spine up the middle of an empty plastic tube.

O'Malley and The Greek and me had The Other Greek Place to ourselves when six or seven dusty Barbarians in ill-fitting camouflage and patterned face paint moseyed in.

With big voices intended to be overheard, they spoke of escape to a silent seaside town, its tall walls bricked with irregular stones.

I gnawed mutely on my dry cut of steak and worked my focus with *purpose* to make out the shape of one particular Barbarian's jawline under his face paint.

He never said a word.

Intently, he watched the others.

His jagged face paint covered the shallow slope of a soft chin.

His worried eyes—*terrified*—lasered on what the other men said.

They all cut each other off and dared each other to one up each other's bad taste.

And this one that I watched closely, he *always* laughed first and loud and awk to demonstrate approval.

None of his friends noticed him, like they saw him only as their necessary audience, like a guy that asks everyone else what they're wearing before he ever leaves the house.

He began to squirm, and I got bold, fixed my stare and stopped glancing away for even a second.

I cut thru my tough steak.

He peeked at me quick and stood up straighter, laughed louder, and drew tighter to his friends.

That Mike leaned toward me from behind the bar and stared at me.

Digging a finger up deep into my cheek, I pulled out a wad of chewed gristle and dropped it on the plate.

I wadded up my napkin.

I got up, pulled on my coat, and announced that I'd be

retiring punctually.

O'Malley and The Greek protested.

"Don't you want to dance with Diana?"

"Eh, Diana, eh? We know how you *love* Diana."

My Diana.

O'Malley and The Greek wanted to dance.

And of course That Mike said, *But you guys only just got here* cuz there went his tips.

Accepting my seriousness, O'Malley and The Greek both ordered tall double shots, needing to reach a particular spiritual apex they'd assumed they'd have more time to creep toward.

Then, it just happened like it does when I'm explaining one of my ideas for a movie, the words *popped* out of my mouth before I knew I'd even had the idea.

I insisted I'd take *everyone* to The Game, my treat, box seats.

O'Malley cheered, and The Greek slapped my back.

I approached The Barbarians in their camouflage and face paint, looking only at the slopey-chinned quiet one who could only nod along, I addressed them, good sirs, *mayhaps* I request the honor of their esteemed company.

I said: "Duh, unga-bunga."

A couple of them hemmed and hawed, didn't think their wives would let them stay out that late.

The others mocked them, and it was all agreed: the big bunch of us—everyone that happened to be at The Other Greek Place that night—would *all* head over to The Game together, my treat, box seats.

I spun to move toward the door and one Barbarian nodded toward Aaron and asked, "Hey, what about Secret Agent Man over there? You inviting him?"

Behind the bar, wiping a glass, That Mike smirked.

Our reunion at the stadium gates was awk.

With their face paints smudged cleanish, darkening their seams, The Barbarians looked like kittens waiting to be eaten.

Especially the quiet one I'd been eyeing, he could've so *easily* been anyone else.

We all made Aaron—standing aside and silent of course—into an object we could all focus on as *outsider* to break the ice and solidify our blossoming bond.

Our crowded box echoed chatter and The Game boomed directly below us.

It took The Barbarians a minute to comprehend that *everything* was on me, they were all free to order whatever and *everything*.

They finally got it when the girls arrived.

Offered iced oysters, the girl on my lap explained she felt queasy, estimating she'd eaten $2,000 in oysters that week.

She ranked the men by spending to the girl on The Greek's lap, who nodded with sympathy between indiscriminate cheers thru halftime.

The girl on The Greek's lap was cute like cute meat.

Some machinist's daughter, undoubtedly a monster, cruel like only *beautiful* people know how to be, I wondered how much had been spent on her oysters that week.

I could never tell anyone's age until she started talking about her major.

A swarthy, chiseled waiter and the girl on my lap kept eyeing each other.

All the different adult smiles at night, there must be a brief window in each dimly sentient blob's life, maybe 26 thru 29, that one knows how to time all those smiles.

The girl on my lap's skin was glossy like a British hot dog.

I sat up to tilt her off and nodded to the girl on The Greek's lap.

She looked to The Greek.

He nodded to her.

She moved to my lap.

The Greek walked off to pee.

Clearly this one, with her hot teeth, told time according to her lipstick.

The largest pizza *in the world* might be an accomplishment to look at, but it's *useless* without the largest *mouth* in the world.

And however you cut it, the ratios will be a mess.

The girl excused herself to the ladies' room.

The Greek returned, making excuses for needing to pee so often to anyone who'd listen.

Then he began his dance alone in the middle of the room, forcing the crowd to navigate around him.

And quickly his dance got serious with pursed lips and furrowed brow.

The second half of The Game began.

O'Malley pulled a girl toward a closet, and when she resisted he promptly fell asleep with his head on a table next to a basket of onion rings and a cup of hot cheese.

The girl who'd been on my lap returned from around a corner, radiating that shared sting of perfect tits moving thru a room.

Pausing for The Greek to spin from her path, she rolled her eyes at his dance, glanced at me and sighed.

And I stood and shouted at the top of my voice, *Time to go.*

"Duh, unga-bunga!"

The room froze.

One Barbarian looked at me, stunned, with a shrimp tail hanging from his mouth.

With the chatter and romp all at once muted, that one Foreigner song surfaced from the background—*he wants to know what love is.*

And that dull-souled Barbarian, the slopey-chinned nodder-alonger who I'd earlier appraised at The Other Greek Place, broke the silence.

"But *we* can all stay, can't we?"

I sauntered over to him like James Coburn and stood face to face.

He held his breath.

My breath heated his cheek.

He cleared his throat and whimpered, "I mean, you wouldn't mind if we stayed, would you?"

The steel spike of my vision burrowing into his forehead, he wouldn't look at me.

No one moved.

Slowly, I raised my hand.

Above my waist, above his elbow, higher than my shoulder.

I inserted my index finger just beyond the cusp of his nostril and held it there.

He didn't breathe.

Lightly, I scraped at the inner walls of his nose with my fingernail, barely breaking apart the crust.

We locked into a stare, not unlike the swollen moment before a kiss.

Aaron came up quick and stood next to me.

"Sir."

With a sudden thrust I pushed a little further up there.

I puffed out my chest.

With my finger inserted into his nostril so tightly, it took very little effort to pull his head this way or that.

In the overlapping indexes of neon lights, Aaron by my side, my finger jammed in the quiet Barbarian's head, no one moved.

Until finally, O'Malley and The Greek cracked open into furious hissing laughter.

We stopped for Polishes on the way home.

CHAPTER 3 Diana Herself

Most commonly, unconsciously, people judge attractiveness according to averageness and youthfulness.

Asymmetry is *not* aesthetically appealing.

People might prefer *slight* asymmetry, but that's not what we're talking about.

People's unconscious assumptions about health and beauty propel evolution.

That person's estrogen is wonky.

That person's got a bad immune system.

Symmetry implies extraversion, openness, lower neuroticism, conscientiousness, agreeability, sociability, intelligence, liveliness, and trustworthiness.

People associate *deception* with twitching, and twitching tenses the face, causing asymmetry.

But I've always found Diana Herself to be nothing less than extraverted, open, not neurotic, conscientious, agreeable, sociable, intelligent, lively, and trustworthy.

If you split Diana Herself's face down the middle with a mirror, she'd undoubtedly look like two *very different* people.

Her eyes aren't only different sizes, but very different shapes set at different angles on her face.

Her nose bends so that mirroring one side of her face would give her a huge nose, and the other side, a tiny one.

And if you did do that mirror thing and she looked like two totally different unattractive people, that wouldn't mean I think she's unattractive.

That mirror thing is no relevant standard.

I *know* about physical asymmetry.

Every morning I needed a big breakfast to soak up the hangover aches.

I never wanted *yogurt and granola* or oatmeal or a fruit

cup.

And every morning, knowing I'd see Diana Herself motivated me to keep my nose hairs plucked and ear hair trimmed.

Someone would know if I hadn't changed my jersey.

I'd roll into The Diner alone by 10 a.m. each morning.

Most mornings, as a matter of disposition, I never much felt like talking, and Diana Herself knew it had nothing to do with her.

I'd sit with my paper and sip my burnt coffee that tasted like a dirty key had sunk to the bottom of the pot.

Diana Herself had a few years on me.

Her three kids, all pretty grown, still lived at home, except when the girl goes missing on a binge.

They'd pilfer her cigarettes and pinch an Andrew Jackson now and then, but what could she do, insist they cough up their painkillers and start paying rent?

Or *what*?

She was proud of her one son, The Future-Barber.

Twenty years behind that counter, she never imagined a day that she wouldn't stand there.

She didn't get maternity leave when her daughter had a kid.

Our routine established our trust.

She had a big honk of a laugh and would forget to breathe when she spoke, which made her voice sound like a barking goose.

And she was the woman I said Good Morning to each morning.

"Duh, unga-bunga."

And she'd ask how I felt before my day had even really begun.

Big cities privilege younger waitresses, pretty women that any man would want serving him.

But I'd been married and had already suffered my insecure *playboy* phase.

The ideal waitress for me was just the same one that I'd come to expect every morning.

25

She knew I preferred breakfasts with limited color palettes—white toast, potatoes, eggs, French toast, pancakes—so she never bothered to take my order, sparing me from having to touch any fingerprint-smudged menus.

When I did feel like talking, she'd listen as long as I needed her to, and she never disagreed.

Her movements always choreographed to the incessant theme of the cheery morning news show on ze Tube behind her.

Her differently shaped eyes moistened at stories of a third grade class buying a homeless man a heavy coat.

Refilling my coffee after every sip, Diana Herself'd spin her wrist, turning her hand over backwards.

Behind the counter, in a corner barely beyond the line cook's reach, above the stack of styrofoam cups and rows of small bottles of Tabasco sauce atop the soda machine, Diana Herself had taped up photos of her kids, each picture dated by a decade.

And next to these, a photocopy of a line drawing—the paper folded asymmetrically—hands folded in prayer, hung sloppy with Scotch tape.

With my paper open on the hard, plastic countertop made to look like marble, my eyes never moved from the news on ze Tube.

A young bank clerk set up her boss and made away with quite a sum, like *Psycho*.

Aaron sat with his back straight at the counter's bend, his eyes blank on ze Tube, his fingers running along the teeth of a fork.

The silverware there did feel as if it'd been chewed on.

The long counter was usually empty between us except for the small plastic cards: *Eggcelent Creations*.

Sometimes other men sat in pairs, often silent, like fathers and sons.

A painting of a bowl of fruit hung above a bowl of plastic fruit.

A monkey-sized statue of a bellhop stood at the door like Aaron.

The decorations blended into a singular density which doubled and doubled again in hung mirrors, same size and same wood as the windows.

This density was meant to mask or at least minimize the smears of grease along the tiles behind the hot grill and the bins of bussed dishes left at the far side of the counter, same color as the countertops, the breakfasts, the landscapes, the dirty water.

But the pride of The Diner, and Diana Herself's *principal* interest, was the wall of framed autographed photos of local athletes, Tube personalities, and stand-up comedians.

And together, me and Diana Herself were good like good bread is good.

We had a simple understanding not unlike a calendar and the weather.

With so much accrued exhaustion in common, we implicitly promised each other to each keep our energy up as a favor to the other.

And she succeeded at this far more often and more *easily* than I did.

I played a long, slow game of *Take Away the Things She Thinks She Likes About Me One at a Time and See How Long She Still Likes Me* but I never settled on a method of keeping score.

We never asked anything of each other, never wanted anything from each other.

I was *all hers* so long as she never asked.

And she was *all mine* so long as we never acknowledged all the ways she wasn't.

Like some old husband or a grown son, a dog or a job, neither of us ever needed much attention, but our keen ability to account for one another's imprecisions remained impeccable.

My Diana disappeared, vaporized instantaneously, if I ever dared look at her straight on.

But Diana Herself and me mirrored each other, resolving

all the simple ways we each differed from our *very unlike* fathers.

And occasionally, depending on the angle, she was the second most beautiful woman I'd ever seen.

CHAPTER 4 Re: Grandfather

The basics of easy internationalism, the air conditioners balanced in The Barbarians' bedroom windows high over the sidewalks, and the aerosol cans that shoot soft cheese *all* depend on oil.

And Grandfather saw this.

He and his *brothers under the skin* knew what Marx knew: The *totality* of a culture's potential expressions and manifestations—easy diet, easy clothes, easy entertainment, easy "government," easy intimacy, and easy easiness—are all rooted in that intersection of material and labor.

A nostalgic cut of jeans; the springs that puncture sweatshop bunk-beds, doors locked from the outside; the dramatic arc of cop buddy films; the rushed hugs at last call: all the outcome of oil and its easy distribution.

Of course, Engels had a trust fund and supported Marx while he developed his ideas about labor and its relations to capital.

And poor Marx died depressed after the death of his wife and the suicides of both of his daughters.

Grandfather was SkullnBones Class of '16.

And he stole Geronimo's skull.

Yes, the fucking skull of fucking Geronimo became a piece of his bric-a-brac.

As an artillery officer in WWI, he had to admit to a lie: He hadn't *really* saved the lives of The Homelan, The UK, and France's top military commanders by diving to ricochet an incoming shell with his bolo knife.

His embarrassed parents had already made plans for their local paper to run the story on its front page.

And *his dad*, as a member of The Homelan's War Industries Board in WWI, made *$200,000,000* manufacturing munitions for Remingtons.

$200,000,000 in '18 is the equivalent of infinity dollars today.

So same as a chimney sweep is fated to oily wrists, and a gardener predetermined to his soily chin, Grandfather got appointed head of DrSSr.

And instead of competing for oil, DrSSr controlled the technology that makes drilling feasible.

Back in '12 Grandfather's bosses The Harrymans partnered with The Ruckafellas to invest $11,000,000 into eugenics research.

That same year Churchill presided over the first international conference on eugenics in London.

In '32 the conference met in NY.

And The Family's train line organized the transit of all the prominent Germans from Berlin to lead the conference.

Given the spontaneous and audacious *hysteria* of investment opportunities at the end of WWI, it's little surprise that Grandfather helped finance Hitler's rise.

Hitler had lost the popular *eleccion* in '32 to an aging war hero.

But almost 40 German business leaders signed a petition to overturn the results.

And in a meeting with Homelan and UK banks—one Dullis Bro was there, I'd guess the one that famously seduced The Queen of Greece—all agreed that Hitler be named chancellor.

A week later The Reichstag burned, and emergency laws *thwacked* into effect.

And a year later The German Prez died, and Hitler merged the offices of Chancellor and Prez.

In '33, Grandfather's bank conspired with agents of Chase Bank, GM, Goodyear, The Ruckafellas, and The PuDonts to attempt to overthrow the "Government" here in The Homelan, hoping to install a fascist dictatorship.

They tried to recruit Marine Corps Major General Smedley to lead the coup, but they failed to consider that Smedley had ardently stumped for FDR in '32, so the plan never got past its initial planning stages.

In '34 Smedley told Congress all about it, and The House McCormack-Dickstein Committee officially acknowledged the existence of the conspiracy.

But no charges were pressed.

And the next year Smedley published his short book, *War Is a Racket.*

Hovver seized Grandfather's bank as a NAZI asset in '42 under the Trading With The Enemy Act cuz Grandfather's bank represented the Homelan business interests of a German industrialist named Fritz.

The NAZIs were still a radical fringe party when Fritz inherited his dad's steel and coal empire in '26.

Fritz bailed out the struggling party on several occasions, was eventually nicknamed "Hitler's Angel" and even titled his autobiography, *I Paid Hitler.*

Grandfather also served on the board of at least one of the companies in Fritz's multinational network of fronts.

This was all quite common and none of it was *illegal-*illegal.

Coca-Cola invented Fanta to continue to sell cola to the German market.

And the NAZIs depended on IBM's punch cards to organize the mountains of census data the holocaust required.

But it didn't *look too good.*

And even more *delicate* for public appearances was The Family's connection to a mining company on the German-Polish border that depended on slave labor from the camps.

We couldn't let The Reds get them first, so The Homelan made a deal with Hitler's intel chief in '45: More than 100 war criminals would be protected and no charges pressed, so long as they all worked for The CIA.

And by '46, The Joint Chiefs gave orders to hire 5,000 NAZI scientists.

NAZI rocket scientists, NAZI Public Relations specialists, NAZI doctors and graphic designers and assassins: with The Catholic Church's help, we found jobs for all of them.

Remember Mengele's nickname among the children at Auschwitz: The Good Uncle.

And in '47 The National Security Act became law.

'47, *what a year!*

The crash at Roswell; that postmodern occultist Crowley died; Churchill coined the phrase "Iron Curtain" and The Cold War began; The House UnHomelan Activities Committee got aggressive, in effect admitting that *culture* is weaponized; and The Dead Sea Scrolls were discovered in West Bank caves, shaking up the history of The Old Testament.

The National Security Act changed the name of The War Dept. to The Defense Dept. and with these ex-NAZIs as its cornerstones, The CIA was founded.

How Grandfather relished the newspaper as a boy!

Tracking the misadventures of Wyatt Earp and Pat Garrett.

He chuckled at Mark Twain's political opinions and marveled at the fantastical inventions of Jules Verne.

Controversy over Andrew Carnegie's philanthropic philosophies crammed the columns.

And Sir Joseph Dalton Hooker kept busy defending his best friend Darwin's ideas against ridicule and slander.

Grandfather was a man born into the *wonders* of The Mechanical World.

Anything could be built.

Anything was possible.

And so it came to be so.

He'd saunter into Nxn's Oval and kick his feet up on the desk and grin and grin and grin recalling one of the last traveling versions of Buffalo Bill and Annie Oakley that he'd seen when he was 7 years old.

Pops and his siblings never did shake their terror and amazement of hard-drinking Grandfather, 6'4", looming over them with vigilant judgment.

Grandma denied his binges, insisted that the children *were not* seeing what they *knew* they were seeing.

And this lesson in denying *Reality* went a long way in shaping Family policy.

The secret of Grandfather's alcoholism made Pops pathologically phobic of personal examination.

And this profound fear of analysis, coupled with his inherited reverence for public image, honed some fundamental spy skills.

Secrecy itself became a fetish.

That constant pressure, the sustained grip like a vice, such tightly coiled *control* takes endurance.

Such repression couldn't possibly lead to any other outcome than the *logorrhea* Pops suffered when his man undressed and sponged him.

And Pops's one *real* power—that blank, prolonged eye contact—that's *simple* after a childhood too afraid to look at your own father above his neck.

CHAPTER 5 *My Diana*

As the years accrue, increasingly I think about *nothing at all* except fucking with The Act of Love, while at the same time, I never feel like *actually* fucking with it.

Still, most nights crescendo the same: grinding my King Charles up against the flimsy closet door at The Other Greek Place.

I'd grunt and throw my head back and howl, biting at O'Malley over my shoulder while he spanked me.

It was all a wild performative ritual for my posse's sake to wedge the slimmest gap between my flushed and fleshy *self* and my self-awareness of my ridiculous irrepressible impulses.

The Greek hooted gruff kudos from a few steps back.

Aaron guarded the door.

That spinning was always the last I remember before Aaron and That Mike would drag me to the backseat of my minivan.

And then the window cold against my forehead, the streets all tilting down on me, rushing at me.

Like some clueless, stuttering, cartoon pig *Casanova* flirting with a spiked hedgehog, I *wrecked* myself into completion for that woman.

That was her simple command.

Like how fire cultivates a forest's floor, she just *appeared*. *My Diana*.

One night, all at once, radiating her weaponized beauty in profile, she was hanging on that flimsy closet door, a sweaty beer bottle dangling from her grip, her slick skin stiff and thick as if she'd gotten a chill in her patriotic bikini, the moon low and huge behind her.

When I was 5 years old, I saw her face in my mind.
When I was 13, I was so confused that I couldn't find her.
I was sick on my wedding day cuz it wasn't her.

Trusted Reader, imagine a public touch between two men, strangers, nothing big, just a glancing touch on a bare forearm.

It's *impossible* to translate even something so simple as *that* into language, to filter the charged *ping* of bone thru the troubled scrim of *wordage*.

But, *I let someone in.*

You ever been touched inappropriately, Scrupulous Reader, an unwanted touch?

It tears you in two.

You partition.

You set that touch moment aside and get on with the moil of your cycling days. It's always *Ash Wednesday* or *Tax Day* or something.

But you never can *integrate* that touch moment into your smiley ho-hum, and *all* your impulses and habits bloom in response to it—everything.

That touch *defines* you.

Let The Barbarians drool.

My Diana was as *real* as anything's *ever* been real to me.

CHAPTER 6 I Got Tapped, But Bolted

As a boy, I'd always found a way to linger at Pops's door.

And every night as his man sponged him, Pops erupted, ranting, disgorging and *heaving* his nefarious admissions—a *spastic* logorrhea.

Proud of his hidden work, he needed *someone* to commend his cleverness.

But every few months, Pops'd get paranoid and slit his man's throat.

And again, he'd muzzle his pride best he could after hiring a new man, but inevitably, when the relentless endurance of constant *appearance* came to be too much, undressing, in transition to nakedness, Pops gushed.

And each new man needed context, so Pops'd retell the old stories.

And my ear to his door, over and over, I'd hear these same stories repeated.

Everyone always forgets, I do also have one good ear.

I completed my long string of C's 10 years ago, Yale Class of '77.

The frat mixers were awfully formal for parties thrown in thick-walled old houses with couches on the porch.

Dozens of people *splendiferous* with restaurant recommendations packed in elbow to elbow, shoulder to shoulder, wobbling cups of punch, and plates of carefully prepared knuckle-sized bites.

The chatter, reflecting back on itself, would aggregate into a dense shriek.

I'd like to buy the world a Coke.

Have a Pepsi Day.

Harrowing social times for me, my cool and self-conscious years, obsessed with underground rock legend Cy Franklin.

The squares all pumped their fists in crowded stadiums, seduced by lasers and smoke, battlefield metaphors to suppress any potential temptations toward inward reflection.

But I *fixated* on Cy Franklin's primal amateurism.

His humble rebellion forced me to confront *head on* what a ridiculous, clumsy, ugly, pathetic, contemptible, and vain wretch I was, attempting to cultivate some contrived *persona* thru superficial stylistic gestures, pitying myself and my mushy ear and the steel spike in the center of my vision and the impossibility of ever being *understood* by The Family, like an iguana in the razor grip of an alligator's jaw.

If I wasn't anxious, I was anxious that I was *about to be* anxious, confounding cause and effect.

The frat mixers would swarm me into their collective unconsciouses.

Fly the friendly skies.

Ajax has the power.

Thru waves of pressing flesh, faces emerged, warped large and leaning in close, chewing and laughing, open-mouthed.

Bet you can't eat just one.

Panasonic: just slightly ahead of our time.

Imagine how the buzz of a swarm sounds to each individual insect wrapped up in the squash of it, all their little eardrums?

That's radar, or its opposite?

He's Family, him—over there.

He's useless. What a waste.

The Family taught us to remember *one thing* about each dimly sentient blob we meet and ask about that one thing every time we see them.

I'd struggle to lift my hand above my waist.

You mean he gets all that money and he never has to do anything?

Oh, how nice to meet you. Any relation to The Hitlers of Boston?

I'd bite at the air, desperate to hoist myself above the throbbing crowd to breathe.

Let your fingers do the walking.

37

Still, senior year, SkullnBones tapped me.

That Tomb was *grimy* as Paris, and musty with mold and incense.

At the initiation, my sneezing fits slashed the drama of the flickering candlelight, my throat tickled until it clenched.

And that's the thing about anxiety: the symptoms confound cause and effect.

The brothers under the skin did *not* appreciate my ruptures of giggling.

With their cold-blooded reptilian erections, those Bonesmen *really do deserve* their exceptional dominion over the expanse of this mysterious and poisoned watery orb.

Here's the SkullnBones initiation ritual: The brothers under the skin surround you, all in their hooded robes, and one guy dressed up like Don Quixote even, and you're lying in this coffin, and you have to wax your alligator while recounting your entire sexual history blow-by-blow as they all watch and listen attentively.

So there I yanked my gelatinous shaft in that coffin, quaggy as King Charles II of Spain.

I told them I wore sweatpants first time I blew my Family seed into a worldly girl's mouth before I'd even discovered the explosion for myself.

"Duh, unga-bunga."

I told them how French kissing on a park bench one afternoon, I massaged some young deb's plentiful bosom while her friend sat next to her, clacking on a wad of gum.

I sprained my wrist when I jut a hand down the front of her tight jeans.

"Duh, unga-bunga."

I told them that my first time thrusting into someone, I was shocked that a *boy* looked back at me when I glimpsed myself in a mirrored closet door.

"Duh, unga-bunga."

I pumped and dandled myself in that coffin, stifling the

tickle in my nostrils, scraping away at my memories, limp
like King Charles II, weighted down with expectation and
tradition.

My *first love* was a townie near Hyacinthignatzi, that
magical land where even the garbage supposedly smelled
delicious.

Summers we'd see each other.

Her older sister had her own apartment and let us hop
into her bed.

My First Love's dexterous generosity in humiliating herself was like erotic charity.

And I was like a horse on a trampoline.

Sitting up Indian style with this skinny bucktoothed poet,
her investing every bit of her tiny tongue, I shocked us both
by shooting up and over my shoulder.

But I froze when it came time to tell the brothers under
the skin this story.

How I must've looked bolting from that tomb, sprinting,
the robe rippling in the wind behind me, my sandals slap-
ping against the pavement.

Panicky that some agent would pounce from a bush and
tackle me, I stuck to the middle of the street.

That final block before arriving home to my marble sty,
realizing that no one had followed me and not wanting to
create a scene, I slowed and lowered my hood.

I waved to an old couple on their porch watering their
lawn.

And not really looking, I had to leap out of the way of a
screeching car turning a corner quick right at me.

CHAPTER 7 Re: The Homelan

The Homelan was originally known as *The New Atlantis*. *The New Atlantis* had been discussed in Alexandria, Delhi, Mecca, and Tibet, long before any European *statesmen* knew of its existence.

Ferdinand and Isabella's Inquisition was a "governmental" agency, not a "religious" one.

After driving The Muslims out of Spain after an 800-year reign, Ferdinand and Isabella wanted a shortcut to Jerusalem to wage more Crusades when their man Columbus smacked into The Homelan.

Thomas Morton and his Maypole—*revelry* is resistance—was like The '60s in The 1620s.

The Puritans called it a cult: consorting with native women, arming native men, celebrating Venus and her lusty children Cupid and Hymen, singing sloppy drinking songs in their tilted antler hats.

Morton was The Homelan's first patron saint of counterculture, like Lenny Bruce or Timothy Leary.

He was starved, banished, held in stocks, jailed, and generally harassed for his utopian leanings.

Upon Capital City's founding, the plots of land were numbered.

And they plopped Le Capital down on plot 666.

Fifty-five out of 56 signers of The Homelan's founding document identified as Freemasons, inspired greatly by the mysterious Rosicrucian philosopher Count Saint Germain.

Count Saint Germain was a strict vegetarian.

And spoke *every* European language.

And he claimed to be Prince Ragoczy of Transylvania, educated by the Medicis and to've had discovered the secret to immortality, The Elixir of Life.

He claimed to've been alive for *centuries:* present when Jesus turned water into wine, just *acquaintances* with Cleopatra, but tight with King Richard The Lionheart.

And he set his friend up to become Catherine The Great, overthrowing Peter of Russia.

He mentored The Rothschilds, deepening their budding interests in the ancient *Mysteries*.

Their fortunes eventually funded The Ruckafellas' oil empire, which went on to create both The CIA and The Kingdom's Royal Family.

The inner core of Freemasonry teaches a hybridizing of science and metaphysics—*as above, so below*—meaning that from the smallest *pinging* bone to the vastest Texasy expansions of the matrix, repetitive geometric law prevails.

Interlocking activities and modes of thinking unify magick, chemistry, philosophy, and hermeticism into sacred geometry, cosmology, and genetic engineering.

Magick and *science* were interchangeable terms until the 18th century.

The founding fathers Wshington, Franglin, and Jufferson were all occultists.

Peyton Randolph, first Prez of The Homelan, Jufferson's cousin, not only foretold The Homelan's fate by dying young of obesity, he was also a practicing occultist.

Open occultists of the 19th century included the chief justice of MA, The Prez of The MA Medical Society, The Prez of Yale, and The Prez of CT Medical Society.

NASA, under the guise of total devotion to *astronomy*, still devotes a lot of attention to *astrology*.

And *Diana* means moon.

CHAPTER 8 Best Chums

I do my best to invest both breath and brain to my greatest capacity each day.

But how do people possibly *do it*—cope with such proximity—the breath right there next to the heart, the eye and ear right alongside the mind?

If *best friends* are conspirators that agree to ignore the fundamental *embarrassment* of the innumerable humbling tasks at the root of identity, then O'Malley and The Greek were my *best friends:* guys you meet and know immediately they're OK, saggy faces with sad eyes, constantly chuckling in small coughs.

O'Malley had an ape's lumbering breath and purposeful blink.

The Greek too, sometimes you catch him suffering to concentrate, quiet, his eyes scanning like a tired monkey.

And *everyone else* were all *policemen* far as we could tell, few *deputized*, but all patrolling the boundaries of each other's acceptable behavior.

O'Malley and The Greek and me felt like fingers, how fingers, each independent, come together to collaborate.

And we were *always* playing games.

We played games together that same way that people help hold an alligator's mouth open to feed it a pill.

I put O'Malley and The Greek up in a nice condo in my building: a common brick building with bushes at its bottom same rusty brown as the brick.

The small concrete balconies all have rusty furniture with cushions that remain dark and wet too long after rain.

A flag hanging from one balcony pledges the whole building's allegiance.

The big tree at the front door, same four stories as the building, is rumored to be planted on the ashes of the groundkeeper's last lover.

And I include O'Malley and The Greek's groceries along

43

with my own.

It simplified things *for me* to get them a car, a cheap thing, used.

And what fun would it be *for me* if they didn't have cable?

I sign their tabs and though, personally, I find it liberating to not have Help, I can't ask my friends to forego.

The groundskeepers never can keep up with the corpses, so O'Malley and The Greek shovel up any that fall into my parking spot.

Pops's best friend growing up was the son of Family friends, The DMs.

The DMs made their fortune on the salty southwest coast of The Caspian Sea, once home to half the world's known oil.

And by the dawn of The 20th Century they'd secured their position smack dab in the bull's eye of global oil.

But when The Red Revolution happened, the oligarchs over there all had their assets seized, so many of them moved here to The Homelan and befriended our own aristocracy, who were all just *smitten* by all the exotic titles.

And these exiled aristocrats made *tremendous* intel operatives: Business provided a simple cover, and the chips on their shoulders made for the ultimate motive.

Pops's best friend's uncle, GDM, came over here in '38, much later than most of these oligarch expats.

He had to first complete his doctoral dissertation on the economic influence of The Homelan in Latin America.

GDM got a job at a home-furnishing company that secretly specialized in blocking Axis Powers access to oil.

And by the mid-'s40s he worked for William F Bukkles's family in Panama.

You know Bukkles: SkullnBones, *National Review*, self-professed CIA.

Thru The '50s GDM worked at CVOVT.

CVOVT's mission was to guarantee continuity, management, and stability of policy in 24 South American oil companies.

It obtained exclusive exploration rights and leased nearly *half* the land in Cuba, millions of acres.

And of course, working with Castro meant dealing with his intermediaries in The Homelan: The Mob.

GDM settled in Dallas, home to his country's large expat population, and he quickly became active in the community.

He joined The TX Crusade for Freedom, which also included the mayor, whose brother was the Deputy Director of The CIA under whichever Dullis Bro was director at that time.

DH Brrrd, owner of The TX School Book Depository, was also a member.

And GDM also served on the board of The Council on World Affairs, along with that most-renowned filmmaker and 32nd-degree Freemason Z'puda.

Z'puda worked with GDM's wife in the garment industry.

Grandfather cofounded another group, The National Strategy Information Center.

And all these groups had one thing in common: they all *hated* King Arthur.

Wall Street hated him for his tax laws that favored The Barbarians; the steel companies hated him after he pulled defense department contracts and ordered his brother to investigate price fixing.

But TX hated him most of all.

The Geneva Accords permitted The Homelan to place 685 military advisers in southern Vietnam.

Eisenhower covertly sent several thousand.

And King Arthur upped this to *16,000,* some of them

45

even participating in combat operations.

But by '63 King Arthur's trepidation became the biggest obstacle to The Homelan's full involvement.

And his intention to withdraw meant *a lot* of money lost for these TX men.

GDM criss-crossed the globe sniffing out business leads in natural resources.

And *everywhere* he went, CIA covert operations happened at the same time.

He married his first wife in '42 when she was only 18, and though they had one daughter, the marriage ended in eight months, with just enough time for him to kick her in the abdomen and hit her on the head with a hammer.

He claimed she was jealous of his dog.

In '48 he married a woman named Fifi, but again the marriage lasted less than a year, ending when she attacked him with a knife.

He hit her so hard, Fifi needed facial reconstruction surgery.

His third marriage, to a woman named Didi, lasted five years, but he did try to run her over once.

They had two children, both of whom died of cystic fibrosis.

In '59 he married his last wife.

They didn't divorce until '73.

GDM's brother—Pops's best friend's dad—worked at *Time* magazine.

And that guy's son—GDM's nephew—was Pops's roommate at prep school.

And then Pops and GDM's nephew served as pilots in The Navy together.

Pops was in his wedding.

And though Pops endlessly gasconaded about his bounteous acquaintances, many of whom he's never actually been close to, he never uttered a peep about this friendship with GDM's nephew.

In '67 GDM's nephew died of an apparent heart attack at only 43 years old.

Pops was a pallbearer.

CHAPTER 9 The Grocery Store Snub

Between The Diner and The Club that afternoon I'd stopped at the grocery store to replenish my Jell-o.

Though I keep very little other food at home, I often browsed to confirm that nothing else looked good.

The Barbarians' pride for their local cream made me embarrassed for them.

And their fish tasted like an oil spill.

It rained as I headed over there in my minivan.

The bare trees, the fences, and the telephone poles all the same color as my breakfast, between pale brown and gray.

Each discrete object faded to a matching hue, obscuring the distinctions between branch, wire, and twine.

The landscape existed as if only to demonstrate the small gestures of fencing that adjacent property requires.

A pigeon-toed young father pushed a stroller uphill.

Someone had invested great energy into covering the entirety of a boxy car in spray-painted flames, each flame's edge fanning and fading perfectly.

The Barbarians adapt to the violent squash on crowded buses.

You never *don't* feel like a stranger walking those streets, stepping over corpses, constantly anticipating a boy will rush from any doorway to walk alongside you, imitating your walk to amuse his friends.

Did you know, Noble Reader, the posh section of Auschwitz was nicknamed *Canada*?

In the grocery store I pawed gummy tomatoes.

I shook a can of nuts and stroked bendy celery.

Some young *Barbarian-ette* bargain-hunting with a baby thrown over her shoulder made for an awk flirt indeed, Maiden.

She thought I'd buy her groceries?

And that aloof look obese people cultivate to return every innocent glance, I was sick of participating.

Hands on hips, pondering all kinds of colors excluded from my breakfast and the landscape, I imagined how sticky ketchup feels on the hair at your wrists, and how sticky maple syrup feels there too, and ranch dressing even after wiping it clean.

Then *whom* should *happen* to turn the corner at the end of the aisle but That Mike.

I didn't recognize him without the apron tied around his waist.

He held a little girl's hand, and they shuffled toward me, him hunched low to hear her murmur.

It *pleased me so* to saunter over.

He glanced up, and I thought he didn't see me.

She was a *beautiful,* blonde little princess gripping a plastic toy horse in one hand, looked *nothing* like That Mike, who looked and talked just like Bruno Kirby, the talkative limo driver in *Spinal Tap* who was also in *Good Morning, Vietnam* last year.

He stood up as I arrived next to them.

All smiles, struggling to bend low, my voice popped up an octave to address the little girl: "Duh, unga-bunga?"

That Mike straightened his back, and, looking down at me bending low, he sighed, "How you doing?"

I nodded and smiled. "Duh, unga-bunga."

Then I turned my attention back to her, "Duh, unga-bunga?"

"She's a pony," she said.

That Mike pulled her by the hand. "Come on, sweetheart. Let's go."

And he walked off, leaving me bent down in the middle of the aisle.

Taken aback, I chuckled and stood up straight to watch him walk off.

"Duh, unga-bunga," I called out sarcastic, truly surprised to see that he exists before four o'clock.

He glanced back. "Yeh, well, I'll see you later at The Other

Greek Place, OK? See you later."

Moving quick, he pivoted at the end of the aisle and nod-ded to Aaron.

CHAPTER 10 Re: Pizza and Cartoons

The simple trust between Barbarians softened me.

You absorb how they tolerate domineering bullies and come to sympathize with the long silences of hostages tied side-by-side.

There are always shots fired at the prom, and still *every time*, everyone laments the *shock*.

Their noses pushed to glass, teary-eyed for sweets or footwear.

You learn to always stand prepared to hand over your watch to a petty official.

Meaninglessness, of course, begets meaninglessness.

Obviously it's funky and puzzling to ponder all the corpses.

Bodies break so easy, dismantling into so many small tearing parts, it's weird we don't all get killed every day.

But it's equally funky and puzzling to ponder that we might live another day at all: with opposable thumbs to pinch, ears to buzz and muffle, eyes to keep closed, knees to lift tall over all the corpses rotting in the rain.

The Barbarian's life is lousy crowded with pizza and cartoons.

All that pizza and cartoons may block out their books and dreams, but at least they don't have to look at all the corpses.

Corpses piled tall along the train tracks that cut across the small downtowns; corpses melting into every curb, their stench on the breeze while you unwrap a sandwich.

I hate how a corpse's weight falls when it's propped up.

Its muscles locked in place, its final facial expression fixed.

And whatever that expression, it's always coupled with confusion: content and confused, terrified and confused, surprised and confused.

Makes you realize how quickly the flip from dimly sentient blob to corpse really happens.

An eyeball bulging four times its normal size cracks the edges of the socket that's always housed it; muscles slackened, the pupils float into relaxed asymmetry.

Face meat gets wormy.

That animating meat-force that'd been held within has spilled out all over its own lap.

Lips recede to reveal teeth, and skin hardens.

Beggar, respectable Barbarian, Good Man: it doesn't matter.

All food to all the birds of the sky and beasts of the earth, and there will be no one to frighten them away.

Having had no say in its final posture, folded in ways that no dimly sentient blob could ever bend, gravel smashed into its skin, it felt rude to even glance at a corpse.

I know it's shocking, Loyal Reader, but it's true: I never even saw a real corpse before moving out among The Barbarians.

I was *30 years old!*

I didn't know about the singular and ultimate weight with which each one sprawls, face down, clinging to the pavement in its own unique way.

I didn't know about the hard edges cut into where, previously, there'd always been skin continuity.

And how pieces shred.

Or the dumb meat of any single face stopped.

No *photograph* holds a *single element* motionless like that while the background continues to bustle about its business.

I didn't know about how sunburn cooks blood into skin.

How little toes, after a lifetime ticklish and tender, get all at once stripped of reflexes, exposed to nibbling critters.

How *neatly* parts detach and get set aside: heads, hands.

Or depending on the weapon used, how *mealy* dermis

can grind.

And other times, you could never *guess* how that dimly sentient blob became a corpse: business casual, with his button-down baby blue still tucked into pleated khakis, no evident sign of distress, leaned against a tree, eyes wide open and rolled back to show only the whites like eggs, mouth agape, tongue between teeth: he died making a silly face at a passing toddler?

I didn't know about purple blood pooling in an ear, how it quiets you for good.

A hacked up, sturdy torso, as independent as a holiday ham, its skin peeled back at the joints to reveal fat and bone: that's humiliating, but no more humiliating than the humble man who died intact losing the kind smile that had always squared his waistline.Both get hoisted the same into the small dump truck.

The lucky ones: it's a whole life's blessing to die face down.

To be charred, ankles and wrists tied, and left a stump on the curb; to be stripped and tied behind a motorcycle to be skinned alive against the rush of pavement; to be hit with pipes and feel each blow shatter bone and watch the witnesses stand around smiling; to be buried alive face down to suffocate, your legs kicking aboveground; to've gone thru medical school and all the hours; to've practiced and refined your eloquent sense of civics; to've been so pretty that everyone yielded to you; to've never even imagined that you could be stopped, in tune with the ancient forces propelling you, but to then be smeared hard against pavement, the path of your last dragging apparent to anyone that passes.

All these are natural causes.

All these are natural effects.

And I'd never seen a corpse before cuz I'd even closed the door and walked away from My Little Brother.

CHAPTER 11 Re: Oil

Ruckafella's Standard Oil brought The Homelan into codependence with The Kingdom after WWII, and that ultimately enabled The Family's *lock* on Power.

But as early as May '11, The Supreme Court said: "Seven men and a corporate machine have conspired against their fellow citizens. For the safety of the Republic we now decree that this dangerous conspiracy must be ended by November 15th."

This dissolution created 33 new companies, greatly *increasing* The Ruckafellas' wealth.

Thirty-three.

As part of The Revenue Act of '13, The Oil Depletion Allowance slashed taxes on *any* income derived from oil production by 5%.

And oil fortunes ballooned.

Regardless of actual costs, automatic deductions were given to compensate for waning assets in the ground.

And by '26 this deduction had risen to 27.5%.

And *The New Republic* reported that Capital City was "wading shoulder deep in oil. In the hotels, on the streets, at the dinner tables, the sole subject of discussion is oil. Congress has abandoned all other business."

As far back as '22 the mayor of NY, John F. Hylan, felt compelled to say: "The real menace of our republic is the invisible government which like a giant octopus sprawls its slimy length over our city, state and nation . . . At the head of this octopus are the Ruckafella-Standard Oil interests and a small group of powerful banking houses generally referred to as the international bankers [who] virtually run the Homelan government for their own selfish purposes."

And by the early '60s scrappy TX had essentially defected from The Homelan.

Far-flung oil empires had long depended on corporate covert operations.

But East Coast Upper Crust privilege + oil fortunes + intel = an *unprecedented* sense of entitlement to other countries' resources.

And by '64 *The NYT* claimed that Dallas had formed an "invisible government . . . [that ran] Dallas without an electoral mandate."

An example of this invisible "Government" in TX is GaDoyla, founder of TX Instruments.

Tight with European oil men and Arab leaders, his career spanned eight presidential administrations.

Chummy with most of these Prezs, *all* of them answered to him.

His son-in-law worked with GDM on The Council of World Affairs.

GaDoyla's son-in-law once sat at Iran's Mossadegh's bedside for *80 hours* working to negotiate ownership of The Anglo-Iranian Oil Company.

The talks turned out unsuccessful.

And two years later a CIA coup overthrew Mossadegh.

This invisible "Government" did *not* like King Arthur *at all*.

His greatest offense, along with his reticence toward Vietnam: his stance against The Oil Depletion Allowance.

CHAPTER 12 My Dawning Sex Life Protected by Thugs

I find it hypocritical, and decisively not *auto-*, if your Man helps tighten your noose when you fix your *alligator*.

My Help and my security detail dwindled until only Aaron remained.

I was a cushy assignment, and no one dared cut any budget that'd strip Aaron of this light retirement.

So I get financed to guarantee his job security, thanks to one line in a dense packet of single-spaced five-point font in the budget of some subcommittee that no one's secretary's assistant has ever glanced at before stamping.

Yes, Stately Reader, The Family has come to possess security so abundant that this security detail itself—with *resplendent* circular logic—supports the bountiful lifestyle of The Family's most inutile offspring, *moi.*

Suited men in dark glasses with ear pieces just always loitered at the perimeter of any playground we brothers toppled around.

I was eight the first time I ever spoke to Secret Service and accepted that I had always known that they did linger for our sake.

This Big Guy, This Thug, stood in position at the gate of the playground.

What depths of insecurity and self-loathing could prompt such a desperate compulsion to dedicate yourself to so *total* a transformation, to warp your own body so that its every detail achieves its most intimidating potential, all the labor oddly on display?

The glum monster had veins up his neck thick as fingers.

And when I forgot my lunch one day, I approached him.

He put a finger to his ear and whispered into his collar, his expression flat.

Without even glancing down at me, he unfolded a crisp bill from his pocket—50 Big Georges—and handed it to me.

He told me to see what I could get in the cafeteria, run along, I'm not supposed to come to the edges of the playground.

Aaron is soft and pokey.

It was honing my erotic manual dexterity and ear nibbles that next provoked me to directly address Secret Service.

And then our contact was suddenly frequent.

They'd insist, *We're parked right over here. No one's looking inside your car.*

Thru those steamy aerobic moonlight grapples, they guarded me while I *blossomed*.

I was an *alligator*, switchblade hard with blood.

Those guys could identify a bone by the sound of its snap.

And they guarded me so that I was free to discern and dissect the workings of the raging dawn of my sexual urges in backseats muggy as tombs, elbows and knees knocking awk as rolling over in a coffin.

My dawning sex life protected by thugs felt like I was the Division A state football champions celebrating The Renaissance.

My dawning sex life protected by thugs felt like I was The Birth of Venus in shoulder pads calling a flea-flicker play after play.

My dawning sex life protected by thugs felt like Myth, History, and the invention of Perspective driving down the field, even faking a punt.

Those were the nights I'd later recall in that SkullnBones coffin, pulling my numb and spongy King Charles with my chalky palm, narrating in candlelight for the brothers under the skin and Don Quixote.

CHAPTER 13 Re: The Bloodline

The blue blood Good Men all established their legacies by running drugs and slave-trading and strategically marrying.

But Good Men can *never be* Bloodline.

Every Good Man a Manchurian Candidate, none of them able to comprehend the scale of the actual project.

The Bloodline built the pyramids.

We are in The Code of Hammurabi.

We count Charlemagne and the leaders of The Holy Roman Empire amongst our own.

I'm cousins with 34 Prezs.

We are related at least distantly to *every* European monarch on and off the throne, kin to *every* member of The British Royal family.

My 13th cousin once removed is the heir to the throne.

In The 12th Century, our guy King Henry I, son of William The Conqueror, along with other lesser-known relations, was formative in the founding and unification of The UK.

And The Jesuits charged with the failed "Gunpowder Plot" to blow up The British Parliament in 1605: they would've been carving our Christmas suckling with us too.

And Churchill.

We were The Dutch East India Trading Company colonizing South Africa.

And William The Orange, creator of The Bank of England, famous for first charting out the global banking industry, of course.

Neanderthals went extinct cuz their eyes were bigger than human eyes.

They expended all that brain-energy struggling to see in

the dark while we Homo Sapiens were figuring out how to skin animals and make advantageous connections.

You know who was selling those coats, and calling in favors for access to fire, sculpting systems and rituals for the evolutionary benefit and psychological survival of the group?

You ever notice The Family's *squinty, beady* little eyes?

Tuck-pointers conceal the seams.

But nothing touches The Bloodline.

The Family often retold a *favourite* romantic fairy tale of a low-ranking SS officer saving the family of a young Jewish girl he wanted to impress.

The Bloodline required genealogical quarterings all the way back to 64 great-great-*great* grandparents, 300 years.

Everyone always checking out those Medici sisters and The Bonaparte girls.

Ha! I should line up to compete for one of *them*?

Pops *loved to* play matchmaker: the *espionage* of romance, the power to steer instinct, the obsession with purity.

Junior habitually lied about being an Air Force officer to impress women.

Master of the backwards compliment, he'd say: *I don't like natural beauties. I've always preferred women like you.*

My Mother George Washington forced Junior to call off his first engagement cuz the girl had a Jewish stepfather.

The girl blabbed to *everyone* re: Junior's vivid insecurities that he'd never amount to anything thanks to The Family's pampering.

Junior got her pregnant in '71, but they didn't see the term thru.

And after the surgery, she never saw Junior again, not once.

CHAPTER 14 How'd It Taste?

Afternoon cards with O'Malley and The Greek with chains of mudslides.

Hands folded across his front, Aaron's mirrored shades reflected the blue pool.

Supper time we'd head to The Other Greek Place: a place where when you sat on the toilet in the men's room, you'd feel a bump when, on the other side of the wall, someone sat on the toilet in the ladies' room.

We'd eat at the bar, smoking between bites of dry burgers and pork-chops with soft fries.

Quiet time with the flicker of The Game on ze Tube.

Aaron stood stationed at the door but sat lonesome at the far end of the bar to eat.

The squeaky bartender, That Mike, lifted himself *up* on his toes when he spoke and grimaced anytime anyone but him voiced a word.

After supper, one of us inevitably deigns to cross the room to the jukebox to play some song that makes you feel young again, cuz even if no one remembers *liking* being young, everyone likes *remembering* it; I mean, you don't remember being *happy* when you were young, but seeing some past version of yourself, naive, is endearing.

O'Malley always danced a concentrated little twist in the middle of the room, his weird arms strong like a small dog's.

The Greek would impersonate him and that was all the permission I required to bop along.

Many of my happiest moments have been standing near people dancing.

And *My Diana* hanging on that flimsy closet door, in pro-file in her patriotic bikini, the moon huge and low behind her.

By the time we got to The Other Greek Place each day, it was always dusk, so naturally the active content of our camaraderie darkened a little.

Primary colors softened and blended.

Daylight no longer stood in judgment.

And always *little things* with That Mike: the semi-weekly joke if *my friend* wanted anything, nodding to Aaron at the door.

And the complaints re: his lower back standing over the sink set at the perfect wrong height.

He'd call me "Mr. Sinatra" if simplifying my math ever caused my tip to peak above 5%.

Every day for years we spent hours together.

I never did get how *and why* O'Malley and The Greek tolerated That Mike.

The thing about That Mike, he just *always* thought about my money.

It's kind of *interesting* what things cost, but I really never *thought* about money.

And however dim our daily energies, O'Malley and The Greek and me were *freed* by our hacking laughter and our rollicking song and screech.

We gave *ourselves* permission to strut and blurt small brags in passing, spinning in the limited palette of beer sign lights and ze Tube, dancing with one another and our empty stools.

I'd shout over the jukebox, "Duh, unga-bunga?"

And they both *fell for it* every time.

You know that old joke, Lewd Reader, where you ask a guy if he remembers his first blowjob and then, dewy eyed, he answers something like, 'Oh, like it was yesterday. It was just magic.'

And then you ask him, *How'd it taste?*

That same gang of us, wishing each other the best with our boredom, said goodbye each night with affectionate gravitas that far exceeded our nods hello each morning.

My *old friends* were all the misfit kids of neo-cons, and I'd ignored messages from most of them long enough, they'd given up on me.

Though I did still sometimes wake to Gore Vidal's desperate late-night messages.

I'd become accustomed to the pizza and cartoons that block out all the corpses.

And The Family was *not*, by any means, a daily topic of conversation.

Occasionally a gregarious stranger cocking his head toward Aaron would be like, *What's up with the spook?*

But when everyone shrugs it off, security fades into the background exactly as it's supposed to.

CHAPTER 15 Pops Visits The Bahamas

Capsizing regimes all over—Guatemala, Iran—The CIA needed middlemen to support its preferred rebels and maintain its plausible deniability.

And by the late '50s it'd exhausted using *esoteric adventure travel* as cover stories.

People will believe only so many quests for Yeti and Eurasian leprechaun gold.

So it routinely set up international businessmen as fronts.

The CIA would invest and sometimes outright *own* foreign-based corporations in Haiti or wherever.

The corporations mostly operated as legitimate businesses, the employees oblivious to the spies they provided cover for.

And the equation simple: Business + Politics + Friendship = Intel.

And with their global sales and acquisition efforts, Pops's companies DrSSr and Zappatoes offered the *perfect* excuses for globe-trotting and question-asking.

Dullis was at Gulf Oil.

Same Dullis Bro that seduced The Queen of Greece or his brother?

Which one helped found The UN?

One is famed for having over 100 extramarital affairs and that's probably the same one whose Cuban Task Force was created to exert psychological, economic, and diplomatic pressure on Cuba.

But I can never keep those two straight.

The Dullises aren't Bloodline, but they and The Family conspired in investment Banking and Law for decades—*generations* even—before both turning to "Government."

And whichever Dullis Bro that was—a master of assassinations, cozenage, and camouflage—after the *hulking* misadventure of The Korean War, he was made commander of The CIA.

Pops and his friend Divine had founded Zappatoes with money from Pops's Grandfather, some from The Ruckafellas, and the rest from various Bonesmen.

And Gulf Oil leased a platform from Zappatoes and kept it parked in the most far-flung cluster of The Bahamans, 54 miles north of Cuba.

The CIA handed Young Pops a list of names of specific Cuban oil workers that they wanted him to hire and train.

In fact, the original code name for The Bay of Pigs Thing was "Operation Zappatoes."

But realizing that was *not* the best cover, Pops changed the name of the secret ship that carried the contraband, naming it after My Mother George Washington, same as both planes he piloted in WWII.

Pops resigned and sold all his shares of Zappatoes when he realized that to become Prez someday, he needed to first get *elected* to "Government."

That Dullis in charge at The CIA put Ruckafella in charge of The Psychological Strategy Unit.

This Ruckafella with his bright green office and bright red penthouse and pet tiger Esso was grandson of the Ruckafella that founded the Federal Reserve.

And this Psychological Strategy Unit he helmed recklessly and enthusiastically explored the use of psychotropic drugs, especially the truth serum Scopolamine, hoping to engineer unwitting assassins like *The Manchurian Candidate*.

But after the *hulking* misadventure of The Bay of Pigs Thing, King Arthur insisted that Dullis resign.

And all parties involved understood this move as King Arthur's divorce papers from The Wall Street-TX-CIA nexus.

CHAPTER 16 Re: Cuba

By the time that The Family moved from Midland to Houston in the summer of '59, it was as much a hub of extremism as Dallas.

The John Birch Society, the anti-communist Christian proselytizers that preached unrestricted Capital-ism, had a grip on the city like a vice.

Some people believe that the ancient Sumerian word that The Hebrews translated into "salt" also meant "vapor," which they take as proof that Lot's wife was *vaporized*, proving that nuclear war destroyed Sodom and Gomorra.

Tolstoy chose poverty, seeing ascetic morality as the only path to holiness.

And The John Birch Society believed that unrestricted acquisition of material wealth was a Christian's primary duty.

After getting booted from King Arthur's administration, Dullis's interest in TX intensified.

He contacted a couple Houston-based officers.

And he visited Dallas just weeks before 11/22/63 to give a reading from his new book for The Council on World Affairs, the only event to promote the book's release.

In 1895 Henry Cabbage Lodge, who would become the first Senate Majority Leader, already foresaw the dominoes of colonial expansion: "In the interests of our commerce... we should build the Nicaragua canal, and for the protection of that canal and for the sake of our commercial supremacy in the Pacific we should control the Hawaiian islands and maintain our influence in Samoa...and when the Nicaragua canal is built, the island of Cuba...will become a necessity..."

In 1898 The Homelan not only supported Cuba's revolt against Spain, but Ruckafella even goaded Spain into the conflict.

Black Gold was oil and White Gold was sugar and access and control of this prized gold yin-yang was solidified by the yellow press.

The explosion of The USS *Maine*, docked in Cuba, was blamed on the Spanish, even though they'd peacefully accepted its presence until then, and Spanish documents revealed that they wanted to avoid war at all costs, knowing that their navy was inferior to The Homelan's.

But Ruckafella, along with Harryman, made *zillions* on The Spanish Homelan War, The Homelan's first war that wasn't in self-defense.

In Cuba's revolution of '59, The Homelan and The Mob both supported the overthrown dictator, Batista.

As far back as the 19-teens we'd diminished Haiti, Santo Domingo, and Nicaragua basically into colonies for our investment banks; Wall Street and Capital City fudging together each other's policies, The Marines on call to intervene when needed.

And this itsy bitsy little island Cuba sat only 90 miles off The Homelan's coast.

Homelan companies controlled 80-100% of Cuba's utilities, mines, cattle ranches, and oil refineries; 40% of its sugar industry; and 50% of its public railways.

And Cuba was the primary operating base for The Mob's casinos.

Three years to the day before 11/22/63, *The NYT* reported that Castro had booted Foreign Oil.

And by the spring of '61, King Arthur had just taken office, and The CIA already had 1,400 exiles armed and trained.

King Arthur told a press conference: *There'll be no military intervention in Cuba.*

And four days later, CIA forces landed on Cuba's south shore for The Bay of Pigs Thing.

Castro's army crushed these CIA forces in three days.

One Cuban Intel official named Pops as the organizer of funding to assassinate Castro.

Official resignation is the most common first step a CIA agent takes upon embarking on a delicate mission.

It creates deniability.

The more sensitive your work, the more *unlikely* you acknowledge even working there.

But on 11/22/63, Hovver wrote Pops at The CIA.

Thirteen years before Pops would be appointed commander there, he saw to it that another man with *his same name* got hired as a gofer in a position so lowly that he wasn't even allowed to talk on the phone.

But the mere presence of his name on the records was all the cover that Pops, the *secret* employee, needed.

The CIA probably first recruited Pops to use him as leverage against Grandfather.

But Grandfather's predominance as a senator was anchored beyond budging.

Grandfather never forgave King Arthur for The Bay of Pigs Thing and firing whichever Dullis Bro.

Grandmother said about King Arthur: "(He) is a very ambitious young man who has neglected his work not only to fill his ambition, but the ambition of his father as well . . . It is fearful to think that a man of wealth can set out to gain an office and let it be bought for him."

CHAPTER 17 Feeling Free

The Family's comprehensive access to alien technologies notwithstanding, *no one* makes Jell-o as *scrumptious* as a Barbarian salad bar.

I cannot *imagine* what they do: substitute water with heavy cream?

I go thru a bucket every night watching my tapes.

I hold it on my tongue an extra second, and the flavor shifts, sharpens, then I melt it with a slurp of my mudslide, and it tingles.

O'Malley and The Greek used to pick it up for me, but I started to get suspicious of my change thanks to their snickering deliveries.

But Jell-o is dense and, with salad bar prices, a bucket does end up about a hundred bucks.

Aaron, even with all his *profound* training to hone his god-given propensity for flat affect, still struggled to repress his sneer from the end of the aisle when I'd stoop to scoop up a bucket.

I'd usually be scraped up and dragged out of The Other Greek Place, sprawled on my couch, gumming my Jell-o by 9 o'clock, reflected sirens always throwing a flashing projection of the bank across the street up onto the silence of my window.

And stationed by the door, Aaron's gaze would lock on ze Tube's static while I knocked at my stacks of tapes to cram one into the machine, the click of plastic against plastic, before the magickal collisions of my chance editing.

I'd watched 2/22/80 a thousand times and my thrill never quelled.

Homelan *college* hockey players trumped a Red team of *professional* players improbably designated as students, engineers, and soldiers to qualify for the Olympics.

The Sports Personality compared it to a Canadian college all-star team beating the Pittsburgh Steelers, who'd just won their fourth Super Bowl in six years.

He said, "That may be the greatest upset in sports history."

It wasn't the gold medal game, but tickets with a face value of $67.20 cost as much as $600 and Jamie Farr, Klinger from *MASH*, attended.

The Homelan team forgot the words and hummed thru the middle of the national anthem.

And I get goosebumps every time when the Sports Personality shouts in the final seconds, "Do you believe in miracles?"

I swat any girl aside for that part every time, doesn't matter how asymmetrical she is, dancing her lazy sexy-dance in the middle of the room.

I always pay her and send her home, climb into bed and light a cigarette soon as The Game ends.

Pops liked to pontificate that The Red Union would crumble all at once at any minute.

And however much he *liked* the idea of letting it collapse and even giggled about the forgotten cosmonauts abandoned to their endless orbits, the potential danger of space junk necessitated this collapse's gentle steering.

Pops insisted that when The Red Union collapses, what happens next will shock everyone.

Police, firemen, bus drivers, all the civil servants won't be paid.

For *years* they won't be paid.

And still they'll all continue to go to work each morning.

Society will continue to function *exactly* the same.

Cuz it will *need* to, of course!

Ground-level corruption will increase, but it's already rampant.

Dentists won't be able to afford soap, but most are already too hurried to get to their hands between patients.

And even more corpses will be left to spoil.

And me and Aaron, same as The Collapsed Red union,

dutifully saw thru my daily routine, carrying on as we always had cuz we wouldn't know how not to.

We got creative with new ways to never address each
other directly and pretend not to see each other.

My best friend growing up got yanked unexpectedly from
his office to The Vatican one day and was made Argentinean
dictator.

I think of him and appreciate how good I got it being
forgotten about.

Exceptional athletes, maybe a song-and-dance man,
know that destiny of feeling set apart.

Of course endless alligator games is the inevitable primitive response.

With shelter and sustenance decisively *not* issues, toler-
ances accrue and thrill-seeking becomes an *endless* chase to
keep ahead of numbness.

And meanwhile, shuttled cradle to grave like confused
students marched dreary thru a museum, beer and The Act
of Love are as close as most Barbarians will *ever* get to feeling free.

CHAPTER 18 Introducing Ozzy

By '60 The Homelan's military budget had reached
$45,800,000,000: 49.7% of its total budget.

And King Arthur, appointed Prez that year, immediately
moved to *increase* that.

Then within 14 months he'd added *another*
$9,000,000,000.

He also launched Alliance for Progress, a program that
claimed to emphasize social reform in South America to
better the lives of The Barbarians.

But in practice it was military aid to keep right-wing dictators in power and fight off impending revolutions.

By '62, based on a series of made-up scares about Red
military build-ups, The Homelan had achieved *overwhelm-
ing* nuclear superiority.

A permanent war economy ensured The Homelan's
wealth distribution remained locked in place.

And when King Arthur presented his budget after his first
year in office, *The NYT* reported ". . . he has been trying to
reassure the business community that he does not want any
cold war with them on the home front."

The conservative giants of Dallas all appointed each other
to each other's boards and intermarried, driven by a *feral*
Capital-ist ideology that transcended party affiliation.

And Executive Order 11905, known as "The Assassination
Ban," stated: "No employee of the Homelan Government
shall engage in or conspire to engage in political assassination."

But *these guys* were absolutely OK with assassinating
democratically elected foreign leaders.

They helped The CIA remove—or attempt to remove—
Guatemala's Arbenz, The Dominican Republic's Trujillo,
Congo's Lumumba, Chile's Allende, Cuba's Castro, Indone-

sia's Sukarno, Iran's Mossadegh, and Vietnam's Diem.

And they had their man inside La Casa Blanca: L-BJ.

L-BJ said re: Diem: "We killed him. We all got together and got a goddam bunch of thugs and assassinated him."

King Arthur opposed The Oil Depletion Allowance.

And he bolstered civil rights, which undermined cheap labor.

Thus he bashed at the crux of these men's wealth and power.

Pops burst into politics in the spring of '62, voracious to obtain the status that Grandfather enjoyed.

Grandfather abruptly withdrew from his own senate re-*eleccion* campaign which was already well underway.

And he pulled aside The Party's County Chairman to solicit a position for Pops.

The Chairman guaranteed him that everyone was keeping their eyes peeled for the exact right spot for Pops to land.

And then The Chairman stepped aside and Pops got *his* position.

In one year, Pops went from the sidelines to Finance Co-chair, then County Chairman, then US Senate hopeful; a career course as likely as shooting a polar bear in Mexico, everyone joked.

As both County Chairman and candidate, Pops had plausible reason to visit wealthy oilmen and assemble a team all over TX.

Pops has recently promised Moste that as soon as he becomes Prez he'll appoint Moste to be the ambassador to Ireland.

This is a gesture of gratitude for Moste having worked on *every one* of Pops's presidential campaigns.

And long before that, Moste also tried to convince Fxord that he should name Pops as his Vice Prez.

Fxord is the only person to've ever been Vice Prez and Prez sans *eleccion* to either position.

Nxn's Vice Prez, Agnew, resigned after being indicted for receiving bribes from Maryland contractors, and Fxord was appointed.

And then, of course, Nxn resigned.

So Pops was *almost* appointed Vice Prez six years before he did get the job under The Actor.

Moste also worked in Nxn's office, Nxn and Deen bouncing ideas off him.

But before that he was CIA, based in Dallas, debriefing people as they returned to The Homelan after time abroad.

He invited GDM to lunch in '62.

Moste made no specific demands or requests of GDM, but he did give him the address of an ex-Marine just returned home from Minsk, suggesting that GDM might like to meet this young man.

He gave GDM the clear impression that he'd appreciate any information he could learn about this young man, Ozzy.

CHAPTER 19 Re: King Charles II

Two hyenas don't muster the energy to fight *every* time they come across each other.

Their every interaction affirms and deepens the established social order until the submissive challenges the dominant.

Nature rewards antagonistic behavior with a dominant social role, access to food, and mating possibilities.

The meek need to weigh the cost-benefit ratio of a challenge.

The top three bonnet macaque males account for over 75% of all mating within their population.

These higher-ranking offspring have a better survival rate, not only cuz they're more physically fit, but they also receive the spoils of being The Prince.

This system repeats in rodents, most carnivores, and the dwarf mongoose.

Whether it's the hopping dark-eyed junco or oystercatchers, the dominant couple in most monogamous bird species *always* gets the best territories with better food and water and less predators.

But even without a hundred pound crown, defending your spoils against the envious many can be exhausting.

High ranking brings inherent costs: a higher metabolic rate and higher stress hormones.

Despite their many extra appendages like gunpowder and telephones, the dimly sentient blobs ultimately remain subject to these same fundamental laws of nature.

Higher genetic variation means better health.

The isolated polygamous communities of Utah suffer incredibly high rates of severe mental retardation.

One study estimated their average IQ to be about 25.

And the Vadoma Tribe in western Zimbabwe mostly have two toes.

I don't know exactly what's *wrong* with having only two toes, but I do know that it's uncommon.

Common physical health defects of inbreeding include:
- Reduced fertility, both in litter size and sperm viability
- Increased genetic disorders
- Autoimmune diseases like multiple sclerosis
- Cancers
- Ciliopathies
- Cleft palate
- Diabetes
- Heart Disease
- Hypertension
- Inflammatory bowels
- Mental retardation
- Mood disorder
- Obesity
- Refractive error
- Infertility
- Fluctuating facial symmetry
- Lower birth rate
- Higher infant mortality
- Slower growth rate
- Smaller adult size
- Loss immune system function

And that *most famous* genetic disease circulated among European royalty: Hemophilia.

These facts attest to The Bloodline's *superlative* power, power enough to *reverse* the laws of nature.

The more purified The Bloodline, the more concentrated the totality of its power.

The effects of inbreeding were *very* personal to Darwin. He married his first cousin.

They had 10 children, and three died before the age of 10.

Of the children that survived, six of them had long-term marriages, but three of these produced no children.

When Darwin first spoke of his ideas re: evolution by natural selection in a letter to his best friend Sir Joseph Dalton Hooker, he said that doing so felt like "confessing to a murder."

In ancient Egypt you'd ideally marry your sister or half-sister cuz women carried The Bloodline.

Jean V Armagnac obtained a papal dispensation justify-ing the three kids he had with his sister Isabelle.

That was rare among Europeans, but he flaunted his brazen eccentricities.

Marriages with aunts, nieces, nephews, and cousins were *perfectly common* among royalty, until finally, the gene pool became so scant, all of European royalty was related to one another.

Francis II from The House of Hapsburg-Lorraine and his cousin Maria Theresa of Naples had several children with genetic health problems.

Five of their children died in early childhood, and their daughter Marie Anne was mentally deficient, her face *hideously* deformed.

And their son Ferdinand suffered hydrocephalus, aka "Water Head," which means he had a *humongous* head and intense mental deficiencies.

He had *daily* seizures.

But *of course* none of that prohibited him from eventually becoming Emperor.

When informed of the revolutions of 1848, he responded with true befuddlement, "But are they allowed to do that?"

The most extreme example of a genetic trait aggravated by royal inbreeding, The Hapsburg Lip, was typical of their bloodline for over *600 years*.

This condition intensified to the point that King Charles II of Spain's tongue was so gargantuan and his underbite *so* severe, he couldn't chew food.

And no one understood a word he said.

And he *constantly* drooled.

And 300 years later as boys, with a sing-song bite, my brothers would call me "*Kiiiiiiiiiiiiiiiiiiiing Chaaaaaaaaaaaaaaaaaa-rrles.*"

My nickname became Chuck, which made mocking me intrinsic to addressing me at all.

Ultimately, King Charles II's impotence led to the extinction of the dynasty, which caused the 14-year War of Spanish Succession, in which 500,000 soldiers fought.

CHAPTER 20 My Ex

At the very least, until recently, I'd retained my alligator health enough to indulge my mild hedonisms.

Minor embarrassments surfaced during my divorce: a fling with a woman with hands as big as shoeboxes, a couple cases of itches picked up from professionals.

What can I say?

Whether it's the struggle to see or the struggle to *not* see, everyone struggles with interiority.

There's bound to be some fallout, everyone butting up against each other, each moving thru our own animal fear, lost in that mysterious hole we each find at our own centers.

A lot of that stuff is simple upkeep.

My alligator made some decisions as if it was a jellyfish with its unified organ that's both brain and stomach.

My ex and I had somehow lost the knowledge of how to even *begin* to touch each other.

And you have to keep the spirit moving smoothly thru its pipes *somehow.*

I've never been the *sensualist* of The Family.

But after my divorce, after a year catatonic, I did enjoy a satisfied return to feeling like the Division A state football champions celebrating The Renaissance; The Birth of Venus in shoulder pads calling a flea-flicker play after play; Myth, History, and the invention of Perspective driving down the field, even faking a punt.

I felt *liberated* from that dank tomb of King Charles, like an alligator scraping along city streets.

There are more relevant matters at hand, however, Randy Reader, than the dwindling health of my regal penis.

True to the institution of divorce, I had very, very little contact with my ex.

Fundamentally, she mystified me, much *stranger* than a

stranger.

I remember she liked old-timey female country singers, meeting people, and being seen.

And she hated how I enjoyed telling The Help to take the afternoon off to go see a movie.

But *who* she actually was, and her ways of being, that was all a mystery to me ever since our shared habit of every day-ness had been severed.

We married young, our marriage one more awk result of my brief flirtation with conforming to The Family's expectations.

I was rehabilitating from my cool and self-conscious years, obsessed with underground rock legend Cy Franklin.

It's basically accurate to say I'm a lifelong bachelor: married at 26, divorced at 29.

And I don't blame her.

She made the decision, and the swiftness and totality of its execution *stunned* me, but us splitting up didn't surprise me.

Mostly, primarily, I remember her as *dull*.

But dullness isn't anything I resent or fear.

I passively *aspire* to it, I suppose.

Most friends I've ever had could be described as dull.

And if anyone leveled that charge against me, I wouldn't feel obliged to defend myself.

Yup, common dullness, *OK by me*.

My ex and me, however, we *exhausted* each other with our dullnesses.

Knowing how I was back then, I can't regret marrying her.

How I was thinking, what I thought mattered, pressures put upon me—she was the *perfect* candidate: pretty hair, slim, smart enough in all the socially acceptable and tasteful ways, but not smart enough to see thru the folly of worrying about social acceptability and taste.

She's from Jackson, Wyoming, *The Joplin, Missouri of The Open West,* with all its nightlife and dazzle.

And she was on track to become the wife of *someone like me.*

And we intersected.

We had the desire to throw a big party in common.

Of course, she came with some *cha-ching!*

Nothing compared to my own, but enough that she could be accepted as *worthy.*

She's since invested all that money into a system of private prisons that she insists is *the future of incarceration.*

It's worked out well for her.

Her name was briefly dragged very publicly thru deep mud.

Isn't it insane how some Contras slaughter a dozen civilians and some doctors at a healthcare clinic and rape some women while their children watch—*horrible* stuff, but *way* across the world—and my ex ends up testifying to Congress?

Luckily, she was on a first-name basis with half the committee.

Nowadays, my ultimate *romantic* goals all involve catching a beautiful woman in a lie.

Catching the same woman over and over no longer interests me.

Ideally, I'd like to catch a beautiful woman in a lie once, then move on to the next beautiful woman.

I'm a punchline in my ex's biography—or *résumé*, I should say.

A *big* gold-star punchline.

She married into The Family, *and* she also knew to walk away from me.

Looks good on paper.

She still looks good for her age in her slim-fit business

skirts.

She never wears too much makeup, but she's never without *some* makeup.

And what's she have to do all day but go from one light-impact workout routine to the next?

I get embarrassed for her when she occasionally attempts her condescending tone with me.

Her true vacancy is on full display when she's stretched, attempting to express *any* emotional depth.

But our semi-annual one-minute conversations are *fine*, friendly enough, always re: our sons, of course.

My brief *playboy* phase fizzled when the simplicity of professionals became apparent.

No risk like when you run into an old senator and with a softened tone he introduces you to his pig-tailed date slurping on a pacifier, her eyes rolling around the corners of the room.

And no shame like some jilted Secretary of Defense that'd fallen in love with The Pass-Around-The-Party-Bottom, raging and pouting as he watches her in The Act of Love with everyone else.

The Act of Love itself no longer interested me as much as my quick escapes knowing that it *could've* happened.

With my deep bellybutton and my tits that ache with every flight of stairs, I'm never King Charles by myself.

CHAPTER 21 Best Chums in Common

As a marine stationed in Japan, Ozzy had been mocked *ruthlessly* by his battalion for being effeminate.

Shaken by this hazing, he mostly hung out at The Operation Bluebird Cafe.

Remember that name, Vigilant Reader: The Operation Bluebird Cafe.

In '60 Hovver himself wrote a memo naming Ozzy as CIA.

In '62 GDM and Ozzy became *inseparable*.

GDM and his wife *devoted* themselves unequivocally to Ozzy and his wife.

Never before had they taken such an interest in overseeing others.

GDM helped Ozzy find work and housing, brought him along to social events and meetings, and even helped with their baby.

At the same time, oddly, *all* of GDM's advice to Ozzy made Ozzy appear weirder, scuzzier, and more unstable, more like a *classic* misfit.

In April '63 GDM went to New York to meet with a CIA agent that he knew, another one that was Chief of Clandestine Operations in Eastern Europa, and The General Manager of The Haitian bank.

Officially, the four men discussed mineral concessions in Haiti.

And the next afternoon GDM met again with that same CIA agent, along with his chief, Divine, Pops's ex-partner on Zappatoes.

Within hours after GDM's meeting with Divine, a Domestic Operations case officer in Capital City created a legend for the entire Domestic Division that they had *no idea* who

GDM was.

The officer requested an expedited check on this purportedly *unfamiliar* character.

He received a report from '58 when Moste, then at Dallas Domestic Divisions, debriefed GDM after a trip to Yugoslavia.

That way, if GDM ever claimed to know Moste, it could be officially attributed to that meeting years earlier instead of the lunch at which Moste suggested he might like to meet Ozzy.

From there, GDM traveled to Capital City to secure approval for a coup against Papa Doc in Haiti.

He spoke to L-BJ's military advisor.

This Haitian coup provided solid reason for GDM to interact with high-ranking officials just months before 11/22/63, and the official trail it created complied with international goals that King Arthur supported.

Five months after GDM left for Haiti, six weeks before 11/22/63, Ozzy got a job at The TX School Book depository owned by Brrrd, a member of The TX Crusade for Freedom, right-wing oilman, and friend of GDM.

And Pops quickly ascended The Party ranks.

The Head of The Party in TX backed him for Senate and Crytin for Gov.

Crytin worked that same intersection as Pops: Military Intel, local police, The Party, Russian expats, and Oilmen.

In fact, Crytin was tight with GDM and Brrrd.

Thru '62 Crytin supervised the establishment of a complicated underground command post for local police underneath The Dallas Health and Science Museum, not unlike the bunkers of my youth.

And on 11/22/63 Crytin's men drove the the pilot car that led King Arthur's motorcade.

And Crytin provided Dallas Police with a Russian translator for Ozzy's wife immediately after King Arthur's very public skull chipping.

Her statements didn't implicate Ozzy, but the translator's sure did.

All our luxuries, The Barbarians do get comforts we'll never have: Lone Wolf Theories, external triggers for internal censors, boundaries of permissible thought.

I envy The Barbarians: their struggles must feel so *real*.

What *depth* of meaning, two people that both *already feel real* on their own, *believing* in their struggles, fucking with The Act of Love together.

Lying awake nights, I imagined: what if I *had to* wake up?

What if I had to wake up and go to that same place I hated 1,000,000 days in a row sans end in sight?

What if I had calloused hands, and my coarse friends and me all had bad nicknames for the boss that we'd whisper and laugh so hard?

However much you may *wish*, you really can only be you.

CHAPTER 22 The Most Beautiful Zoo in The Middle East

The Garden of Eden sat between the Tigris and Euphrates rivers in Sumer, which was later named Mesopotamia and now Iraq.

According to The Sumerians, their civilization existed for 500,000 years, fallen from a previous Golden Age.

Sumerian culture blossomed all at once out of nowhere.

Its influence reached as far east as The Indus River and all the way to The Nile.

Their citizens traveled frequently and widely.

Their queen, stylish by contemporary standards, wore modern wigs, large earrings, necklaces, and makeup.

She died in a ritual suicide 2,150 years before the founding of Rome, 2,000 years before Moses started writing.

Around 2,000 B.C the first Codes of Justice were written in the halls of Sumer's metropolis, Babylon.

The Sumerians also invented: the first writing system, the wheel, schools, medical science, written proverbs, the idea of history, the bicameral congress, taxation, the concept of social reform, cosmogony, cosmology, coins, the 360-degree circle, spherical astronomy, 60 seconds in a minute, 60 minutes in an hour.

Their accurate knowledge of the movements of the sun and moon led to the inventions of the first calendar and the Zodiac, whose horoscopes The Barbarians still sweat each morning.

Diana means moon.

Sumerians described and diagrammed Uranus, Neptune, and Pluto, none of which are visible sans telescope and weren't *rediscovered* until 1781, 1846, and 1930, respectively.

Sumerian civilization lasted *2,000 years,* 100 times longer than The Homelan has currently existed.

And then it disappeared all at once.

And though their culture lasted 2,000 years, they observed and recorded a cosmic cycle that takes 25,920 years to complete.

Sumerians described *beings* that came from the sky to enlighten them and establish civilization, but they didn't use the word "gods."

"Gods" was a later translation by The Romans and The Greeks, like how Lot's Wife "vaporized," and The Family teaches that Jesus wasn't a Red.

These *beings* are *very* similar to The Nephilim in The Book of Genesis.

When Genesis says: "Let us make man in our image," that's a heavily redacted version of The Sumerian creation story.

Those first Barbarians Adam and Eve *needed* to remain ignorant, *lest ye shall become gods*, you know?

One Nephilim was named Nazi.

The British took Baghdad from The Ottomans in WWI and made it the capital of The British Mandate of Mesopotamia.

WWI ended The Ottoman Empire after 600-something years.

Six hundred years is *ten times* longer ago than the end of WWI until now.

Six hundred years is *three times* longer than The Homelan has officially existed.

In The '20s, 40% of Baghdad's population was Jewish; it was the city's largest single community, with a *2,600-year* history there.

In '32 The British granted Iraq formal independence.

And in '41 a pro-German and pro-Italian "Government" replaced the pro-British "Government."

They surrendered power back to British forces less than eight weeks later, but in the chaos, there was an organized massacre of Iraqi Jews: 175 killed, 1,000 injured, 900 homes destroyed.

Over 80% of Iraqi Jews emigrated in the next decade, mostly to Israel.

Throughout The '50s The UK promoted Baghdad as The Crossroads between East and West.

It moved at a modern clip with the bustle of young people, its cafes crowded with ambitious men pontificating big ideas.

Late in his career, Frank Lloyd Wright developed his grandiose Plan for Greater Baghdad, which included a cultural center, a university, an opera house, and museums on an island in the middle of The Tigris.

But due to yet another political fluctuation—Qasim dethroning The Hashemite monarchy—the project never got realized.

In Feb '63 a CIA-authorized, six-man squad assassinated Qasim in a Ba'ath Party coup.

The CIA also provided The Ba'ath Party with a list of suspected Reds to round up and kill.

One young thug, Saddam, made especially frequent visits to our embassies.

The CIA supported and trained him in Beirut in '59.

He was *our man*, appointed leader, overseeing the construction of The Baghdad Zoo in '71, the largest and most beautiful zoo in The Middle East.

CHAPTER 23 The Cinema and Me

Back when I first arrived, still struggling to fit in, I tried to be a *Realist* with The Barbarians, but doing so was *Idealistic.*

"Duh, unga-bunga!"

The Barbarians so deeply *believe* the easy dreams of their programmings:

Nerd wins beautiful girl's heart!
The bully is defeated!
See A-List Celebrity boobs!
Small town guy goes big time!
Eat all you want and lose weight fast!
Parent and child switch bodies and learn lessons walking a mile in each other's shoes!
Positive Male Role Models!
The underdog wins the game!

O'Malley and The Greek would draw out a one-minute dialogue from *The Treasure of The Sierra Madre* into an *hour* of hyperventilating chuckles.

When they took turns out-doing each other the way Paul Newman says "Mendacity" in *Cat on a Hot Tin Roof*—"The mendacity." "No, no, no—the mendacity."—I knew better than to invest my one good ear too attentively for fear of being appointed referee.

If their collaborative synopsis of a movie began at noon, we'd be lucky to approach its climax by the time we moved over to The Other Greek Place for supper.

Top Gun, Crocodile Dundee, Platoon, Inchon, The Karate Kid Part II, Star Trek IV, Back to School, Heaven's Gate, Aliens, Eddie Murphy in *The Golden Child, Cafe Flesh, Ruthless People, Ferris Bueller's Day Off, Dead Zone, New Wave Hookers, Down and Out in Beverly Hills, Plan 9 from Outer Space, The Color of Money, Stand by Me,* all the *Emmanuelle* movies, *Legal Eagles, Cobra, Police Academy 3, Peggy Sue Got Married:* We loved them all!

But consistent with The Family's fetish for secret knowledge, I loved *obscure* movies most of all: Monte Hellman, *Bad Timing*, *Weekend*.

You ever seen *The Great Gatsby,* Bob Redford and everything pastel?

Or *Fahrenheit 451?*

The Man of La Mancha with Peter O' Toole as Quixote and Sophia Loren as Dulcinea del Toboso?

A Catcher in the Rye starring Leo DiCaprio?

Obviously as a body of work, Kubrick *speaks to me* like no other filmmaker.

2001 not only made me smarter, it taught me how time passes.

He goofed The Family in *Strangelove* and The Barbarians in *A Clockwork Orange*.

And *The Shining*, *that* is the movie I would've made.

But my *favourite* Kubrick film has always been the moon landing, obviously.

Diana means moon.

And above all others, my single *favourite movie ever* is *River's Edge*.

A teen melodrama like *Rebel Without a Cause* but with thrash music, it had a limited release 18 months ago.

You know it, Principled Reader?

Keanu, Ione, Crispin, Dennis Hopper.

I never won't watch it when it's on.

As much as I loved seeing movies, and I loved O'Malley and The Greek's role-playing and context unravellings, most of all I loved *making up* movies.

I *always* thought—or felt—I should've been a director.

That's the chips down, final curtain, ultimate disappointment of my life, at the root of my identity.

Any time a small crack of quiet arose as O'Malley and

The Greek transitioned from their real-time synopsis of one film to the next, they were always happy to hear out my next ideas for a movie.

"Duh, unga-bunga. Duh, unga-bunga. Duh, unga-bunga. Duh, unga-bunga," I'd say.

And they *steadfastly* encouraged me, nodding, *very interesting, very interesting. Good idea, good idea.*

But The Family made it clear: *by no means* would they accept me putting my name on movies.

With movies, each generation gets remembered according to the limitations of its technologies, how the representation most obviously differs from *lived* reality.

Long ago, silent people bumped around slightly more quickly than we do.

After them came new people who inhabited a world with sound but lived so much slower than us, we could see their punchlines and hokey morals broadcast from too far out to hold our attention.

And they still all lived in just shades of gray.

Now turning channels is the apex of peace, way different than seeing any one channel, and not unlike my collage tapes.

One channel now even strives to do 24-Hour News.

Tomorrow's dominant technology of representation will be *Life on Earth* itself?

Ha!

A mirror-world simultaneous and symmetrical!

The Family's ultimate victory.

I bristle whenever someone says *Oh, this is just like a movie.*

Saying that means you've inverted the whole symbiosis of art and life, and catharsis, confounding cause and effect like anxiety.

That it *cannot* be communicated is exactly what makes

Life on Earth what it is: irreducible, subjective, durational, experiential *being,* etx.

Working unpaid for years while honing your craft is the *real* secret of *The Arts.*

But of course, The Family would've had *requests*: *your villain should have this or that kind of accent.*

Just imagine their arduous lean on me if they had any inkling I'm penning My Report you now hold in your hands, Agile Reader!

I should've coached basketball.

Re-watching my tapes *always* reveals deep strategies.

But My Report here intends to invest my *Life on Earth* with meaning.

Just wait until they see how I deftly contradict the spin of that droll and schizo so-called *Objective* biography.

CHAPTER 24 Soda Pop, Etx.

Cuba's sugar interested Kendill, the Head of Pepsi.

And Harryman also had extensive sugar holdings there.

Like oil, The CIA used both Coke and Pepsi bottling plants as commercial cover.

Local franchises were often gifted to crucial military and ruling elites in each country.

Of course, it wasn't *only* Soda Pop.

The CIA doled out international marketing monopolies for *all kinds* of products: cars, sewing machines.

But Soda Pop was big.

They probably chose it for its irony factor, its sweetness and disposability a perfect cover.

Kendill would later be identified by *The NYT* as a pivotal player in the overthrow of Allende, the elected Socialist Prez of Chile.

A Soda Pop Convention in Dallas the week of 11/22/63 brought *8,000* outsiders to town.

The Army Reserves, led by Pops's chum Crytin, volunteered for a strange extracurricular activity the night of 11/21/63: it was very *nice* of them to load orphans onto trucks and bring them to a rodeo that the bottlers hosted, but it also got a lot of army trucks out on the streets.

One Soda Pop Convention attendee met Ruby for a drink that same night.

And the convention accounted for two of the three future Prezs in Dallas on 11/22/63: L-BJ was keynote speaker that night and Nxn was invited as a guest speaker at the last minute, taking the opportunity of the spotlight cast by King Arthur's visit.

And coincidentally, Pops was there campaigning.

The Soda Pop Convention reserved a large venue early, which consequently determined King Arthur's ultimate destination and his motorcade route.

When he first returned to The Homelan, young effeminate Ozzy joined a Civil Air Patrol Unit founded by two Ruckafella brothers and Brrrd.

You Remember Brrrd: owner of TX Book Depository and an associate of Crytin and GDM, active in The TX Crusade for Freedom, along with Dullis's Deputy Director of The CIA, and the mayor of Dallas whose brother played a key role in The Bay of Pigs Thing aka Operation Zappatoes.

I can *never* remember which Dullis Bro is which: one of them ratted on the other for doing The Act of Love with The Queen of Greece and I don't know if the rat is the same one that had over 100 extramarital affairs.

Anyways, just weeks before tying himself to Ozzy, GDM incorporated a charity devoted to the study of cystic fibrosis.

And he put Brrrd's wife on the board so it certainly wouldn't look weird that Brrrd and GDM knew each other.

The TX Book Depository doesn't sound like it, but it's the name of a private company.

Its board members were all military men *highly* critical of King Arthur and involved in many CIA propaganda campaigns.

The CIA *adored* publishing.

The Senate concluded that The CIA published or subsidized over 200 titles in just '67.

The TX Book Depository building sat almost completely empty—*sans* tenants—until about six months before 11/22/63.

Thanks to The Soda Pop Convention, King Arthur had only two possible routes to his destination.

And The TX Book Depository stood along one of them.

Anyone could've determined the route long before it was made official.

Brrrd was away on his first-ever African safari on 11/22/63, but he later removed the window that Ozzy supposedly fired from and had it installed it his house.

According to witnesses, Nxn went *bananas* when he heard the news on 11/22/63.

Pops, on the other hand, stopped mid-speech at The Kiwanis Club but retained his poise.

A couple hours later, Pops called The FBI from Tyler, TX, 100 miles from Dallas, to report a *suspicious* young far-right character that'd been coming around The Party, mumbling about killing The Prez.

At the *exact moment* of King Arthur's skull being so publicly chipped, Pops's own top employee stopped by the house of this *suspicious* young far-right character to ask him to help paint campaign posters.

So Pops's phone call to The FBI officially established:

1) Pops was in Tyler, TX, not Dallas.

2) He was trying to help the investigation.

3) He was wide-eyed naive re: any larger conspiracy.

4) He provided an alibi for the same young man that he made the call to accuse.

Kitchelle had helped Pops get his start in politics and was also chums with GDM.

His brother at The FBI was the *specific* agent that Pops called to report his intel.

So, the man that helped start Pops's political career shortly before 11/22/63 was at the same time chums with Ozzy's handler, and his brother created a paper trail for Pops.

Pops named witnesses that could provide further info re: this *suspicious* young far-right character but spelled all their names barely wrong.

Pops left Dallas that morning.

He'd spoken at The Homelan Association of Oil Drilling Contractors the night before.

And when he called Kitchelle's brother, he told The FBI that he was going to Dallas that night from Tyler.

This slippage creates confusion when the story is told

later.

He did, in fact, fly back to Dallas that afternoon on a private plane, only to catch a commercial flight to Houston.

But this misleading trail was akin to a magic trick, the magick of Political *Realism*.

Though an aspiring TX politician at the time, Pops has never written one word or spoken publicly re: 11/22/63.

Years later, in her own official biography, My Mother George Washington published a letter she said was written on 11/22/63, before, during, and after the announcement of King Arthur's very public skull chipping.

I wonder if this latest, best-selling, so-called *Objective* biography of The Family alludes to that.

Effectively this letter serves as an alibi for her and Pops's entire day, though it's not apparent who exactly the letter supposedly addresses.

The couple they tooled around with that whole day—The Ummers—the husband was known OSS and CIA and oversaw multiple coups.

"We went all over the world and we did what we wanted. God, we had fun," he once said.

For example, a couple years later in '65, Ummer orchestrated the CIA-backed coup that brought Suharto to power in Indonesia.

Freeport, the largest mine in Indonesia, was well-known to be closely linked to the CIA coup.

And King Arthur's policies on Indonesia were decidedly not in the interests of Freeport.

CHAPTER 25 Cocooning with The Barbarians

Later, everyone else claimed to've known all along that my marriage was a joke, but I really did believe in it.

Apparently my lovely ex had been hinting for a couple years, occasionally dropping my keys in the blender.

Still it shocked me—*shocked!*—one morning when I cracked my eyes open and she announced her departure.

Seven months pregnant, and our other son had just turned one.

And she no longer wanted to wait around for her husband to decide what he wanted to be when he grew up.

The shock triggered what I took to mean *retirement.*

I wasn't 30 yet, hadn't begun to build anything in either Politics or Business.

But in response, I certainly didn't cultivate my best self or get vengeful.

I slackened, exceeding her worst fears for my potential slovenliness.

Moving day, one of the movers, a big guy in a weightlifting belt, held me in his arms while I *sobbed*, hysterical with long snot, unable to catch my breath

And that's when I moved out into the corpse-strewn wildernesses of The Barbarians.

The first months, it took all my energy to wrangle the aching, no surplus energy to move, let alone conceptualize a next move.

Sipping mudslides with a faraway look, I might've *appeared* immersed in concentration, pondering my brewing inner life, but that wasn't the case.

I'd shut down, been burned clean, the sum of my limited energy conserved to invest in repair.

I lived alone with yesterday's breath always hanging in the room.

Thru the dull ache of my morning skull, I'd wake up already *ashamed.*

In the neon hum of a grocery aisle, two Barbarians, skating thru their days, would bump into each other, smile and struggle to summon each other's names, and witnessing it would be enough I'd have to scuttle home to center myself.

My senses seemed rented and a step detached—living like a robot's digital sneeze—like I'd been substituting for someone else's *Life on Earth*.

One more man alone on the streets, not breaking stride to step tall over the corpses piled at the curbs.

My late mornings made the days dark early.

And the days stacked into a dizzying repetition, a hypnotic minimalism.

Lost in watching my reflection on the surface of the bus window while the outside world zipped past me in reverse and flipped over—the reflection of a reflection—I was *startled* when another passenger I hadn't noticed before stepped out from behind my own shape.

A bare tree revealed a beehive, unlit Christmas lights strung to its boney branches.

And one day at a time, I began to eat breakfast at The Diner every day.

Diana Herself served me plenty of times before I noticed her.

When I emerged from this state, after that first winter, I didn't tear thru the skin of a cocoon.

No crust crumbled from my eyes.

Just slowly, I intuited how to get on with the simple business of everyday maintenance.

And a year later I was better than ever.

I'd learned to sleep in and wear shorts every day, blissfully free from anyone else's expectations.

And I could *see*.

That classic blessing of all of history's misfits—even with the psychedelic glare of that steel spike at the center of my field of vision—I could see *everything clearly*, from the *outside*.

The days stabilized, each as much like the previous as possible: Diana Herself for breakfast; playing cards at The Club with O'Malley and The Greek; all of us heading together to The Other Greek Place for supper, sitting at the bar with that cocksucker That Mike serving us.

I didn't need to see The Great Wall of China.

When I visited Europe as a teenager, the natives seemed determined to confirm every stereotype: The Parisians terse and snooty, The Italians boisterous and overbearing with their affection, no respect for boundaries.

Living among The Barbarians I'd achieved our great national ambition: *comfort!*

Any of my brothers in that same situation, spontaneously single, would've hopped the next flight to Beirut to party with The bin Ladens and Mötley Crüe.

But I, Unflappable Reader, I went to live among The Barbarians.

And *that* has made all the difference.

CHAPTER 26 L-BJ

Newly appointed Prez L-BJ called the investigator in Dallas and said: "You have your man. Let it go."

Then after Ozzy got shot, L-BJ called the Parkland operating room while they still had Ozzy blobbed open on their operating table and ordered the doctor to take a deathbed confession.

L-BJ's mistress, the mother of his secret son, went to a party with him on the night of 11/21/63.

When they arrived, Hovver and Nxn and Gather—who would go on to lead The Plumbers in H2oG8—were all already there.

L-BJ snuck off with them to a private room.

And afterwards, he whispered to her, "Those motherfucking King Arthurs will never embarrass me again. That's not a threat. It's a promise."

And the party fizzled out.

Of course, L-BJ claimed loyalty to The Other Party, but he worked within the network for years.

The TX Gov in '63 was L-BJ's campaign manager in the stolen *eleccion* of '48.

L-BJ enjoyed a reputation for *total* ruthlessness for many years, but it was that *eleccion* that earned him the nickname he's retained in back rooms ever since: Lyin' Lyndon.

An assistant to L-BJ's Attorney has gone on record saying that L-BJ killed King Arthur.

L-BJ's Attorney *himself* would never make such a claim.

But all of L-BJ's Attorney's partners agreed: L-BJ's Attorney *took care of things* in Dallas.

They claimed he was the *secret ruler* of TX since the late '30s.

But he got a chance to relax finally when L-BJ appointed him ambassador to Australia.

L-BJ's business partner, Estes, testified on record that L-BJ killed not only King Arthur, but also his own sister: a promiscuous druggie and gossip that he couldn't trust.

One investigator looking into corruption charges that threatened to lead back to L-BJ was found remote in the woods.

His death ruled a suicide: he'd banged his head in his own car door a few times, then shot himself five times while unconscious from carbon monoxide poisoning.

King Arthur's brother, RKF, invested deeply in an investigation of a corrupt network of TX military contractors, and everything pointed right back to L-BJ.

Then, at the time of his own assassination, RKF was investigating L-BJ's closest associate, The Senate Secretary, for corruption: real estate schemes, call girls, bribes.

One week after taking office, L-BJ reversed The Homelan attitude toward Vietnam and intensified it.

Brown and Root, which would later become part of Halliburton, had largely financed his political rise, and now won a $380,000,000 no-bid contract for Navy facilities in South Vietnam.

L-BJ met with his 14 advisors *daily*, 12 of them CFR.

CHAPTER 27 Fortune

Alan Rufus is commonly believed to be the wealthiest Briton in all the history of The British Isles.

He accompanied William The Conqueror's Norman invasion, and received 250,000 acres of land as a reward for his allegiance.

By the time of his death in 1093, his estimated worth was the equivalent today of over 80,000,000,000 pounds.

The Medici Family of Florence was among the most illustrious noble families of European history, hereditary holders of the titles: The Grand Duke of Tuscany, The Duke of Florence, and The Duke of Urbino.

Other family members included multiple popes and queens.

Giovanni di Bicci de Medici, founder of their family bank, was appointed The Pope's banker in 1410.

By 1457 his son had expanded the fortune to the equivalent today of over $22,000,000,000.

Heshen, a Manchu official of The Qing Dynasty, lived from 1746-1799.

His fortune included the equivalent today of $42,000,000,000 in silver alone and his total wealth equaled the total imperial revenue of *15 years* of the Qing "Government."

His 8,000-acre estate included 3,000 rooms and his treasures included:

220 pearl bracelets, each pearl comparable in size to a large cherry and 10 *humungo* pearls, each the size of an apricot

40 tablefuls of solid-silver eating utensils

40 tablefuls of solid-gold eating utensils

20,000 sheets of fine sheep-fur wool

56,000 sheep and cattle hides of various thicknesses

He had 7,000 sets of fine clothing; 361,000 bronze and tin vases and vessels; 100,000 porcelain vessels made by famous masters; 24 highly decorated solid gold beds; 460 European clocks; 606 servants; and 600 women in his harem.

Jakob Fugger, a German banker and merchant, achieved monopolies in the European silk and copper trades, and became chief financier and creditor to Emperor Charles V.

He died in 1525 and left his nephew the equivalent of $438,000,000 in gold.

Tsar Nicholas II of Russia was born in 1868.

By 1916, the year before The Reds overthrew him, he was worth the equivalent of $290,000,000,000 in today's money.

Not only the wealthiest monarch or head of state in history, he and his wife were declared martyrs after being murdered by Bolsheviks in '18, making him the wealthiest saint ever.

Osman Ali Khan was the last of seven Nizams to govern the Hyderabad State in India between 1911-1948.

Time magazine put him on its cover in '37, regarding him as the richest man on all of this watery and poisoned mysterious orb.

He owned *dozens* of Rolls Royces.

He had his own mint, literally printing his own money.

His private treasury included 100,000,000 pounds in gold and silver; 400,000,000 pounds in jewels, including The Jacob Diamond, valued at $126,921,500 in today's rates.

He used it as a paperweight.

The last Pharaoh of Ancient Egypt, Cleopatra, lived from 69BC-30BC.

She was a member of The Ptolemaic Dynasty, a Greek family that ruled Egypt after Alexander The Great's death, and the first of them that didn't insist on only speaking Greek.

It would've been tough for her to present herself as the reincarnation of Isis like she did if she didn't speak Egyptian.

After ruling jointly with her father, Cleopatra married one of her brothers, then the other, ruling jointly with each of them.

But really just she ruled.

Her romance with Julius Caesar solidified her power, then she made their son her co-ruler.

After Caesar's assassination, she took up with Mark Antony against Caesar's legal heir, Augustus.

Her and Antony had twins, but The Romans colonized Egypt before either twin had a chance to reach the throne.

In the '30s, King Abdul Aziz ibn Saud, founder of the modern Kingdom, was advised by former British intel agent and ex-pat St. John Philby.

An eccentric orientalist, Philby called The King "the greatest Arab since the prophet Mohammad."

And he even got Churchill to consider making ibn Saud the King of *all* Arabs in exchange for supporting pro-British policies, such as accepting the Jewish state in Palestine.

In '43 Philby helped negotiate The Kingdom's first contract with The Ruckafellas.

The Ruckafellas had already controlled 95% of all oil produced in The Homelan by as early as the 1880s.

But *this* deal was the mother-load.

WWII had established both oil as the matrix's *preeminent* strategic resource, and The Homelan and The Reds as its rival superpowers.

In '44, a member of The Homelan's official delegation

to The Kingdom said, "The oil in this region is the greatest single prize in all history."

Not unlike I feel re: *My Diana*.

CHAPTER 28 Re: The Kingdom

To circumvent Congress, The Zionist Lobby, and the press, the "Government" ceded relations with The Kingdom to the oil companies.

Diplomats became oilmen, and oilmen became diplomats, dealing with those *strange men* in their flowing robes.

Simple self-interest determined The Kingdom's policy; their National Interest, *Realism*.

They supported international Muslim concerns when it looked good to do so, so long as the issues bore no real consequence to them—Uganda, The Philippines, Russia, China, but *never* Arab Muslims.

And The King habituated himself to his unlimited power.

He claimed to've deflowered several hundred virgins and gave each one away as a gift afterwards.

He kept four wives, four concubines, and four slaves and he swapped out these groups of four frequently.

He married into more than 30 tribes.

One tribe spread the rumor that his alligator had dwindled into King Charles, so he paid them a visit to deflower one of their girls in front of everyone.

But he wasn't always so showy.

He kept his harems in windowless basements so no one else could see them.

Internationally, his habits looked a little less good.

He was eventually exiled to Kuwait, and other than that only left The Kingdom one other time, to visit Egypt.

While there he didn't recognize The Kingdom's national anthem being played in his honor and didn't know what to do when told what it was.

And he awk inquired about buying £100,000 worth of pretty women to bring home with him.

When he liked a married foreign woman, he often rewarded the husband with huge business contracts.

And though ibn Saud himself had four wives, his 42 sons

had *1,400* wives between them: 33.333 wives each.

Forty-two sons but he never counted his daughters.

And he also never educated them, so we can't know if they ever learned to count themselves.

The King's habits proved contagious, and his many princes fanned out all across this watery and poisoned mysterious orb with the assumption that all women could be bought and sold.

One prince went so far in a long game of one-upping the open abuse of outsiders, he assassinated The British Vice-Consul in Jeddah for not giving him more whiskey.

From the '40s to the '70s, the seven biggest oil companies were nicknamed The Seven Sisters, together controlling 85% of all oil reserves on this mysterious and watery poisoned orb.

Top-level visits between chums preceded every major meeting between the companies.

And by '72 The Federal Trade Commission proved that the eight largest oil companies were interlocked thru large commercial banks, meaning, when the board of any one of the six largest commercial banks met, the directors of the top eight oil companies met with an average of 3.2 directors of their largest competitors.

This baby octopus was born in Feb '45 when King Abdul Aziz met FDR to cement one of the most consequential agreements in all World History: the trade of oil for security.

In '57 The Eisenhower Doctrine deepened this commitment.

King Arthur pressured The Kingdom to release their 4,000 slaves, but that didn't happen.

He understood how to balance The Homelan's founding

pretenses against its energy dependency, so he never criticized their human rights record publicly.

The Nxn Doctrine of '69 declared that The Homelan would no longer bear the main responsibility of defense and would instead send billions in equipment.

And all this opened the door for Pops's covert Privatized Security Agreement.

This support doesn't go to The Kingdom army, but specifically to protect and sustain The Royal Family.

As long ago as the '30s, The Kingdom gave verbal support to Palestine while withholding any material support.

When the Arabs lost the Arab-Israeli War in '48, though officially allied with the defeated, The Kingdom remained unfazed cuz Arab unity represented potential trouble for The Kingdom.

In '67 Israel launched attacks on Egypt, then Syria, then Jordan, defeating the Arab armies in six days.

And this *inflamed* Arab nationalism.

Between '67 and '73, The Kingdom faced the greatest number of attempted overthrows in its history.

In The Arab-Israeli War in '73—The Yom Kippur War— Nxn supported Israel.

So The Kingdom nationalized its oil.

The Israeli victory prompted The Arab Oil Embargo of '73.

But thanks to a covert agreement, The Kingdom's petrodollars poured back into The Homelan in the form of business and real estate investments.

In effect, The Kingdom used gas that The Homelan bought to buy The Homelan out from under itself.

The Royal Family even strutted in their robes into soul and funk label Stax Records in Memphis and tried to buy it.

And Pops sat positioned *perfectly*.

In the two years leading up to the Oil Embargo he served as ambassador to The UN.

By the time of the embargo, he was national Head of The Party, which dealt with politics and public perception, but also with The Party's top funders, the TX petroleum refiners staring at their own dwindling domestic reserves.

In March '75, one of The King's nephews pulled a gun out of his traditional headdress and shot The King dead.

Pops dispatched his former #2 man at The CIA to work full time with The Royal Family to improve security.

Using their fear against them, Pops got The Royal Family to secretly subsidize *everything* that he and his chums wanted: billions and billions and billions and billions and billions and billions and billions and billions of dollars.

The Homelan encouraged The Kingdom to spread the extremist Wahhabi version of Islam to stir up Muslims in the Red-controlled countries of Asia, which it believed at the time to be the world's greatest undeveloped oil reserves.

The Homelan elevated this radicalized element of Islam, with military training, over the largely moderate and insular Muslim population.

The Oil Price Shock of '73 had the greatest persistent economic effect on The Homelan since The Great Depression.

Those with the oil used their leverage to stabilize their *real* incomes by raising global prices.

And thanks to the dramatic inflation, the effects of the accrued momentum dug in.

New permanent economic policies deepened dependency: cause and effect constricting the bonds of "The Brutal Friendship."

The Brutal Friendship meant that The Kingdom would *never* assert Arab or Muslim rights at the expense of its relationship to The Homelan.

Consequently, relations with its own Barbarians would *always* remain stressed.

This meant greater repression, which meant greater dependence on The Homelan's security.

Unlike The Homelan with its repressive tolerance, its battlegrounds psychic and spiritual, The Kingdom adopted *unrestrained* totalitarianism.

There's more phone sex in The Kingdom than anywhere else, contact between unrelated men and women being illegal and all.

CHAPTER 29 My Report

GDM had known The Bouviers since the late-'30s.

They spent the summer together at a Long Island Cottage: GDM; his brother from *Time* magazine and his wife, and their son—Pops's best boyhood chum.

They were the guests of Jackie Bouvier and her mom.

Jackie grew up calling GDM "Uncle George."

And Onassis, Jackie's future husband and hater of RKF, nearly started a Haitian business venture with one of GDM's closest partners.

There was a dinner with Jackie's mom right after 11/22/63.

Dullis joined them, whichever Dullis, the one that ratted the other out for The Act of Love with The Queen of Greece, who may or may not be the same one that founded The UN, but I don't know if he also had over 100 extramarital affairs or which one was the rat.

But at this dinner was GDM and his wife, whichever Dullis, and Jackie's mom.

And they talked about 11/22/63.

Jackie's mom said she didn't want *any* investigation.

But not me, Conscionable Reader!

I've found *purpose!*

A singular *ambition* motivates me to pen *My Top Secret Report* that you now hold.

You're no doubt aware of this latest, best-selling, so-called *Objective* biography of The Family that The Personality asked Junior about.

I shall correct every one of its outlandish and unfounded claims!

Yes, it's Family policy to not write *anything* down: no breadcrumb trails, no shredded evidence to tape back together, no games of telephone.

But *My Top Secret Report* that you now hold, Venerable Reader, shall lift the spell of that ludicrous and deranged so-called *Objective* biography.

And the primary, most *gargantuan* and outrageous fallacy that *My Top Secret Report* shall set straight is re: My Mother George Washington.

The totality of the durational *scrape* of my days I've endured this ridiculous myth that *I* am supposedly My Mother George Washington's *favourite.*

Me!

All the dumb biographies claim the same thing: *Me,* My Mother George Washington's *favourite.*

Part 2

HALLOWEEN'88

CHAPTER 30 Re: Me

Isn't it weird how all of us, all the ways we all *weird* each other?

Me and Aaron's *chilly* relationship had grown *chillier* over the years.

Of course it's difficult to read a Secret Service guy, *unreadability* being a fundamental skill of their employment.

But I'd learned to read a twitch of his lip or a flared nostril.

And he did unabashedly sneer when he almost came into bodily contact with one of my sandals.

Down the counter some mornings, his lips would hardly part when he spoke.

But Diana Herself, pouring his coffee, would snort a laugh and glance to see if I'd noticed.

When the timing worked out, it always pleased me to stand and pull my coat on to head over to The Club before Aaron had time to finish his breakfast.

The hushed edges of his manner sharpened.

My gym shorts and muumuu jerseys didn't mean that I didn't see other people's margins of error.

Had my fecklessness become contagious, his collar untucked a quarter inch and his gestures broadening?

"There's a car out front," Aaron said.

Rusty leaves floated the bright blue surface of the pool.

My chair's leg caught on the astroturf.

"I'm sure," O'Malley said, "it's just a matter of what's-it-called?"

He tapped his cards neat.

"National Intel," The Greek said cool with a smile.

"Yeh," O'Malley said. "I'm sure it'll only take a second."

Citing only each other as sources, hack scribes circularly perpetuate those fanciful musings that *I* am My Mother

George Washington's *favourite.*

Same as all those photos posed clearing brush and fly-fishing, it humanizes The Family to assume that the matriarch must *most* love her *least* ambitious.

It flatters her maternal instincts to protect and nurture.

Years I've tolerated this farcical excrement.

The statistical data of my existence would hardly fill a baseball card—hardly fill the *edge* of a baseball card:

Born Jan '55.

One mushy ear.

Steel spike seated at the middle of my field of vision, swirling whatever I look at into conical depths.

Graduated Yale '77.

Married Sept '81.

Divorced Sept '84.

Only witness to My Little Brother's death.

And though that new best-selling biography touted as so equitable and *Objective* refers to me, of course, as My Mother George Washington's *favourite,* Pops *disabused* me of this sentimental notion.

I did see him once only a year ago.

Fully submitted to my drinking, Pops and I *finally* had a thing in common.

I visited his country club, a formality to clarify the expectations of my invisibility throughout his campaign.

Deep into his campaign, he shaved compulsively—three times a day his aides claimed—and shed pounds fast.

He preferred to hold court while pacing behind the bar, the blinding shine of his big square and compass behind him.

One of his own commercials looped on ze Tube, all my brothers and their kids in it, everyone except me.

Stretching and contorting, manic with *eleccion* personality, he'd perfected his menacing way of calling everyone *friend.*

I was 32, divorced, grubby, and jauntily at home among The Barbarians.

In grimy tennis whites behind that bar, he looked me over like I maybe looked *familiar.*

And with that grinding *peel* of his voice he said, "You know, I always thought it rather lousy form of your mother. It really was never fair of her."

And I responded calmly, "Duh, unga-bunga?"

I didn't understand.

"How she never even *pretended* to like you, how she never really even *tried.*"

Pops insisted that each of us makes his own way in the world, The Family wouldn't give us *a dime.*

Of course, who needs *a dime* when you got The Family name.

Growing up at picnics with The Kingdom's Royal Family, we had the *freshest* blue eggs and tomatoes beyond what The Barbarians could even imagine.

There was always falafel alongside the dollops of macaroni salad, and tabbouleh with the Jell-o.

I'd *Gone Native,* adopting O'Malley and The Greek, foraging for omelettes at The Diner and gorging on thick Jell-o from the salad bar.

Though the native population I lived among had been colonized psychically, emotionally, spiritually, and materially, my condo still represented the *greatest* distance I could possibly escape.

I no longer lived with any sense of suspense.

Like a bicycle buried in snow in a small mountain town and no thaw coming.

CHAPTER 31 Re: My Brothers

Junior's been groomed since birth to be Prez.

So if I maintain my current rate of unravelling, I should expect to soon be appointed *intergalactic cosmic commander!*

Junior's anxious to run for TX Gov, but he can't until after Pops's second *eleccion,* so that it doesn't appear to be a referendum on Pops's Prez time.

So instead, after *el eleccion,* Junior plans to buy a baseball team.

Even as a young man Pops was self-conscious and austere.

Junior wears high-heeled cowboy boots and stages photoops standing next to people shorter than him.

His eyes glaze over when he's spoken to.

And until his recent sobriety, he was *always* sleeping off a hangover while a meeting carried on around him.

But I'll give him this: I really never have known anyone so *decisive.*

Deep down, Pops and Junior have both always felt the need to not only *rule the world*, but to be *liked* while doing so.

That's Democracy's fundamental *appearance* thing.

It was *love at first sight* when Rover met Junior in '73.

Pops became aware of Rover when Rover served as National Chairman for The Party's College Committee.

Rover attended four colleges but never graduated.

His rivals within The Party complained about his dirty tricks, so Pops investigated.

He cleared Rover of all charges, lectured the complainers on loyalty, and gave Rover a job.

Rover was a *true believer* in The Art of War.

He planted bugs in his own office to accuse his opponent

of doing so.

Once, as a child, Junior was praised for taking initiative when he ticd a bucket to his opponent's boat before a race.

It was Rover's idea that Junior should buy the baseball team.

Like donating to an art museum, owning a winning sports team goes a long way in exonerating deficiencies.

Golf's highest prize is named after Pops's grandfather.

You do remember The Family invented golf, right?

It electrifies the team's investors to transform Junior from a *Nobody,* in the eyes of The Barbarians, into a *Somebody.*

And make a bundle doing so.

Most investors, especially those from The Kingdom, prefer to remain anonymous.

And that works cuz Rover *insists* that The Media refer to Junior as the team's "owner," even though he'll be one of many and won't devote two hours a week to team business.

His partners understand it'll lead to cushy appointments as the ambassador to Switzerland or seats on foreign intel boards.

And the bonus, beyond public perception: Real Estate.

And somehow it was *just fine* with The Family that Junior produced and financed movies.

Junior and his chum Betts have financed *every* Disney movie in the last few years, updating the company's anti-semitic tradition into quieter, more subtle means of constructing limiting racial identities.

Betts became the Yale equivalent of Stone from Harvard.

Robert G. Stone, not *Clement* Stone.

Not Roger Stone.

Robert G. Stone, Chairman of the seven-man Harvard Corporation, Oil and CIA connections, used to be partners with Divine.

You remember Divine: Pops's partner at Zappatoes, on record as CIA under commercial cover since '63, etx.

As commodore at the exclusive NY Yacht Club, Stone's intimacy with oligarchs flourished.

And most impressive, he was a 32nd degree Freemason.

But I mention Robert G. Stone only in comparison to Betts.

It's Betts who's buying the baseball team with Junior.

Of course, Junior's name doesn't *appear* on those Disney movies.

To him, selling movies is the same as selling hydraulic systems, bombs, or subcontracted black sites.

Pops had a glamorous streak, sneaking out to make the rounds with his producer chums, liked being photographed with movie stars.

Junior just wanted Scrooge McDuck's magic coin.

My next brother after Junior has been in Miami about eight years.

He's been The Party Chairman for Dade County, and just this year became the state Secretary of Commerce.

He's going to be Gov.

The Family had *zero* history in Florida.

But my brother saw The Barbarians' local culture of Nascar and motorboats and intuited how he'd appeal to them, inflaming their sense of *The Local:* God, and guns against the outsiders that come rushing in each year come Season.

And name recognition alone will *elect* him.

He moved down there after a shark-fishing expedition, bought a condo complete with glass-inlaid glass—literally a glass tower—and fell in quick with the Cuban exile community.

A good city for him since he's always assumed it his privilege to squeeze the ass of *every single* woman that he's *ever* seen.

My next brother *under him* is the prez of a Kingdom bank and never leaves his private outpost on the northern tip of Paraguay, sitting atop the world's largest supply of titanium.

After oil's depletion, titanium will be the world's most valuable resource, but it'll be another 25 years before anyone notices or cares.

A few dozen people live in my brother's little sovereignty.

The Family doesn't like the press to snoop cuz it really *does* look an awful lot like Jonestown.

My brother always points out quick that Jonestown was in Guyana, "very different climate, different political system."

Basically he's The King of a Kingdom outpost.

It's his old VW minivan I drive.

It was 10 years old when I got it but had only 2,000 miles on it, and no rust.

No snow-salts cruising around a humid rain forest.

So there's Prez Pops, Future-Prez Junior, Future-Gov Brother, King Brother, and *Moi*.

My Little Brother died at 11, a long life given his circumstances: rushing clunky into a corner whenever anyone entered his room, longing to be able to sleep lying down like a *normal person*, playing dumb as people talked in front of him, *I pray to God he's an imbecile* and *notice his genitals are perfectly normal*.

Every account of The Family, both sympathetic and critical, refers to his death as *The Tragedy*.

I was 13.

I remember him as the blinding embodiment of the present tense of speckling ancient star light.

Every account of The Family's history includes me only to say I'm My Mother George Washington's *favourite*, and I was there when My Little Brother died.

They all fail to mention inbreeding.

Two things truly define the character of the *super-rich*.

First, tantrums happen.

Often and sans bashfulness or restraint: papers floated, glass crashing, and guttural screams.

That's part of, once in a while, very rarely, being forced to delay gratification.

And secondly, the *endless* indoctrinations to comprehend!

All that pomp and ceremony and shadowy magick: *this* effigy you're bowing to seems to contradict your vow to *this other* effigy; ill-fitting robes over your suits, incense in bank vaults.

It's a *lot* of mumbo-jumbo to keep straight.

And then the subtler hereditary curses of privilege: off-spring *doomed* to become performance artists or DJs.

And the big open secret *at the root* of keeping domestic class structure intact and preserving the perpetual dream of *Middle Class* consciousness: the oligarchs are *exactly* like what The Barbarians commonly call *Hillbillies*.

Obviously there's the inbreeding.

And everyone always threatening to sue each other.

Paternity cases, afternoon naps, ubiquitous bleached blondes in skimpy outfits, and grown-ups screaming like children.

Always lots of desserts.

Lobster is sloppy, no matter *how much* you practice, you end up using your hands and make a mess of your bib.

The Hillbillies' finger foods and our hors d'oeuvres aren't dissimilar, we just know to eat stuff loaded with the same B12s that get diminished from drinking all day: liver pâtés, caviar.

You know who *always* comes across like bad actors when being themselves?

Aristocrats.

And Hillbillies.

And what *slobs!*

Oligarchs disrobe when they get home, throwing their clothes to the floor behind them as they pass thru their long halls, their Man trailing to pick up behind them.

That whole *never picking up after yourself* thing, that's the big difference: rich snobs and privileged fleabags can *afford* to be bonkers and each live in our personal dream world.

I've told you, Trusted Reader, that I haven't kept Help in years, so my condo's piles of crumpled papers and stacks of smeared plates should come as no surprise.

Hiring a maid to come a couple times a week would not make any difference.

And I got my deadbeats dependent on me, same as Hillbillies.

And finally there's the God stuff and the sex stuff.

Only The Middle Class bourgeoisie refuse to acknowledge The Illuminati.

The Hillbillies *feel* how true it has to be.

And of course we *know* how we operate.

And the God stuff: wouldn't *you* have strange gods *too* if you were more powerful by factors of infinity than anyone, *anything* else, on this mysterious and poisoned watery orb, floating in infinite yet paradoxically expanding space, feasting like gangsters, like prison guards?

Junior's always been the least imaginative among us, so what gets him off is simple: a ballerina skirt and Rommel's personal field jacket.

Death, present and personified when possible, is his biggest turn-on.

A lot of autoerotic asphyxiation cuz he doesn't like to be touched too much.

Future-Gov Brother always behaves all playful ashamed, referring to himself in the third person as a dastardly "bad boy."

It's like there's no blood's left for his brain when it all rushes to his alligator.

He likes common cross-dressing, doesn't need that military element that Junior does.

But he does like people to wear leashes, likes to pull people.

And he likes it a lot when people shit themselves.

He likes to scold them.

King Brother likes hermaphrodites.

He's the ruddiest and most athletic of all of us, always out in the sun on his golf cart between gold mines, eating mangoes off the ground, in his dashikis and safari hats.

He looks like a quarterback.

But hermaphrodites, that's a Bloodline thing.

Hermaphroditic species often suffer lower degrees of inbreeding depression, the repeated generations of *selfing* purging the problematic recessive genes from the population, so his hermaphrodite kink is really just a health kink, the desire to scrub away his own genetic grime.

That I know so much re: the sex lives of my brothers discloses another thing in common with Hillbillies: The Family *loves* their audience.

No reason The Act of Love should be any exception, the thrill of deep-rooted caveman pain shown naked.

Look out when one of them begins to feel his alligator purr.

He'll pull his bare ass out of his tuxedo pants and hoist the nearest Help onto the island in the middle of the kitchen, or flip someone over the back of an exercise bike—especially in weight rooms with all those mirrors.

Junior once got dozens of slivers up and down his arm when he pushed over a pile of firewood during a Family party.

Junior's bed is hundreds of years old and wider than a two-car garage.

126

He claims it gives him the surging power of Min, Egyptian god of alligators.

And when it's finally his turn to be Prez, the bed will travel with him.

It has pillars like a museum entrance, each one carved with a bull, a lion, an angel, and a lamb.

And a live girl grinding on each post.

CHAPTER 32 Bunkered Youth and The Chuck Norris Wars

They never allowed us time to pack, but leaving my teddy behind, I'd find his warped clone waiting for me in the bunker, this one's button eye stitched to pull its nose to one side asymmetrical.

My Mother George Washington would insist: *it's Teddy. That's Teddy. The same goddam Teddy.*

Most often we'd stay a couple days, playing cards with Secret Service, never able to differentiate between drills and emergencies.

The Family never spoke re: these excursions, then or later.

O'Malley and The Greek *love* it when I mention stuff like secret bunkers.

I realize, Exalted Reader, that you've never been in an underground bunker, let alone a secret base.

But it's not just Idaho, Wyoming, and Montana.

Half the land in California is federally owned.

You're never far.

You ever snooped around under The Astrodome?

That new Denver Airport being built, smack dab in the middle of The Homelan.

When King Brother came along, our two older brothers occasionally teamed up on him.

With the cushion of years between us, even back then no one noticed me.

But Junior and Future-Gov Brother were *fierce* rivals.

Junior, being the oldest, beat up Future-Gov Brother relentlessly.

The burden of all of History's little brothers weighing heavy on him, Future-Gov Brother learned to brood and drag his feet, his every action dictated by a push from behind, a pull of his hair, or a hard punch on the arm.

But about twice a year this thing would happen, always when Future-Gov was backed into a corner.

Future-Gov, balled up, down and defeated, anticipating The Incredible Hulk, which wouldn't exist for another few years, channeled his rage to cast a spell.

With a *howl* deep down from his gut where all the shamed ghosts of ancestors nested, his breath hard thru his nose like a bull, his eyes red and intense, channeling the *spirit* of The Party's warrior, he would growl loud and slow, low in his little throat: "*Chuuuuuuuuuuuuuck Noooooooooorrrrrrisssssss!!*" and charge Junior.

Junior would hear no more than the initial "*CH*" in "Chuck"—like the lighting of a fuse—and he'd throttle off into retreat, mowing over anything in his path.

He respected Future-Gov Brother's spell, instinctually comprehending its leveling power.

But Future-Gov Brother *always* caught him.

And The Chuck Norris Beatings became extreme enough, I'd estimate the boys got an equal number of punches in on each other annually.

The difference was how they each *used* these punches.

Junior benefited each day, using them regularly and sans hesitation, but the threat of violence was usually enough to guarantee his dominion over us brothers.

Future-Gov Brother, on the other hand, saved up all his punches and settled the score twice a year with severe beatings.

Beyond the immediate satisfaction of vengeance, he benefited little from his punches.

Junior was the more obvious spawn of The Family.

Infinite parallel, or slanting, *harmonizing,* quaquaversal micro-realities, and *still* all my earliest memories involve being scolded or bullied.

CHAPTER 33 The Abduction

The long limo, parked diagonal and flanked by two SUVs, barely fit in The Club's lot.

My Mother George Washington reflexively shielded her eyes from a blast of blinding sunlight; her hand up against her face and open palm turned out toward me.

She had a giant neck like a mayor, fleshy as a turkey.

Decades of daily public smiling, and she *still* couldn't get it right.

Her eye contact was like a vice grip, afraid she wouldn't be able to cope with the massive lumpiness I'd acquired or the mascot on my jersey if she let her eyes drift.

When I was a boy, she was *already* an old lady—not day-time TV and not smudging your cheek with a spitty thumb—but an old lady nonetheless.

We did not stop back at my condo to pack.

Billboards zipped by: Pepsi has Madonna and Diet Coke has Demi Moore.

Just Do It.

We passed mall after mall set back behind parking lot after parking lot.

Roddy caught my eye in my reflection in the window and I dropped my gaze to count my toes wiggling past the grill of my sandals.

My Mother George Washington's lawyer Roddy'd been by her side since the day his father, The Prince, first sent him to The Homelan from The Kingdom for being lady-like.

And by that time, he was in junior high and it'd already been decided that My Mother George Washington would be his only client.

He steadfastly *dripped* with earnest and deferential awe.

With a single long scratchy whistle of the straw, I finished the bottom half of my mudslide and placed my empty glass on the tray.

We all learn the best and heaviest lessons over and over.

Your brain's settings cannot be *undone* or won over with appeals.

All your *incredible* efforts to change yourself only establish you as *more* yourself, someone prone to incessantly appealing himself for change.

Kinetic *You:* the one who flips and contorts in endless variations seeking some new sense of stabilized *selfness*.

My Mother George Washington, the sullen queen mime, *performs*.

You're expected to simply *soak in* the dynamic diminish-and-swell of her pursed lips.

Her sighs give breath astounding gravity.

My haphazard *Life on Earth* boiled over in her proximity.

If she were ever to smile, would she still look like George Washington, or was it only the strain of her resting frown that twists her face into his august likeness?

The dexterity with which the growl low in her throat moves *way up* into her nose and then eases into a soft purr.

But she remained silent.

Roddy explained, "It being *Eleccion Time*, The Barbarians and The Media, they're getting nosey."

I nodded.

"And now with *Le 24-Hour-News Channel* . . ."

My Mother George Washington, her face turned toward the window, closed her eyes in the sunshine.

It's *common sense* physics how gossip spreads among The Barbarians: short and quick waveforms in denser populations, but in the country, everything so spread out, information and ideas rebound in longer, slow cycles.

I watched the waist-high hickory smoke of the controlled

burn of a prairie, stunned by how flames carved thru brush, flabbergasted to grasp how flowers existed timelessly before we dimly sentient blobs appeared to trace our fingertips along them.

"There's no joy," Roddy pontificated, "like the joy a mother feels when giving her child a gift."

I looked out the window at the long cycles of common sense physics, the smoke thinning neck-high above the prairie.

I traced the path the capillaries carved across the backs of my hands.

"Hyacinthignatzi," Roddy smiled.

My Mother George Washington lowered her eyes and drew a breath as if the mere mention of its name commanded respect.

"We remember how happy you always were there as a boy," Roddy said, though he and I both knew that he hadn't even moved to The Homelan by that time.

A rusted cylindrical gas tank off in a field looked like a haystack at sunset.

Roddy assured me that they all understood I didn't like Help around, so the estate had been evacuated.

But soon they'd start setting up for the *Eleccion Night* party and I might even like to make myself *useful* and help.

My Mother George Washington caught herself snorting and cleared her throat.

I nodded, careful to neither confirm nor reject anything.

It can be subtle in some contexts to distinguish and distill the witness from the victim, and I wasn't quite sure yet which role I played here.

Some *human* part of me wanted to *squawk*.

Could they possibly understand the tremendous series of troubled surfaces I'd passed thru in those intervening years since they'd seen me, hour-by-hour, the struggle to remain upright, endlessly whacking away at all that *language* anchoring the knotty roots of my brain?

At the center of a small downtown, on the stone steps of a municipal building darkened with wetness, couples lined up to marry in ill-fitting formalwear.

Roddy's mannerisms had always reminded me of a daytime-Tube historical reenactment actor.

He'd learned English with a British accent, and you know, Committed Reader, how when people with smart-sounding accents say anything less than incredibly brilliant, it sounds stupid?

He spoke with the rounded bark of a dolphin, not loud but landing heavy on the punctuation.

My Mother George Washington clicked her 19th-century nails across themselves.

I knew that she had to have a sleeping fox inside that sleek purse of hers, so I listened for stirring, and watched for an outline to roll across its surface.

In a park, half a dozen homeless men had organized mid-afternoon calisthenics in the shadow of the public gallows.

We passed two giant feet in dirty basketball shoes poking out from under a fence, with two heads popping out its top: baby waving to its first passing motorcade.

Maybe this whole movie we were trapped in was in slow-motion.

I steeled myself: Do *not* even mention the *sting* of personal identity.

Weeds bloomed green and shot up tall between cold stones in a flooded cemetery.

The distances between small houses increased.

The very first initiation rituals of The Bloodline all involve spiral candlesticks leading melting wax along specific and circuitous paths.

There's The Homelan's genesis myth of gunfighter holy

men *selflessly* trekking across the ever-expanding frontier.

We are all expected to *always* stand ready for bare-knuckled service to the throne.

Roddy read a contract out loud to me.

A search party in neon vests moved between trees thru long tape, brushing the muddy forest floor.

Roddy handed me a packet printed in *obscenely* small type.

The Family's *impenetrably* dense system of coding had evolved as slowly as the genetic defects of inbreeding, layers of 17th-century cryptography layered upon obscure layer.

Logic was no more relevant to these encryptions than aesthetics determine a key's teeth.

I asked Roddy to help me with the codes and he apologized, "I'm sorry. I just can't do that."

I thought perhaps I'd misapprehended, why shan't he elucidate these codes' cracking?

And I said, "Duh, unga-bunga?"

"I'm sorry. I wish I could. But you understand that the reason these are written in this code is so that only *you* could understand them."

I nodded cuz certainly I got that, yet I failed to ascertain their meanings.

"Duh, unga-bunga."

"I promise it's really not a big deal. Once you know the code it's really very simple."

"Duh, unga-bunga."

"Right. And I can't *tell* you the code cuz I'm not allowed to tell *anyone* the code cuz only *you* are supposed to know it."

"Duh, unga-bunga."

"Well then, I'm not sure that I can know for sure that you are you."

"Duh, unga-bunga?"

"I'm sure I don't know. But that's not the point."

"Duh, unga-bung—"

"But I can't *know* that you are you, cuz if you were you then you would know the codes."

I sat silent, reduced to my *Real Self,* the self
that my brothers were correct to mock as a child,
"*Kiiiiiiiiiiiiiiiiiiiiiiing Chaaaaaaaaaaaaaaaaaaa-rrles.*"

King Charles II: apex of the famous Hapsburg Lip, typical of The Hapsburg bloodline for over six *centuries.*

The condition worsened until King Charles II's tongue was so fleshy it filled his mouth.

His underbite too severe to even chew food.

My Mother George Washington's famous party trick was she could differentiate between currencies and denominations by sniffing bills while blindfolded.

And at 33 years old, I remained destined in perpetuity to be that same runt I'd *always* been.

I cleared my throat and sat up tall.

I couldn't just be kidnapped.

They must know, *Mother, I have taken a lover.*

I told them, "Duh, unga-bunga."

My Mother George Washington rolled her eyes, and Roddy sighed.

CHAPTER 34 *HATCH YA ZINGY NIT*

The motorcade stopped at an unmarked single lane road off the interstate, barren in every direction.

My Mother George Washington's peck goodbye missed my cheek by a good five inches.

Aaron got out of the SUV behind us.

My VW minivan sat waiting.

The two of us got in, and I drove.

The road was straight, *Ahead* and *Behind* immediately indistinguishable.

Moving thru vast emptiness, there was no sense of progress or movement with which I could orient myself within the still prairie.

Turning around would mean turning my back on terrifying silence, so I continued to move along the dirt grooves of tire tracks.

The road diminished to nothing, the prairie glistening, licked down like cat fur.

In the distance, strange ruins stood tall above the pasture: a short run of highway overpass, 100 feet or so, straight drop to straight drop, high overhead like Roman aqueducts.

After some minutes of bumping silence, we came upon the knotty old tree that our rope swing still hung from.

Grandfather used to make us boys guess the tree's age.

Whatever number we'd say, he'd say, "more, more, more."

We'd laugh, "infinity," and he'd say, "more, more, more."

Then his tone would hush like Aesop emphasizing the moral of his story.

"Our family," he'd say, "has been working to get the power we enjoy since before this big, old tree was just a seed fallen on the ground."

We all nodded that we understood.

"This tree has been here since long before electricity. No

one could turn on lights then. And the nights were dark, dark, dark. And this tree has been here since before our people even arrived here to begin The Homelan. Naked Indian boys and girls were climbing this tree and living to watch their grandchildren climb this tree before our people first stepped foot here."

We all nodded that we understood.

"And even then, our Family was planning this."

We all nodded that we understood.

I felt magnetized moving thru majestic silence, approaching that totality of my looming loneliness, approaching The Family's *favourite* holiday house where I hadn't been welcome in some years.

Was it memory or premonition, the bunker?

Sport-coated with spritzer in hand, I'd visited Hyacinthignatzi dozens of times since being down in that bunker or even thinking of it.

But this time, with a bolt of awareness, somehow I knew *this was the place.*

And confirming the setting meant confirming the memories.

And confirming the memories, something in me—something in my deepest and most hidden motivations—blew open exposed; the molten ore from which my decision-makings formed, the dream-network of my fears and associations.

Maybe the bunker would turn out to be no more than a big supply closet.

But I *did exist* in that moment.

I had existed.

I will exist.

First, only the occasional rusted signs to ignore, *Warning "Government" Land: Restricted.*

In that length of road from the gate thru the prairie, the

light shifted inexplicably from darkening dusk to lighter dusk.

The trees thick along both sides, I could see very little beyond the bouncing beams of the headlights.

I stopped to lift a rusty gate in my path.

Ankle-high thorns in damp brush stuck me.

The gate's wet rust stained the long cuffs of my jersey red.

The air startled with the singsong and clicking of insects and birds.

A single anomalous leaf the size of an elephant's ear was spotted minuscule with disease.

And we continued on, the trees opening up again into shocking dusk prairie, the road straight ahead appearing endless.

My throat constricted, I worried I'd gone too far and had passed the house.

But I couldn't have missed a *mountain*.

Agitated and impatient, I drove fast for such a bumpy road, fighting my gut's *screams* to turn back.

Shotgun, Aaron gasped.

In the distance: the four-story tall Owl that stood at the door, backlit.

The road came to an end at a bent-up gate.

I hit the brakes hard, almost careening right thru it.

Hyacinthignatzi was a goose-poopy estate like a red-mud, tin-scattered cabin town.

The knee-high merry-go-round we'd bang our shins against as kids must've been too rusty to spin.

A long footbridge made of unravelling rope and splintering planks hung creaky over a ravine.

The statue in the center circle of the driveway still invited climbing: a bull, a lion, an angel, and a lamb playful twisted up into a chimera.

And I couldn't see it, but I knew that behind those doors, the candy counter in the lobby of the private movie theater must still be stocked with the chalky sweet-tarts of my youth, powdering away in their wrappers.

The sign on the gate had been vandalized, Hyacinthignatzi anagrammed: *HATCH YA ZINGY NIT
Hatch!*

CHAPTER 35 Re: Lopsidedness

By the summer of '64 Pops felt totally confident he'd win the TX Senate seat.

Twenty TX newspapers endorsed him, including both Dallas papers, both papers in Fort Worth, and *The Houston Chronicle*, and he'd even formed a statewide organization, The Other Party for Pops.

In the end, he got The Party nomination, but didn't win the seat.

L-BJ won in a landslide: the #1 most lopsided popular "vote" victory *ever*.

Of course, the popular "vote" doesn't mean much: Samuel Tilden beat Rutherford B. Hayes in the popular "vote" in 1876, and nowadays Tilden is most widely regarded only for his *world-renowned* porn collection.

L-BJ brought Dullis back into "Government" soon after 11/22/63 as a member of The Warren Commission, officially tasked with investigating the many mysteries of 11/22/63.

The doctor that performed King Arthur's autopsy had never performed an autopsy on a gunshot victim before.

And he burned his notes from the autopsy.

The emergency room doctors had a very different sense of the bullet's trajectory than The Warren Commission later determined.

The autopsy didn't happen in Dallas as law dictated.

The Secret Service flew the body to Bethesda on Air Force 1.

Arriving in Bethesda, King Arthur's body was in a body bag in a different coffin than when it was loaded on the plane in Dallas.

The front right side of his head had been cut and pulled back, obfuscating any entrance wound.

Two FBI agents present at the autopsy noted in their

report that this head surgery was performed before the autopsy, between the Dallas emergency room and the Bethesda coroner.

Not Mob, not *Cubans*, not The Reds could touch the body on that plane.

CHAPTER 36 A Jellyfish with a Cartoon Billygoat Gut

By mid-century—like I explained re: DrSSr—The Family controlled the technology that made drilling for oil feasible.

And drill-bits quickly became hydraulic-actuating assemblies, airplane landing gear, wing flaps, and bomb doors, unifying the Energy and Military-Industrial sectors.

And I mentioned Grandfather owned Geronimo's skull?

In his farewell address in '61, Eisenhower famously said: "This conjunction of an immense military establishment and a large arms industry is new in the Homelan experience. The total influence—economic, political, even spiritual—is felt in every city, every statehouse, every office of the federal 'Government.' We recognize the imperative need for this development. Yet we must not fail to comprehend its grave implications. Our toil, resources, and livelihood are all involved; so is the very structure of our society. In the councils of 'Government,' we must guard against the acquisition of unwarranted influence, whether sought or unsought, by the military-industrial complex. The potential for the disastrous rise of misplaced power exists and will persist.

"We must never let the weight of this combination endanger our liberties or democratic processes. We should take nothing for granted. Only an alert and knowledgeable citizenry can compel the proper meshing of the huge industrial and military machinery of defense with our peaceful methods and goals so that security and liberty may prosper together."

In 1856 British Prime Minister Benjamin Disraeli said: "It is useless to deny, cuz it is impossible to conceal, that a great part of Europe—the whole of Italy and France and a great portion of Germany, to say nothing of other countries—is covered by a network of these secret societies . . . and what are their objects? They do not attempt to conceal them. They do not want constitutional 'Government' . . . they want to change the tenure of the land, to drive out the present owners of the soil and to put an end to ecclesiastical establishments."

In 1909 Walther Rathenau of General Electric Germany said: "Three hundred men, all of whom know one another, direct the economic destiny of Europe and choose their successors from among themselves."

Joseph Kennedy, patriarch of that idealistic and decapitated dynasty, said: "Fifty men have run The Homelan and that's a high figure."

Woodrow Wilson: "Since I entered politics, I have chiefly had men's views confided to me privately. Some of the biggest men in The Homelan, in the field of commerce and manufacture, are afraid of something. They know that there is a power somewhere so organized, so subtle, so watchful, so interlocked, so complete, so pervasive, that they had better not speak above their breath when they speak in condemnation of it."

Supreme Court Justice Felix Frankfurter: "The real rulers in Capital City are invisible, and exercise power from behind the scenes."

1933, elected Prez, FDR wrote: "The real truth of the matter is, as you and I know, that a financial element in the large centers has owned the 'Government' ever since the days of Andrew Jackson."

He also wrote, "In politics, nothing happens by accident. If it happens, you can bet it was planned that way."

And his son wrote: "There are within our world perhaps only a dozen organizations which shape the courses of our various destinies as rigidly as the regularly constituted 'governments.'"

Colonel L. Fletcher Prouty, liaison officer between The Pentagon and The CIA '55-'63 said: "The Homelan is run by a 'Secret Team,' an 'inner sanctum of a new religious order' answerable only to themselves. The power of the team derives from its vast intra-governmental undercover infrastructure and its direct relationship with great private industries, mutual funds and investment houses, universities, and the news media, including foreign and domestic publishing houses . . . All true members of the team remain in the power center whether in office with the incumbent administration or out of office with the hardcore set. They simply rotate to and from official jobs and the business world or the pleasant haven of academe."

He wrote: "It is big business, big 'Government,' big money, big pressure . . . all operating in self-centered, utterly self-serving security and secrecy."

James Forrestal, the first Secretary of Defense, collected over 3,000 pages of notes for his tell-all exposé, but he unfortunately *killed himself* before getting the chance to write it.

He said: "These men are not incompetent or stupid. Consistency has never been a mark of stupidity. If they were merely stupid, they would occasionally make a mistake in our favor."

Jellyfish have a single unified organ that's both brain and stomach.

And The Family with its complex layers of security-eye-balling-security is no more sophisticated in its motives and operations than a jellyfish.

It devours *anything* within its territory.

And it *expands* its territory endlessly until some barrier stops it.

And then it pressures this barrier until this barrier shatters, eating and thinking only of eating without distinguishing between the two.

A jellyfish looks like a thrown fried egg, and The Family is like a jellyfish wrapped in the flag.

Like a cartoon billygoat, a jellyfish can digest *anything*.

Remember how cartoon billygoats ate dented tin cans and bent-up crowns, fish spines with their heads intact, and neon green nuclear sludge?

I couldn't devote my life to *charity*.

That's what The Family would want if one of us ever bolted awake, stung with that clumsy appendage, a *conscience*.

Whatever social good I *ever* did for The Barbarians, it'd only contribute to the impression of The Family as public servants.

Machiavelli invented The National Interest: *Raison d'État!*

A country no longer needs to evoke moral justifications or religious reasoning to start a war.

Its economic, military, or cultural goals are justification enough for whatever it deems necessary.

Realism.

"A mean between what conscience permits and affairs require," Jean de Silhon said.

Remember, Intimate Reader, wars don't need to be *won*. They only need to establish chaos so that no other regional power rises, like how The Homelan recently supported both sides in The Iran/Iraq War.

This is just as true for psychic wars as it is for resource wars.

The Family never pursues libel and slander charges against its critics.

They can't risk a court validating a critic's claims.

So critics are usually offered millions in hush money and if they turn that down—however much The Family *wants* to display the dissenter's head on a stake in the mall's food court—the punishments are quieter: Anonymous letters are sent to break up marriages, bank accounts are frozen, borders uncrossable, planes unboardable.

Ultimately an illusion holds social order in place.

Not force, but the *perceived threat* of force.

CHAPTER 37 Hyacinthignatzi

Arriving at some specific geoposition, eight years later or so, knowing that you're in this exact same spot, there's a *bolt* of experiential knowledge: so *that's* how a decade feels.

Like a pig sniffing the spring breeze, I hung a couple dry knuckles loosely on the rusty fence.

The cicadas blared as loud as big city traffic mid-day: the screams of all the chopped-off hands buried wrist-deep in these fields, the brittle plant-life blooming from the innumerable ground-up bones in the soil.

Up a shallow slope, the house itself appeared as just more forest wall.

My nose burned, the odd dusk air like how cat piss slashes thru the sweet smell of verdant green.

I attempted to sequence every woman I'd ever bedded, then collapse them all into a unified, singular entity.

Like a security guard strutting the library when his walkie-talkie squawks, owls returned the gate's long wail.

It was impossible to determine *where* the ice castle was its widest.

Jagged, it bulged like pillowy canyons or a cliff-face thru clouds.

Patterns inside patterns cut away to contradict the clean lines of its many doorways and windows, no two the same size or set at the same height.

Insects popcorned about, arhythmic and constant.

I felt like a dumb cow hypnotized by a powerline's hum, unable to defend my own wide back against the bites of berry bugs and fleas.

It looked like a child's cut paper design; like a primitive flying machine; like an Alaskan explorer's pre-fab lab constructed to mimic a sailor's navigational star; like a Mormon church painted in the color schemes of Pennsylvania Shaker crafts, the accrued spiritualism evident in its labor, like some desert temple for a living sky.

The shore had climbed high, waves breaking at the back of the house's lowest windows.

Absorbing me proved to be The Family's most expedient form of banishment.

Lit by the beams of my minivan, the decrepitude stunned me.

At some point that last summer, if not more recently, *someone* in The Family must've camped out there for some holiday: reptiles do need shade to cool off.

But left unattended, things do degrade quick.

Aaron moved thru the gate and up the slope across the tall lawn toward the door.

One sunflower stem thick as my thigh clung to the fence.

Its gargantuan flower had grown too heavy for its stem and, in its attempt to fortify itself upright, pulled the whole fence down.

I didn't move thru the gate but instead stepped over the fence at that point.

The grass was damp with dew.

On the porch Aaron leaned a forearm against a rickety pillar, a gesture incongruous with his Secret Service discipline.

Never before had I seen a movement of his expand so sing-song and broad.

Such a *classic* lean on a country porch made me realize that I had no idea re: Aaron.

He could just as likely have been a Manhattan kid as a Nebraskan.

I stepped up on to the porch with a long, loud creak.

"Dusty," Aaron said, and I nodded.

Inspecting the jagged angles of the porch in the headlights, my hands cast shadows that prohibited me from seeing the very spots I tried to touch.

"Sir, I have worked for The CIA and Special Forces for 35

years," Aaron whispered.

I could've been more patient, but except for mastering the art of sleeping standing up, I can confirm indubitably that it'd been at least five years since he'd applied a single one of those *special* skills, so I hissed back, "Duh, unga-bunga."

"That is *not* true, Sir."

He stood up straight and puffed his chest out. "*A lot* of what I do, Sir," he continued, "is *very* subtle work, very subtle. I would be surprised if you *did* notice it."

"Duh, unga-bunga?"

"Yes, Sir. In fact, if I am doing my job properly, it means you *won't* notice it."

The only threat to my life he had to watch was my cholesterol and I don't remember him ever *diving* across The Diner to knock an omelette out of my hands.

"Duh, unga-bunga?"

He rolled his eyes.

"Duh, unga-bunga."

He swallowed a lump in his throat.

"All I am saying, Sir, is that we can stand here all night if that's what you like. Or we can speed the fuck back home to the condo."

He gestured to the minivan.

Not exactly a *ringing* endorsement of his warrior spirit.

"My job is I go where you go. I don't *consult* with you. I follow."

I nodded. "Duh, unga-bunga?"

Aaron threw his hands in the air. "Sir, I say it's late . . . and . . ."

"Duh, unga-bunga," I said.

From the porch I stretched down to glance my fingertips along the surface of the pooling water, and remembered Marco Polo as a boy, the waves breaking high against my chest, bald and taut.

A Mountain Dew bottle had been bludgeoned into the ornate grates of the old iron door.

Used as an ashtray repeatedly, the syrupy soda spittle made the ashes into a gunky gelatin.

As boys, we wore our magnets everywhere on the grounds.

Officially, 11 bedrooms, six sitting rooms, a couple offices, a den, a library, a dining room, a big kitchen, a little kitchen, and various patios and decks all together made up the central house.

Attached to this main house, a six-car garage made it look even bigger.

And a pool area, and, even with a private nine-hole golf course, the overgrown tennis court came to be used primarily as a putting green.

There was the dock, the boathouse, and a few small guesthouses that looked like troll cottages.

That's *Officially*.

Gravity Anomaly Maps betrayed the cavities underground.

CHAPTER 38 Old Obediah and His Cousins

Entering the house, the air was thick.

The mice didn't bother scuttling off.

Still water in the kitchen sink stank rank.

Every surface a little sticky like someone had brushed a thin coat of syrup over everything.

In my immediate census of insect species, I preferred the ones with exoskeletons, complex and shiny, tiny suits of armor.

In the mucked-up glass of the chandelier, big as a small car, my reflection flipped over and reversed, opening and repeating *endlessly* like a child's run of cut paper dolls.

I hollered up into it, only to hear the bounce: "WOOP–WOOp–WOop–Woop–woop–woo–wo . . ."

Lamps bolted to the walls extended out like streetlights with keys intended to give the impression of their mechanical necessity, but there were normal light switches.

Stacked wooly mammoth husks filled the first bathtub I came upon.

Testing its faucet, bugs and squadrons of more bugs climbed up the drain, undeterred by the cold stream.

Built on Old Obadiah Newcomb's land, Hyacinthignatzi had been handed down thru a distant line of cousins, cousins I knew by reputation, always a punchline.

These cousins were reclusive, backwards yokels, cross-eyed and double-jointed, muttering in an accent understandable only to each other.

They died off about 20 years ago, their strain of The Bloodline coming to an abrupt dead end.

And though they often bragged that their melatonin and serotonin harvested from menstrual blood was the same anti-aging compound that Dracula himself swore by, those last two brothers lived out their bachelored days bearded in crumpled tuxedos, their toenails far too long for shoes, with wads of each other's semen clumped up in each other's hair.

Still, The Family found inbreeding jokes a little less funny than your common oligarch does, ever since My Little Brother's death.

The estate landed in Old Obediah's hands in the late-19th Century and he built the ice castle around '03.

Then he passed it on to his daughter and her husband, Grandfather.

Most often it's been the site of private gatherings both small and large, holidays or hosting dignitaries for informal off-the-record meetings.

I always loved to break away for an hour to ponder the bent feathers and crumbling shells of the rocky shores.

That's the experience of severe beauty: how to measure it.

But I'd never been there alone before.

Grandfather and Grandmother—Old Obediah's daughter—never did live there, but they let Old Obediah's cousins stay as a condition of the inheritance.

These two never stepped foot off the grounds.

We'd gawk at those cackling skeletons.

It hurt my young bones just to glimpse their dandruff and scratch.

One wing of the house was surrendered to them and we tolerated their howls like mournful coyotes impersonating sirens.

The Family often joked that these old cousins were the only *real proof* that I had one ounce of Bloodline in me and I do bump along like a crippled bear same as they did.

You'd think it odd that they kept a corpse on ice.

Then you'd see it blink.

Old Obediah himself was like an *opposite* Noah: his life's goal was to kill one of every known species.

Various furs and bones still might explode from any door

one opened.

Odd taxidermy crammed up narrow staircases, rare species *in-between* species, like how a parsnip is both a carrot and a potato.

But Obediah's cousins lacked his nuance.

They'd smash the pelvises of dogs into the forest floor with sledgehammers just to watch the dog's front legs contort and laugh with mad glee at its howls.

They had contests: how many throws it took each of them to explode a kitten against a wall.

They pulled guns on each other daily, their warning shots wrecking every ceiling in their wing.

Carpentry and spackling kept the groundskeepers busy, the insides of their water buckets stained red.

Well after The Civil Rights Movement, Obediah's cousins continued to prefer the *old traditions* with their Help.

And as a boy, I once came upon an older man I'd never seen before tied to a tree, stripped naked, one of his legs skillfully skinned from the knee down.

A raccoon nibbled his shin.

I threw stones until that audacious raccoon sauntered off, but the man insisted it'd be better if I didn't untie him.

CHAPTER 39 The Warren Commission

The Warren Commission consisted entirely of conservative insiders that despised King Arthur, all chums of L-BJ and Nxn, not *real* criminal investigators.

Still, the conviction and gut-shot of Ozzy, along with The Warren Commission certifying him as the lone gunman, fabricated closure for The Barbarians.

So many strange bustlings embroiled Ozzy in the 18 months leading up to 11/22/63, investigators found his path tricky to trail.

His character became *so* convoluted, he could stick to *any* theory, and sticking to any theory serves to confirm none.

In Moscow he theatrically visited The Homelan embassy to renounce his citizenship.

Well aware that The Reds recorded him, he offered to gift them radar secrets.

Compared to the underworld scumbags Ozzy hung around with in New Orleans, GDM was positively *respectable* company.

And most oddly, someone impersonating Ozzy popped up in Mexico in Sept '63 to visit both the Cuban and Red embassies.

By six weeks before 11/22/63, there were obviously only two potential parade routes.

Any insider could *easily* have placed Ozzy in Brrrd's depository.

Whether he was actually *responsible* for King Arthur's very public skull chipping or he was framed, clearly Ozzy was gently shepherded to his destiny, likely without ever knowing *who* he really worked for.

The Warren Commission's McCloy served as Prez of The World Bank, The Homelan's High Commissioner to Germany, The Chairman of Chase Manhattan Bank, Chairman of The CFR, and a member of The Wise Men.

And Ruckafella kept him *pinned* under his thumb.

The Warren Commission went to Dallas and set up offices in The Republic National Bank Building, a hub of the anti-King Arthur aristocracy.

Pops's business, a few corporations and law firms allied with The CIA, and GDM all had offices in the building.

GDM testified to The Warren Commission.

And they concluded that he was a "highly individualistic person with varied interests," basically meaning that The Warren Commission decreed GDM to be officially *eccentric*.

The fact that GDM was neither the first nor last person to spend time with Ozzy between Minsk and 11/22/63 went a long way in The Commission's mind in determining that GDM wasn't part of the plot.

And GDM was in Haiti that day.

Right after 11/22/63, GDM visited NYC and Capital City to meet with CIA and military officials including L-BJ's aide and Divine.

I don't know much re: Jack Ruby.

I know he worked for Congressman Nxn in '47, that big year that the UFO crashed in Roswell; Crowley died; The Cold War began; The House UnHomelan Activities Committee got aggressive; The Dead Sea Scrolls were discovered; and The CIA was founded.

I watched a made-for-ze Tube movie in '78, *Ruby and Ozzy*, but it only dramatized the testimonies of The Warren Commission.

Michael Lerner played Ruby.

No one knows his name, but he'd look familiar to you as a guest star on *MASH*, *The Brady Bunch*, *The Odd Couple*, *Rockford Files*.

He was also in another made-for-ze Tube movie re: 11/22/63 playing King Arthur's Press Secretary, Salinger.

And within a few years, both King Arthur and RKF were dead, all threats of their dynasty averted.

And a dozen years later, The Family's dynasty *blooms*.

CHAPTER 40 Slithering Thru the Maze

SkullnBones have either established or penetrated *every* significant research, policy, and opinion-making organization in The Homelan.

At Yale, its members are nicknamed "spooks," same as CIA agents.

Bonesmen are required to leave the room if anyone mentions SkullnBones.

Of course, SkullnBones is just the recruiting arm for the larger network.

And like *sly* Ulysses's eminent tiptoe past the cyclops, the *most powerful* groups remain nameless so that it's impossible to prove they even exist.

Every CIA Director *ever* has been a CFR member.

CFR protects CIA: CIA protects CFR.

CFR, The TriC, Bilderberg: none of them receive any "Government" funding.

They're all financed by the same names you'll find all over your household appliances, the food in your fridge, and the beauty supplies you rub into your skin.

The CIA-sponsored Bilderberg was founded to steer the evolving international order with a focus on "reeducation," for the sake of long-term global planning.

Royalty, Media, and Finance mingle sans fear of scrutiny at their annual meetings, everything off the record.

Extremisms make The Barbarians anxious, so these groups all represent themselves as moderate.

When *The Wall Street Journal* criticized The TriC in '80, for example, Ruckafella responded: "Far from being a coterie of international conspirators with designs on covertly ruling the world, The TriC is, in reality, a group of concerned citizens interested in fostering greater understanding and cooperation among international allies . . ."

But Admiral Chester Ward, former Judge Advocate General of The Homelan Navy, and longtime CFR member said: "The CFR, as such, does not write the platforms of both political parties or select their respective presidential candidates, or control Homelan defense policy or foreign policies. But CFR members, as individuals, acting in concert with other CFR members, do."

Initiates take blood oaths, agreeing to punishments if they reveal any secrets: a slashed throat, your tongue torn out at the root, burying you alive, your children.

Operating covertly to guarantee they're impervious to The Barbarian's occasional outrage, they manipulate both sides of a conflict to ensure their preferred outcome.

One side demands more than they really want.

The "other side" makes a show of indignation, and then they compromise, and balance is maintained.

Hegel conceptualized it as Thesis + Antithesis = Synthesis.

Create a problem so that the solution presented achieves your ends.

SkullnBones' *only* agenda is to plant members into positions of power so that these members can hire other members into positions of power.

No creed to spread, no specific mission, simply big appetites to protect.

Luce, the founder of *Time-Life,* was renowned in his day as "the most influential private citizen in The Homelan."

And Jackson, The Vice Prez of Time Inc. from '31-'64, who'd helped CIA Director Smith recruit the first Bilderbergers, served under Eisenhower as "special consultant on psychological warfare."

Jackson was also interested in movies.

He arranged for *Life* magazine to buy the Z'puda's famous film and keep it from being seen.

And it's literally *not possible* to trace corporate ownership and power structures.

The slithering between private and governmental appointments *can't* be traced thru stockholdings, regulatory agencies, or public decisions.

It's a *maze* of tacit understandings and handshake contracts, solidified in locker rooms, officers' messes, faculty clubs, embassy conference rooms, garden parties, squash courts, and board rooms.

Anyone that *does try* to detangle this gets hounded, hunted down, tortured, and destroyed.

CHAPTER 41 Making Myself at Home in The Dream War

Big pipes, rickety, ran jagged across the low ceiling.

Cramped unlivable with a small table jammed between a water heater awk in the middle of the room and a wall, the kitchen was like the engine room of a run-down, dusty spaceship.

Wide floorboards tilted all topsy-turvy like a pirate ship's deck stressed in a storm.

All the wood, metal, and glass made the plastic kitchenware and the shiny frame of a folded up futon appear alien.

A locked door had no handle but wadded up newspapers filled the hole.

Large heating lights, a humidifier, child-sized handcuffs.

Aaron appeared giant in a tiny room, the top of the closet door reaching below his chest.

On a leather radio, I tuned in an old country station.

The music felt correct, contemporary to our setting.

A bird's nest had exploded in the freezer.

The Family loved muscly cuts of white fish, thick sauces on everything.

As a boy, my *favourite* was the anteater steaks and their chef from the Guangdong province.

Standing around a corner, we'd watch the anteater waggle in its cage.

The chef would enter, chest puffed out, not deigning to acknowledge us and never saying a single syllable before hammering the terrified beast unconscious.

He'd cut its throat and drain its blood with a ballerina's grace.

Boiling it to remove the scales, he'd finally speak, explaining how his wife collected them for quilts.

The blood broth had *astonishing* medicinal qualities.

I never felt so sharpened.

Aaron hummed the theme to *Man of La Mancha* with
Sophia Loren and Peter O'Toole while I heated up a can of
soup.

Where could I *possibly* order a pizza from?
Back among The Barbarians, I'd developed an instinctual
voodoo to cope with leftovers, everything from egg-rolls
made better with melted cheddar to just boiling water.
The trick is to imagine you're cooking for Sophia Loren.
And she's *beaming* and tossing her hair.
A green old sandwich and a muddy sock sat in the drawer
next to the stove.
Maybe Aaron knew how to decode that packet Roddy
had given me, but when I asked, he stifled a chuckle and
pretended to clear his throat.
Sophia Loren might enjoy a can of soup.

The Personality flashed on ze muted Tube, looking as if
he'd driven overnight, crackling with gas station coffee.
When dream logic failed to crack the packet's code, I
stuffed the crumpled pages down into the garbage disposal,
choking it to a halt.
The buzz of ze muted Tube harmonized with the growling
rev of the garbage disposal's thwarted motor.

Where I expected the old cousins' wing to be, it was not.
Between two lamps, I balanced my shadow in yellow
lamplight.
A gas heater the size of a big trunk, big enough to fit a
magician in with his wrists handcuffed to his ankles, heated
that entire wing.
And another big screen Tube, the exact same size as the

heater, looked awk set down in that same room, mirroring it perpendicular.

Flipping back and forth between Le 24-Hour-News Channel and Le 24-Hour-Sports Channel, I hit *Record*.

I'd fast forward, rewind, hit *Record* again.

And again.

A breakaway slam-dunk interrupted an aerial survey of tornado damage.

A slo-mo replay of a blocked shot reflected off *eleccion* soothsaying.

A man-on-the-street eyewitness pontificated about a celebratory sideline dance.

Recall, Keen Reader, that spectral evidence was admissible at those long-ago witch trials in The New Jerusalem.

Such evidence rendered normal systems of defense useless.

Sensitive issues are still mostly handled thru the channels most difficult to even prove the *existence* of.

That's the *real* backchannels and *back rooms of* political dealings.

History overflows with agents unknowingly responding to directives given in dreams.

Effeminate Ozzy, shaken by Marine-hazing while stationed in Japan, hanging out at The Bluebird Cafe, Operation Bluebird *coincidentally* the name of the precursor to the MKUltra Program.

Rudolf Hess parachuted unannounced into the estate of Duke Hamilton to broker a peace deal between The UK and Germany, explaining that he'd been commanded to do so in a dream.

Pops appeared to me in a dream within weeks of me moving into my condo.

He said, "OK, if you *insist* on living out here among The Barbarians, you know the consequences."

Those dream psy-ops of The Family that'd pinned down *countless* generations of The Barbarians were suddenly aimed at me.

In my dream, The Actor appeared and stared into my eyes.

No one was immune to the spell that his *appearance* of power cast.

We stood in his Oval, and up in the rafters, all the scaffolds, lighting, cameras, and sound equipment.

Staging the background of a dream requires surprising amounts of crumpled gauze.

And recalling this dream made me remember My Little Brother, his erector set exoskeleton like a full-body retainer, propping up his head too big and heavy.

He passed his days building dioramas of the estate perfectly scaled for lizards to live in.

The true master thespian of us all, he pretended to never notice when any visitor was struck breathless at the sight of him.

Four large carpets defined distinct spaces in the library.

My Mother George Washington chose literacy when she needed a public cause and filled Hyacinthignatzi with books for photo ops.

Prior to that, The Family had one unanimous and unofficial favourite book, *The Fart Book*.

I picked up Twain's *Mysterious Stranger,* frayed along its edges and beaten soft. Its cover image of a classic hermit wizard with a long white beard and pointy hat carrying a lantern sent a rush of adolescent mystery crashing thru me.

While my brothers read Machiavelli and Ayn Rand, this was my favourite book as a boy.

I read it over and over and over, never quite sure what it meant.

Huck Finn famously faced the moral dilemma of social

injustice, but *Mysterious Stranger* more ambitiously and obliquely, impossibly even, questions whether ethics are instinctual.

I carried *Mysterious Stranger* along with me, fearing it'd crumble if I opened it.

The halls revolved and unfolded around me quaqua-versal.

I think I paced, but maybe treadmilled, as the halls scraped beneath my feet.

The flooded yard there, the minivan parked there, I gave up on stepping outside to reorient myself.

Entering back thru the same door, I'd always step into a different hall than the one that I'd stepped out of.

I didn't notice exactly when I lost track of Aaron.

Families are like systems of gutters set up all wrong.

Channeled thru complex piping, thoughts drain into feelings and feelings drain into thoughts, and water damming weird spills over.

Hyacinthignatzi's *amazing* giant drain pipe was shaped like a dragon.

Was Aaron's lean on the porch the night we arrived a country lean or a city lean?

Stocked as all the closets were, the jerseys and shorts I prefer could not be found.

All the slacks cinched against my gut and held folds of flesh in a breathless stress position as I yanked up on the zipper.

Pondering the pliable limits of my own pudge, psychologically and philosophically, how could I *ever again* feel like the Division A state football champion celebrating The Renaissance; The Birth of Venus in shoulder pads calling a flea-flicker play after play; Myth, History, and the invention of Perspective driving down the field, even faking a punt?

What *presumption* to *enter* the rich and complex interior of another dimly sentient blob.

Pressing my nose to the glass, a dead crab had been trapped between layers of a window.

Suffocated or overheated, dropped at a party, or the shore had climbed that tall in a storm?

O'Malley attributes his flat nose to a boyhood of pressing it against bakery windows.

Hiking the halls of my hideout, or my trap, my temple, or my sanitarium, the foggy maze of my own perception. . .

A swath of cut carpet from Honest Abe's boyhood bedroom, a splinter of Genghis Khan's jawbone; *nothing* could replace my back scratcher.

Catching dust drifting thru dusk-light was a concentrated task, felt like attempting to catch Lot's vaporized wife.

But simple compared to accepting your *self,* common as a hammer or an artichoke heart, pressing against the limits of your self-awareness like Alan Arkin in *Catch-22*.

CHAPTER 42 Enter *River's Edge*

I held my breath, until, again, *yes*, a howl cracked the night, pulverizing everything decent and good.

I kneeled on a bed, the tip of my nose cold against a cold window pane.

I did *not* like the look of my own face reflected, registering the shock of what appeared before me.

Below the window, sauntering toward the house: *Locals*.

I can only report to you, Purposeful Reader, journalistically, fair'nbalanced as I can, sans hyperbole or descriptor, fleeced of extrapolation, cuz what I saw, I, too, still cannot believe.

There, in the flooded yard of Hyacinthignatzi, I saw *River's Edge*.

My *favourite movie ever,* that *perfect* melodrama, like *Rebel Without a Cause* with thrash music, *River's Edge* played out before my eyes.

Sitting beside Jamie's naked corpse, the big guy, John aka Samson, was howling by the river's edge, *guttural* howls.

Jamie, *the corpse* I see when I think "corpse," right there in front of me.

Little Timmy, 12 years old, played out a parallel and miniature version of John's scene.

Little Timmy threw his sister's doll off a bridge above John aka Samson bellowing and smoking on the bank below.

Little Timmy and John aka Samson had the same big jowls, like brothers.

I watched Little Timmy watch John aka Samson.

The first lines of dialogue after all this howling was John aka Samson's conflict, trying to buy beer.

The Pizza Delivery Guy from *Fast Times at Ridgemont High* demands ID.

I should've reread *The Stranger,* instead of *Mysterious Stranger.*

Keanu gets introduced defending his little sister, whose doll Little Timmy has thrown off the bridge.

Keanu is Little Timmy's older brother.

They wear the same denim vests, Keanu's over leather and Little Timmy's over a sweatshirt.

Crispin's first line is: "Hurry Your Ass Up."

How to *possibly* understand his acting style?

We see Feck's blowup doll before we see him, Feck, Dennis Hopper.

There's the howl of bad saxophone.

Feck, Dennis Hopper, has one leg, some near-rhyme with the blowup doll.

Feck, Dennis Hopper says, "Women are evil. I killed a woman once."

"You're my friend?" he says twice, first to Crispin, then to the blowup doll.

Then he puts his empty gun to his own head.

Their first conversation as a big group is a classic teenage runaway thing: one kid mentions *Easy Rider* right after Feck, Dennis Hopper's appearance.

Ione is beautiful.

John aka Samson is totally open with everyone: "I killed her."

Keanu's jacket has a peace-sign over a skull.

"Why?"

"She was talking shit."

They talk re: Portland like a utopian escape.

That music when they walk away from her body, after they all go to gawk at her body.

"It's like a movie, testing loyalty against all odds."

Their social studies class is about subculture.

Their teacher talks about the potential power of youth movements, knocking pigs on their asses—*meaning* in the madness.

A third of the movie passed before I snapped out of my trance.

I never won't watch it when it's on.

I could go downstairs, introduce myself and crack open some beers, but crashing into their plot could throw them off-course.

Did they *know* they were in a movie?

Shattering those boundaries might provoke retaliation, and, especially John aka Samson, Crispin, and Feck, Dennis Hopper, these were not stable guys.

I turned from the scene outside my window.

Every whistle of breath thru my nose felt like the first faint alarm of my doors smashing in; every shade of perpetual dusk, the shadows of intruders moving in thru the window.

My clothes hung next to the bed on hooks looked as if I'd been zapped into obliteration—atomized à la Lot's Wife—and my clothes remained hanging in the air a split second before dropping into a pile.

Panic confounds cause and effect like I can't say if I can't *breathe* cuz I can't breathe or if I can't breathe cuz I can't *breathe*.

Those people—locals, *River's Edge*—had stormed *the grounds*.

CHAPTER 43 Diana Herself on the Phone

The phone was sticky against my ear.

Really I pined to call The Other Greek Place and ask That Mike to hold the phone up to *My Diana* in her patriotic bikini, sweaty beer in hand, in perfect profile, silhouetted by the moon low behind her, hanging on that flimsy closet door.

But it made me sick to imagine That Mike eavesdropping.

And I never knew if she wouldn't vaporize upon being directly addressed.

I looked out over the prairie, my ridiculous *self* reflected expansive on the cracked glass patio doors, the dark grounds rolling and spread out under my reflection, the kitchen bright behind me.

Those stone walls that cut across those fields older than The Homelan.

Diana Herself's answering machine picked up, a classic monster movie clip, a villain with a sinister voice low in his throat *delighted* by the pleas of a young woman, corny organ music swelling ominous.

Beep.

I did my impression of Pops.

The only acknowledgment of The Family between us, she always found it hysterical.

I said I'd target her house with satellite missiles if she didn't call me back.

But lingering, reconsidering my reflection—my ridiculous *self* matrix-bound—my charade fizzled.

I told her it was me.

I told her I was thinking of her, calling to talk, no big deal.

I knew she was busy.

Call back whenever she had the chance.

She wouldn't have the number at Hyacinthignatzi, and she'd know something was up, just that I called at all without a Super Bowl potluck to organize.

I pulled long on my cigarette.

And she picked up, out of breath and hurried, she said, "Hello, hello."

I muted the game flashing behind me on ze big screen Tube as a diving save replayed in slow-motion reflected across the cracked patio doors.

I flinched touching the tacky receiver back to my good ear, then cringed holding it there.

I said "Duh, unga-bunga."

She sighed.

I dabbed out my cigarette in a baby-skull ashtray.

The drawn-out photosynthesis of our shared history, so perfect when immersed in it, proved difficult to dip back into.

And in that small pause, each waiting for the other to speak, she detonated into tears.

I swiveled, my bare feet sticky on the kitchen tile, and lit another cigarette.

"Duh, unga-bunga."

"Yeh, I do."

"Duh, unga-bunga."

"Pfft," she chuckled. "Yeh."

"Duh, unga-bunga?"

"Oh," she punched thru her pauses with emphatic exhales. "Just stupid power stuff at work. *Stress.* My daughter's gone thru my coffee can and took like more than half my tips for the week."

I nodded.

"I don't know how she expected me to not notice."

"Duh, unga-bunga?"

"It's not the money. I don't care."

"Duh, unga-bunga."

"No, it's not that. I mean that's nice of you to offer, thank you, but I don't want your money."

"Duh, unga-bunga."

"No, for real thank you, but no. I just mean, if she's stealing from me again, that means I have to worry about other stuff."

"Duh, unga-bunga."

"Yeh. And I just thought—I mean, I *knew*, and I *hoped*—you know?"

"Duh, unga-bunga."

I drew out the syllables to their fullest expansions, testifying to the depths of my empathy.

Pulling the phone cord back around what I thought to be the same corner, I stepped into *another* living room instead.

I thought to follow my smoke back to the other room, but it'd dissipated.

With a fluttering snore, Aaron slept sitting up in a tiny recliner.

I couldn't guess how many days it'd been since I'd seen him.

He farted loudly, bolted awake and gasped.

He looked to me to help him locate the emergency.

I rolled my eyes and motioned to the phone.

He gestured an apology and closed his eyes again.

I asked, "Duh, unga-bunga?"

"What?" she said.

"Duh, unga-bunga."

"You called me. It's not even 6 a.m. Obviously I'm up for work. So why are *you* calling *me* so early?"

"Duh, unga-bunga?"

"No. I was up."

Looking out over the prairie, I took a long slow swallow of my mudslide, scrutinizing my reflection as I did so.

Local legend says they drew the borders of these counties according to the clouds; where the rush of light comes barreling down, they called it a new county.

"So do you have a *private kingdom* now? I've read about your brother."

Neither of us said anything for long enough to count to 10.

Count to 10, Faithful Reader.

"Or I could come visit you?" she said. "I mean, if you

want."

I sighed, stood up, and walked back to the kitchen, the phone cord slackening as I approached its dock.

"Duh, unga-bunga," I said finally.

She inhaled deeply, said, "Mm-hmm."

CHAPTER 44 The Dusty Bunker Does Exist

I plugged in an extension cord and grabbed a lamp from the next room and, carrying it like a torch, I stepped down into the dark staircase.

It smelled sweet, how rain on wood smells like cinnamon.

The dimensions of rooms-*inside*-rooms, it's always slippery.

The silence made the margin of error inside my mushy ear audible, like a chorus of chirping frogs.

But after only a few steps, my plugged-in torch pulled taut.

The struggle to sleep is the struggle of convincing the mind to submit to the body.

That dark stairway hidden in the back of that pantry must've been the entrance to that space that, until then, I'd never known for sure actually *existed.*

And when I considered that it *may* exist, I never knew for sure that it was there, in that shape-shifting, decrepit old spaceship ice castle.

The dusty bunker, the location of the emergency hide-and-seeks of my youth.

Like a reptile hides under human skin, like The Vice hides at dusk, the entrance to the bunker was hidden in the back of that pantry, behind the stacks of innumerable soup cans.

CHAPTER 45 Rectify the Language

It's Genesis 1:26—God gives the dimly sentient blobs dominion over all creation.

And so too, The Family has dominion over all the dimly sentient blobs, cultivating scapegoats and reffing beauty pageants.

A utopian rupture similar to The '60s, The Great Awakening of the early 19th century was a *culture-wide* madness, revolutionary and romantic, putting society itself up for grabs.

It was a split between those that had *emotional* conversion experiences, aka *New Light* believers, and those that had experiences of religious awakening motivated by reason, *Old Light* advocates.

Any conversion experience is *certainly* emotional and *unarguably* contains a shift of reason.

So was the distinction between Old Light believers and New Light believers simply a matter of cause versus effect?

Matthew 11:27: "No one knows the Son except the Father, and no one knows the Father except the Son and those to whom the Son chooses to reveal him."

Meaning: these teachings are complex and the channels to understanding them are patrolled by The Chosen and *you* don't get it cuz *you* aren't among The Chosen.

And if you *are* among The Chosen, you're exempted from common moral reasoning cuz John 15:3: "You are already clean."

The New Testament conceals an exposition on the *regeneration* of the human spirit, the means of elevating consciousness one degree at a time up the 33 vertebrae of the spinal column.

"Leper" and "Blind" represent what we now call The Barbarians.

Early Christians lived like Reds.

In the first century Christians split into two big camps: who was the *real* messiah, Jesus or John The Baptist?

Political factors determined which camp flourished.

In the ancient past, the gods walked with men and left the keys to their wisdom with the *illuminated* chosen.

They ordained the anointed and appointed those worthy to mediate between themselves—the gods—and The Blind and Leprous Barbarians, who hadn't developed *eyes to see.*

Hidden knowledge *remains* hidden.

What's known to The Barbarians of one era gets hidden *more deeply* in the next era, control gripping down like a vice.

And knowledge gets lost.

The Library of Alexandria was built in the third century BC, long before the printing press, and only a few copies of any one book existed, all copied by hand by monks.

The partial or complete destruction of The Library of Alexandria happened on four occasions: Julius Caesar's men set it on fire in The Alexandrian War of 48 BC; the attack of Aurelian in the third century AD; the decree of Theophilus in 391 AD; and the Muslim conquest of 642 AD.

Religious crusades have historically made a *great* cover for Capital-ism.

Once empire is established, who cares what covert *means* established it?

God wants his followers to be rich, and *anything* that restricts that intrudes on *Freedom;* Freedom meaning the freedom to *exploit* others.

Two gospels say that John The Baptist baptized Jesus, but Luke said John The Baptist was in jail then; Matthew and Luke give different accounts of Jesus's birth; Exodus 20, Exodus 34, and Deuteronomy 5 all have different versions of The 10 Commandments.

These ultimately superficial contradictions still create the need for interpretation.

Of *greater consequence,* however: is God vengeful or forgiving?

He'll attack you with locusts unprovoked and willy-nilly insist that you slaughter your firstborn.

But he'll also blot out your transgressions and make your scarlet sins white as snow if you ask politely?

Unsure how to resolve the paradoxes and nuances of *His* all-holy mood-swings, The Barbarians cede power to those men that claim the power of correct interpretation.

People in crisis are susceptible: mid-divorce; lost your job; startled by the grief of death; dipsomaniacs; cokers at dawn, cutters at dusk; can't shake the ghost of Uncle's touch and scent every time someone sits close enough to bump thighs.

With its exaggerated promises and tricks of the light, conversion is seduction.

The primary text of The Religious Right, *The Institutes of Biblical Law,* written by R.J. Rushdoony in '73, teaches that biblical law should replace the secular legal code and education and social welfare should be handed over to the churches.

Murder, rape, incest, kidnapping, adultery, blasphemy, homosexuality, astrology, striking a parent, and any women who fuck with The Act of Love before marriage all merit the death penalty.

Rushdoony's literal reading of The Bible believes that slavery should be reinstated, "deformed" individuals can't be priests, and women should have no legal rights.

Leviticus 21:17-21: Everything menstruating women touch is unclean.

Exodus 21:7-11: Men can sell their daughters into sexual bondage.

Reading The Bible from certain angles can illuminate philosophy, art, literature, poetry, and music, expanding your world.

But, of course, that's not the politically expedient reading of *Present Circumstances*.

39% of The Barbarians believe in the looming mayhem and generalized cruelty of Le Grand Finale *A-poc-a-lypse:* monsters with scorpion tails guard the borders of their *Weltanschauung*.

Choirs roar rousing Christian hymns while pictures of Homelan troops battling in far-off lands flash across huge screens; prayers somberly honor men in uniform; *gigante* flags have crosses superimposed on them; The Founding Fathers kneel, swords by their sides, praying to a Jesus with glistening six-pack abs.

Like a hermit crab, The Family took Saint Orwell's play-book and stealthily moved into common language, inverting words.

Words like "truth," "death," "life," and "love" no longer mean what they mean to the uninitiated.

"Wisdom" means obedience to a belief system.

"Liberty" is defined as the extent to which you obey Church Law.

Confucius stated the first thing *he'd* do if *he* was the head of state is he'd *rectify the language*.

CHAPTER 46 Pops Ascending

In '66 Pops finally won a seat in The House of Representatives, and he immediately joined The House Ways and Means Committee, writing tax laws including The Oil Depletion Allowance.

No other freshman had gotten on that committee in over six decades.

But Grandfather cajoled the committee chairman, minority leader Fxord.

You remember Fxord: Warren Commission member, future Vice Prez and Prez sans *eleccion* to either office.

In '67, the day after Christmas, Pops traveled to Indochina with Divine.

The Phoenix Program began at the same time as their visit.

Rape with eels, snakes, and hard objects; electrocution to the genitals and tongue; tapping 6-inch dowels into your ear until it penetrated your brain: The Phoenix Program did *not* lack imagination.

Pops's Cuban exile chum was a known organizer of The Phoenix Program.

By '72 they'd assassinated at least 20,000 "suspected Viet Cong," maybe 40,000.

Pops and Divine got out of there just in time.

Three weeks later The Tet Offensive began.

But eighteen months in office, Pops had already grown restless with his position's limited powers.

So he and Grandfather teamed up to persuade Nxn to make Pops his running mate in '68.

Within days, Nxn got letters from 35 of The Party's most important members imploring him to do so.

Nxn was only 39 years old when Eisenhower named him to be his Vice Prez, and he significantly changed the role of

the office, taking on critical foreign and domestic issues, so
he took the position seriously.

Though enamored by Pops's corporate clout, he chose
someone else.

But Nxn's first month in office he did set his daughter up
on a date with Junior, even sending a plane from Capital
City to Georgia to pick Junior up.

In '67 Pops was a TX State Representative and L-BJ sent
him a birthday note.

The next year L-BJ's decision not to run made room for
Nxn and Nxn's consistent sponsorship of Pops's escalation
to power.

Pops left Nxn's inauguration party to accompany L-BJ to
the airport, an uncommon move for a State Representative
from the other Party.

L-BJ returned to his TX ranch and suffered severe depression.

His lawyers paid a psychologist $1,000,000 to guarantee
that L-BJ didn't talk.

And he soon hosted Pops as a guest at his ranch.

In '70 Pops left his House seat to run for Senate and Nxn
made Pops a promise that if he lost, Nxn would appoint him
a high post in his administration, Head of Small Business
Administration or something bereft of specific duties.

Pops lost and was devastated.

But very quickly Nxn began to catapult Pops forward,
often over better-qualified candidates.

Nxn named Pops ambassador to The UN.

Grandfather had helped the populist Nxn early in his career, and, in turn, Nxn helped position The Family dynasty.

But the higher Nxn ascended, the more he begrudged his
handlers.

He continued to answer to them assiduously, but his anger festered.

He was frustrated re: the extent to which he was beholden.

The Family's oil associates fared *far better* than *any* other group in Nxn's first term.

It was a *cabal* of The Family's camp.

But Nxn also often backed conservative members of The Other Party, and this made The Family livid.

In a letter to Nxn's treasury secretary, Pops wrote, "I was also appreciative of your telling how I bled and died for the oil industry."

CHAPTER 47 My Five Senses and My Memory Persist

A little bug trekked epic across a glass shower door.

How *staggering* the perspective of that vast transparent landscape.

Given its 12-hour lifespan, what a fate to invest a full *half* of one's adulthood in crossing a crystalline surface to approach a vertical horizon line.

Did it know it could fly?

Aaron, *compelled* to demonstrate his *ninja-like* foraging spirit, like a deer's pounce on a berry, wandered the halls more like a Christmas ghost from a Dickens movie, dragging chains down the long, resonant halls.

But that *whoop* at the moon was *not* him.

Stepping lightly, the floor creaked, and I moved quick.

The door groaned open like a voice thru its own skull.

The moon hung large and dim in perpetual dusk.

Yonder comes *more dusk*, like thick cheese down a throat.

Diana means moon.

My days, no longer crushed into modular particulars, no longer neatly severed by units of sleep, *smeared.*

Drifting shaky thru a singular, shapeless, and unmeasurable *betweenness*, only my dread of the reappearance of *River's Edge* grounded me.

My five senses and my memories *persisted* in conspiring to create this *profound* illusion of subjectivity, like a cloud trapped in a box.

The Barbarians would never *believe* how grubby and overrun by bugs big houses get.

Like how skin layers; the slippage that meat allows bone; the flashing static of dandruff and scratch; I moped the fractal wings, mirror-image rooms, and architectural near-rhymes, scooting old trunks and chimera skeletons aside to swat at bundles of cobwebs and mice turds.

Sometimes I heard far-off stomping, the clang of armor, and Roy Orbison singing.

Aaron must've heard my scrape and moan from afar same as I heard him.

Moving thru slumbering steel appliances, wooden bowls, and severe-looking chopping devices coated in syrup and stuck with fuzz, I steeled my nerves in anticipation of a cat leaping out like in *Alien*.

CHAPTER 48 The Invitation

Diana Herself didn't mention confronting her daughter re: the money missing from her coffee can, and I didn't ask.

She'd picked up all the extra hours she could at The Diner, and, disoriented with over-extension, felt awake inside a dream same as I did.

Every time the bell above the door jingled, she hoped Kris Kristofferson had come to sweep her off her achy feet.

Instead, a recently divorced stand-up comedian, a regular at The Diner, had pushed a signed headshot on her for The Diner's Wall of Fame.

He'd sat brooding about performing his one-man show to an empty room every night, so on her birthday Diana Herself decided to wrangle a few of her friends to go and surprise him.

She smiled along best she could for 20 minutes, while her friends rolled their eyes, until the recently divorced stand-up comedian started riffing on a "lopsided" waitress.

I sighed and stood up and stretched.

"One side of her body hangs a foot lower than the other side," he chuckled, affecting an exaggerated stance.

"When she takes my order, she stands at an angle like she's hiding it."

He spun in place.

Me and her listened to each other sigh.

"When I walk out and she waves thanks, she spins so the same side remains facing me. I don't think she even knows she's doing it."

She paused a long time.

I tapped my ash in the sink and took in my jagged reflection on the cracked patio door.

"It's like watching a competition, how many different angles can she spin and keep it hidden," he said, squirming.

Her story took long enough to tell, I had to clear my throat to speak but had no idea what to say.

"Duh, unga-bunga" I said.

The Family had always expected I'd drag them into the

scandal of a *left-handed* marriage, so I poured myself a mudslide and invited her, insisted, *please quit your job, come join me.*

Even expecting it to feel long, the drive back to the main gate felt longer than I'd expected.

After the woods near the house, thru all the dry brush of the open prairie, I imagined *River's Edge* like land-pirates charging over the shallow slopes, howling with spears raised overhead and muskets.

I hit the brakes hard.

The guard held a bright light to my window, blinding me.

"Ex*cuse* me," he barked with a squealing twang. "Ex*cuse* me."

I held the back of my hand up to my eyes.

He tapped his flashlight against the window.

He suffered that specific dry skin of having cracked pecan shells with nails that need cutting.

"Ex*cuse* me, Mr. VW Van, you *cannot* be out here. This is protected wildlife *ecosystem* land here, Sir. I don't know where you *think* you're going. You must be lost, but you *cannot* be here."

I lowered the window and told him my name and he lowered the flashlight.

He leaned close to study my face, his breath like shrimp Chee-tos.

He looked like a gold rush cowboy that'd been camped remote and solo too long. I noted that I'd approached from the direction of Hyacinthignatzi.

"No one's come 'long this road for a *long time*," he said, then leaned in for added drama, "except some nosey people weren't s'posed to."

"Duh, unga-bunga?" I asked. "Duh, unga-bunga?"

He twisted his scraggly mustache, gray with red tinges of nicotine at the tips, squinted at me.

"Well, Sir," he said, "I serve The EPA wherever they see fit set me down."

I wanted to say something like 'Good Man' or something and imagined how Junior would say it like a cowboy boss: *Good. Man.*

He saluted me and stepped back toward the gate, but I called out to stop him, and turning back, now he was blinded in the beams of my headlights.

"Duh, unga-bunga."

"No problem, Sir. But you will have to 'scort her past this point, Sir. That's procedure."

We agreed that he'd call up to the house when Diana Herself arrived and I'd come fetch her.

As he sauntered off, I called him back again to ask about *River's Edge*.

He hadn't seen anything but promised to keep an eye out.

I nodded thanks, and he fixed his stare on me.

I waved terse and got the window half up when he shouted, "Funny—"

He approached the car, arms swinging and eyes downcast.

"It's *funny* I should keep an eye out for you."

"Duh, unga-bunga?" I said, not shifting the car into park, my foot on the brake.

"Well," his voice lifted. "I was gonna just say it's *funny* I should keep an eye out for *anything* for you."

He paused, staring, both of us silent.

Finally I asked, "Duh, unga-bunga?"

"Oh, just ironic I guess, seeing as I'd been turning a *blind* eye for The Family so long—"

"Duh, unga-bunga," I cut him off.

And he shouted quick as I pulled way, "My old aunt, her sister went blind in a *painful* way, her eyes burning for years. And all the birds fell from the sky and looked like they died of sunburn when they made *my family*'s river a toxic dump."

I drove off.

"Just two guys talking," he called out. "Not much company out here."

I was beginning to guess how he got this remote appointment.

CHAPTER 49 Foreground and Background Reverse

That steel spike at the center of my field of vision extended like an endless swirling whirlpool as deep as the limits of my depth perception itself down the ice castle's long, long halls.

Touching my fingers to the closest wall, the wallpaper's foreground and background reversed in my vision, quelling the vertigo a moment.

Pushing my fingers thru my thin hair, I considered my reflection in a convex crystal lamp and drew stripes across its dust.

Extinct jellyfish specimens, bronzed exoskeletons, and various animal skeletons jumbled together into impossible hybrids cluttered my path.

I stepped out the nearest door into the dusk air and took a long, steaming piss on the bushes.

Dusk can look a lot like dawn.

You can*not* escape your own privilege.

The overgrown green tennis court needed trimming.

Piled next to the course's last green, someone's abandoned intention to dig a sand trap.

It'd been *years* since I'd seen a sand trap without a corpse in it.

Ring Ring By the time Diana Herself arrived, a day or who knows how long later, I did *not* go to the gate.

Ring Ring The line rang over and over and over and, gulping mudslides, motionless at the counter in one of the innumerable kitchens, I never answered.

Ring Ring I wished I could map the ice castle in my mind to locate that cramped entrance to the bunker again so I could escape the incessant ringing, but I couldn't find it with all that ringing and ringing and ringing.

Ring Ring The phone rang and rang like the never-ending echoes of some defining and inappropriate touch that's torn you in two.

After eventually, it rang less often.

Each time it stopped, I hoped it wouldn't start again.

Ring Ring It would, finally stretching to an hour between the two final calls.

Shortly after the last string of ringings, *My Diana* let herself in.

Standing in perfect profile, silhouetted by the moon low and huge behind her, she dropped a six-pack of sweaty beer on the counter and gave me a peck on the cheek.

She told me an asymmetrical woman sat in her car, parked at the gate.

I nodded, careful not to look at her straight on.

She said the woman's whole backseat was crammed full of stuff.

I lit a cigarette.

The Mustachioed EPA Cowboy had warned her that she might not want to come up here alone.

I nodded.

A mudslide and a cigarette sutured my bifurcation.

My Diana called The Mustachioed EPA Cowboy at the gate.

As she quickly confirmed to him that all was fine in the ice castle, I placed a long sleeve shirt over her shoulders, concerned she'd get a chill in her bikini, and she nodded thanks.

The phone did not ring again.

CHAPTER 50 State of Grace

In his recent *State of Grace*, Junior felt wakeful love for every man, woman, child, alpaca, shrew, platypus, lamprey, prairie rat, genome, coral reef, algae, iceberg, nightshade, bay, dental hygienist, octogenarian, crawfish, trout, pilchard, periwinkle, mealy redpoll, black-gloved wallaby, snotty-nosed giraffe, Woman Engineer, and pygmy hippo— *every single solitary* dimly sentient blob and mighty cockroach stuffed and huddled on this mysterious, poisoned, and watery matrix.

He could see the yin-yang in a head of broccoli.

Remember Pious Reader, The Buddha had a trust fund.

Junior spoke only in parables and obscure riddles.

If you sighed and said: "Man, that makes *no* sense," he'd nod with a smirk, like an arrogant Obi-Wan Kenobi, and say: "*Exactly.*"

It certainly didn't harm The Family's long-standing program to dumb down The Barbarians to arm their chief imbecile with koans, some glassy-eyed monk carrying his roller-skates along a pier at dusk.

Maddening as his babble of *Light* and *Holiness* was, I do feel a little sorry for Junior, The Family forcing him to suppress his *State of Grace* for the sake of appearances.

You know that Peter O'Toole movie *The Ruling Class*?

My *favourite* movie of his is *Man of La Mancha,* of course.

He's Quixote and Sophia Loren is Dulcinea del Toboso.

Junior failed to recognize that *The Ruling Class* was a comedy and social critique.

He so identified with the aristocrat that thinks he's Jesus, Junior even memorized the prayer that spontaneously overwhelms Peter O'Toole and named it "Junior's Prayer."

"Junior's Prayer"
My heart . . . Rises with the sun.

I am purged of doubts and negative innuendos.
Today, I want to bless everything.

Bless the crawfish with its scuttling walk.
Bless the trout, pilchard and periwinkle.
Bless Ted Smoothey of 22 East Hackney Road.

Bless the mealy redpoll,
The black-gloved wallaby and W.C. Fields . . .
Who's dead but lives on.

Bless the snotty-nosed giraffe.
Bless the buffalo.
Bless The Society of Women Engineers.
Bless the pygmy hippos.
Bless the mighty cockroach.
Bless me!

In Junior's defense, it really is powerful when Peter
O'Toole spreads his arms wide and his eyes roll back.

CHAPTER 51 If Tati Had Directed *The French Connection*

As UN ambassador under Nxn, Pops had Vietnam, the China-Taiwan dispute, and the Middle East to keep him occupied.

Nxn wrote that he gave Pops the appointment cuz he "not only had the diplomatic skills to be an effective ambassador, but also cuz it would be helpful to him in the future to have this significant foreign-policy experience."

Nxn upgraded the position to full ambassador status and made Pops a member of his cabinet.

The official salary was substantial and came with a *splendiferous* residence in NYC and a staff of 111.

And Pops could finally, *truly* speak to Grandfather like his peer.

Pops had been taught that when he thought Grandfather was angry, Grandfather was actually being protective of him.

Wrenching in the vice grip of his *feelings* at Grandfather's funeral in '72, Pops *howled* a coal black sob, sudden and hard as a reptile claws itself free thru human skin.

He was *overwhelmed*, liberated from the *only* oppressing force he'd ever known.

And it *terrified* me, this one second crash, cracking open the silent room.

Pops sobbed like a bird with its wing torn off, like a half-eaten mouse escaped from its predator and hobbling, understanding all at once how to make a wish.

Grandfather, the energy baron and war profiteer whose hobbies included experiments in sterilizing The Barbarians, was painted rosy and laid out in his casket.

His teeth variations on a theme: fangs with dry blood compressed deep in their seams, the edges in need of bleaching.

Nxn's chief of staff said that whenever Nxn referred to "The Whole Bay of Pigs Thing" he was actually referring to King Arthur's very public skull chipping.

Nxn and The CIA were at war cuz he wanted records of The Bay of Pigs Thing.

He became *obsessed*.

Obviously he was *acutely* aware of King Arthur's feud with internal elements that led up to 11/22/63.

Governments *everywhere* historically endured systems of state security keeping the king himself in their crosshairs.

Nxn asked to see *lots* of documents, all of them re: the violent expulsions of heads of state.

But The CIA wouldn't show him anything.

Pops's "Townhouse Operation" was like if Tati had directed *The French Connection*.

Its sole intent was to set people up to blackmail them later if necessary.

Nxn's personal agent collected campaign checks from Party donors, raising a $3,000,000 slush fund of covert campaign money to be funneled thru dummy committees.

They flew a guy around to bump into unsuspecting senators and awk hand them wonky amounts of cash: $6,728 cash in a fat envelope of crumpled and irregular denominations, for example.

This purposefully confusing accounting made it so only a small portion of these bumbling handouts ever showed up on public records.

The totally unspoken agreement was: you took cash, you do what Nxn wants or face exposure.

The guy that ran the distribution of handouts from a townhouse basement assumed that Nxn, or at least loyalists to him, had authorized it.

Wiekest received one of these surprise handouts.

And when someone leaked this to *The Washington Post*, Wiekest believed that Nxn intended to blackmail him.

Pops called Wiekest the day after the story ran and said that he had the Townhouse receipts in his possession, and that he, too, had received some funds.

What should he do with the receipts?

Should he *burn* them?

Wiekest knew that burning evidence was a criminal offense.

And he figured that Pops, who'd become Head of The Party by that time, must've been calling on behalf of his boss, Nxn.

So Wiekest told him *No* and got in touch with a federal prosecutor.

Wiekest saw a *fake* trap, *exactly* the trap that they meant for him to see.

Pops stoked Wiekest's anger at Nxn.

Suddenly, Wiekest's own political survival was at stake.

At the H2oG8 hearing, he immediately launched into a speech alluding to a conspiracy against him.

The Townhouse Operation provided Pops a perfect cover: if he was a recipient, how could he be the perpetrator?

Jowarsky, Pops's chum who helped push Nxn from office, was put in charge of investigating The Townhouse Operation.

And he decreed Pops was "clean, clean, clean."

Pops was a pallbearer at Jowarsky's funeral.

I had an idea for a play, once, too.

At first it appears to be a stage adaptation of *TX Chainsaw Massacre*.

But then two-thirds thru, the actor playing Leatherface pretends he's fed up and protesting his role as being beneath his skills and calling, he recites a dramatic monologue from *Raisin in the Sun,* to puncture the suspenseful silence.

Thru and thru I'm a *Movie Man*, you see!

193

CHAPTER 52 Infinity with *My Diana*

When I was 5 years old, I saw her face in my mind.

When I was 13, I was so confused that I couldn't find her. I was sick on my wedding day cuz it wasn't her.

Then *finally,* the moon low and huge behind her, she *appeared.*

When I first heard her voice . . .

"I love you more than I've ever loved anyone."

She told me Not good enough.

"I love you *twice as much* as I've ever loved anyone."

She told me Not good enough.

"I love you *10 times* more than anyone else."

She told me Not good enough cuz I love you *100 times* as much as I've ever loved anyone else.

"That's not good enough cuz I love you *1,000 times* more than I've ever loved anyone else."

She told me Not good enough.

"I love you *10,000 times* more than I've *ever* loved *anything.*"

100,000?

We were living in the perpetuity of *Dream Time.*

You think I was *born* Mr. X-ray Crutch?

Mr. Oil Painting of Shattered Glass?

We couldn't be bothered to account for imprecise language.

She and me mirrored each other's *illumination.*

We wouldn't notice when we were touching each other's faces or not, both groggy all day and happy about it.

Her smile got even bigger.

She took my arm in hers and rested her head on my shoulder.

In the springtime the new fronds simply *unfurled* from their tight buds.

Meeting each other, each of us found ourselves.

She'd call me *Belmondo*.

She'd crack up at my Pops impersonations, a clumsy cowboy lost in The Middle East: *Which one of you sheiks has gone on and hid all my oil?*

Day by day, we'd live in moonlight, often intuitively choosing to sleep outside.

Diana means moon.

We'd float downstream lazily on a raft constructed of junk, and when we tired, we'd hide out in our fort constructed of junk.

Like *Pierrot Le Fou*, we'd kill her parents and run away with the inheritance.

In a small town gas station, no one would recognize me and snicker.

I'd remain unfazed by every man spinning to sneak a glance at her.

I'd chase a man around his car with a tire iron and wrestle him to the ground to carjack him.

We'd have to pull over and make out to save ourselves from veering off the road, across the beach and into the tide.

In her sundress and sunglasses, she'd put on my dusty wide-brimmed hat when we had to pass on foot thru expansive pastures.

I'd chew a cigar all day, reading out loud to her when we stopped to rest.

We'd dawdle thru our ever-expanding *Present Circumstances,* our quaquaversal best selves running unrestrained.

We'd be one, while also each retaining a constant sense of

Wonder re: other.

She'd gnaw my cigar's wet end to get a sense of how it feels to be me.

Five senses and memories—redeemed like a jellyfish shedding its exoskeleton.

Realism is: when she *appeared*, I stammered for hyperbolic descriptors.

I could *foresee* it all: suddenly, I would die a long and painful death.

CHAPTER 53 Infinity 2

Like a starfish regenerates its severed appendages, *I'd let her in.*

My Diana.

Like how fire cultivates a forest's floor, she *appeared,* all at once, freed from that flimsy closet door, her patriotic bikini replaced by worn-in army duds, severed free from the moon that I'd always known to backlight her, low and huge.

And I *wrecked* myself into completion for her.

Her smell.
Like a handstand on a hill.
I could *see.*
My hearing balanced.
A *bolt*—total identification all at once.
No more questions and nothing more to understand.
The moon.

Me: redeemed, transformed, no longer the inutile trust-fund chubby drunk I'd become with The Barbarians.

My surface buzzed as it hadn't since my Yale days.

But I was certainly no longer *that* ridiculous, clumsy, ugly, pathetic, contemptible, and vain wretch, pitying myself and my mushy ear and the steel spike in the center of my vision, always anxious I was *about to be* anxious, confounding cause and effect.

She redeemed and transformed me simply by being Sophia Loren playing Ione's part in *River's Edge.*

I never needed to ask her backstory cuz I had watched it hundreds of times.

As a kid she took black and white photos in cemeteries: her shirtless skateboarder boyfriends with long bangs swooped to one side and ugly plaid pants, climbed up on tall graves with the easy-going un-self-aware eroticism of a deer.

She was an *Artiste* with an intuitive sense of formalism, bristling with joy lining up angles in relation to the corners of the frame.

She squinted when she smiled.

And the front of my skull *pinged*.

She sold paintings to the old ladies at her mom's church.

Among tables of frozen fish sticks and bulk pierogis, she took commissions: dead husbands, poodles, grandchildren.

She worked at a grocery store, then a record store, then a temp agency, different offices stuffing envelopes or alphabetizing files.

The department store, a warehouse, the periodical desk at the library, a parking garage, a barista, a janitor, teaching, more temp whatever, seasonal window displays.

But somehow she'd still be a clumsy lover, unsure what to do or how to move, just as I preferred.

The scale of the impossible promise to quell the shattered and lacerated psyche with a singular and *total* answer.

Only *I* could understand that incessant sense of solitary confinement she carried along with her everywhere.

My biorhythms buzzing, like a parakeet that *happened* to flitter into The Super Bowl Half Time.

Like a pig snoring in his afternoon wheelbarrow.

A glow expanded to saturate the barren *moments* between surfaces.

Those territories of *mind* from which our extraterrestrials bloom out of hives of tangled wires and blinding light, must be the same territories of mind from which the tenant farmers of the past birthed hobgoblins bursting into *the world* from out of mud.

And *Yes,* Heedful Reader, I've seen *Solaris.*

What authority might pardon me?
I'd been prosecuted, maybe, certainly *charged*.

Allegiant Reader, if we agree it's *impossible* to translate
even something so simple as that glancing touch on a bare
forearm between two strangers into language, to filter the
charged *ping* of bone thru the troubled scrim of *wordage,*
then how could I possibly comprehend still being the same
man that had always smiled dully and dim-eyed, unsure
what to say, friendly even when unable to *conceptualize*
another rich and complex interior besides my own even
existed to look back at me?

I'd been *seen*, seen and *understood*, a part that can understand itself as a part of the whole.

Something *lifted* inside me—a *blooming*—while at the
same time, some *other* element inside me dropped hard and
took root.

This counterbalanced expansion, my sense of *self in
world*, shifted into a deeper unity, an embodied *collapse* of
noun and verb into singular perfect action.

Her eyes made the color wheel obsolete: blue-green-
brown-pink-orange-purple-song, but brighter.

She'd evaporate when I'd attempt to look at her straight-
on.

And she obviously possessed x-ray vision.

She told me that she'd overheard a surprising amount of
laughter for a man wandering around alone, and she liked
that, she said.

We agreed: your dreams define you.

Pure undifferentiated ache, not pleasure, not pain, just
throbbing.

Everything burned clean: motive and its residue, effort,
plan and impulse.

She explained to me if you hang the smaller of two parts of something sculptural—for example, the skull of a field mouse hung high above the skeleton of a beaver—the scale corrects itself in the viewer's eye dependent on the relative scale and the viewer's positioning.

She called it "Corrective Perspective."

These hybridized forms appear natural only cuz of how we see them, when actually, if we were to inspect their components from any perspective except the exact angle that the *Artiste* shows us, it would all ring hollow and false.

My *Realism* is the moon.
Diana means moon.

CHAPTER 54 How to State of Grace

When The Actor began his second term and time came to organize Pops's race, everyone camped out at Hyacinthignatzi.

Wead first approached Pops cuz ghost-writing Wiekest's memoirs, he felt Wiekest portrayed Pops unfairly.

Like the Old Light advocates of The Great Awakening of the early 19th century, Pops was refining what he officially *believed* or not.

And Wead, being Born Again, wrote briefing memos on The Religious Right.

Junior, helping Pops, read Wead's memos.

Ironically, the pro-choice and socially liberal Peanut Farmer was the first Born Again Prez.

Beyond the *obvious* social and business opportunities that religion presented, it also presented the ideal counterweight to balance any *questionable* behaviors of one's past.

Ruckafella and Dullis both did this.

Honestly, I don't know which Dullis.

I don't think we should assume it was necessarily the same Dullis Bro that had over 100 extramarital affairs that seduced The Queen of Greece, cuz really, you have to have *something* to prove to rack up those numbers and the same guy that had so much to prove would rat on his own brother out of envy, and I've never *seen* The Queen of Greece, but being a queen implies some standard of *quality* over quantity.

With 39% of The Barbarians believing The Bible to be the actual word of God to be taken *literally* word for word, Junior's awakening was a big selling point.

Junior, that same guy that used to smash chandeliers with a baseball bat to show off when high and bragged about getting pulled over for drunk driving all the time and being let go when the cops identified him.

It's Bloodline tradition that one son becomes a priest and

the other an attorney, and then you have God's Law *and* Man's Law on your side.

Party Boy Junior represented a potential burden for Pops's campaign.

But they flipped this into a blessing waiting to bloom.

Spiritual conversion *wiped the slate clean.*

With a *complete* reinvention, *anything* snorted or penetrated was erased, and no longer a threat to any ambitions.

The Barbarians didn't care what you did for *40 years,* so long as you got reborn.

Alcohol served as Junior's delegate sin, metonymy to avoid details.

And overcoming weakness even *attracts* voters; it looks like strength.

In the official story Junior swore off booze the morning after his 40th birthday.

He woke up hungover and decided to never drink again.

Good Theater, right?

Easy to remember, and, a 40th birthday dinner, who wouldn't have a couple drinks to celebrate?

Arthur Blessitt, the internationally renowned "Pilgrim with The Cross," first kindled Junior's spirit.

He had no scraggly beard, and he didn't *rant* like an arcane poet.

He's in *The Guinness Book of World Records* for "The World's Longest Walk."

Blessitt came from the Deep South—Mississippi, Louisiana—a revivalist Holy Man for years before he even hit puberty.

He made his way to Hollywood to preach to street kids, fried hippies, Hells Angels, junkies, runaways, teenage prostitutes, failed actors, and aspiring rock stars.

And by '68 he began carrying a 96-pound cross up and down The Strip.

They called him "The Minister of Sunset Strip."

He had six kids with his first wife, whom he married

within three weeks of meeting.

He named all his sons after himself, so they all went by their middle names. Christmas '69 he left for his first walk: L.A. to Capital City.

'71 he did his first international walk.

In the years following, he lugged his big cross over 40,000 miles across more than 300 countries, often thru war-zones to promote peace: Russia, Lebanon, The Baltics, Ukraine, Iraq, Iran, North Korea, Afghanistan, Somalia, Sudan, China, South Africa, India, Antarctica, Palestine, Israel, Cuba, Libya, Yemen, Vietnam.

Along the way he met The Reverend BG, The Pope, Yasser Arafat, and Muammar Gaddafi.

He was arrested 24 times.

Back in The Homelan he'd recount his adventures as if *Jesus-Superman*: saved by miraculous shifts of wind, conking gunmen over their heads with his Bible.

In a dramatic publicity appeal to sci-fi geeks, he launched his cross into space.

April '84, Blessitt passed thru Midland TX, and prayed with Junior to accept Jesus.

And so began Junior's *State of Grace*.

And suddenly he couldn't *not* see the yin-yang in a head of broccoli!

But Blessitt was obviously a *wee* bit eccentric for The Family's official narrative.

They insisted that Junior repress his *State of Grace,* and asked Wead to please explain more to him.

The Family arranged that The Reverend BG be enlisted for Junior's *official* conversion story, a *demotion* from his *State of Grace* to "Born Again."

Just *associating* with The Reverend BG gave Junior a sense of moral legitimacy in The Barbarians' eyes.

Junior liked to tell the story of how just being in The

Reverend BG's presence, walking the beach together here at Hyacinthignatzi, made his spiritual conversion inevitable.

They lunched on the patio overlooking the ocean, then that night sat around a fire and The Reverend BG answered everyone's questions re: spirit.

Junior said he made you feel *loved*, not judged.

The Reverend BG had been a chum of The Family a long time, and even urged Nxn to make Pops his running mate in '68.

In '70 he was part of a small group that visited The Actor when The Actor was The Gov of CA, to tell him all about Le Grande Finale *A-poc-a-lypse*.

They joined their uncalloused hands in prayer, and one man shook and pulsated, prophesying The Actor's appointment to Prez.

The Actor asked The Reverend BG to address The CA Legislature, to tell them all about Le Grande Finale *A-poc-a-lypse*.

The lanky Reverend BG took up too much space anywhere he went, like he couldn't fold his own limbs up enough to keep them out of the way.

He permed his thin hair to counterbalance his brushy eyebrows and thick ear hair.

Vain, petty, corrupt and arrogant, with ostentatious taste, he always gave me the impression of being a bad actor.

But he mastered Political Theater in his way.

Anytime you'd see him on ze Tube, he was stuffing his face, a napkin tucked in his collar, like he couldn't make time for an interview except when gorging, like he was *always* being interrupted while attempting some grotesque stunt involving portion sizes.

And for the right price, he'd convince his followers that *whatever* agenda The Family needed was biblically justified.

Restricted labor rights, expanded mining rights, exploitative international trade agreements, all cuz *The Bible told me so*.

It was impossible to say if he actually knew the Bible passages and chose to warp them or if a vague, impressionistic reading sufficed for him.

He spoke so *passionately,* people *loved* his readings, however mangled.

The Reverend BG didn't remember the story of Junior's conversion.

He said, "I don't remember what we talked 'bout. There's not much of a beach there. Mostly rocks. Some people have written—or maybe he has said, I don't know—that it had an effect, our walk on the beach. I don't remember. I do remember a walk on the beach."

Junior's *State of Grace* kicked his poor team of lawyers into turbo-overtime, anticipating where he'd drift to next and hurrying to advance the scene, casting actors in roles as converts.

And in the event that Junior's blessings so moved any actor to a degree that performance and actor obscured, confounding cause and effect, the lawyers had to follow up immediately with waiver forms explaining that his blessings were in *no way* legally binding.

CHAPTER 55 In Infinity My Diana Listens to My New Movie Idea

We skipped thru the quaquaversal halls, her arm thru mine like an escort down an aisle.

The unmitigated *shock* of her smile and her smell, like an inter-dimensional agent on a mission to rectify the inherent margins of error in corporeal form itself, an answer to the promise of form, brimming *completeness* and faultless fulfillment.

Perhaps my ribs had been kicked in, splintered into a lung.

The lawn tickled my toes across the open tops of my sandals.

She hung on my every word as I explained my latest idea for a movie, her eyes closed as if she watched the movie projected on the inside of her skull.

I explained, I have *no idea* where the ideas come from.

I don't *try*.

They just pop out.

I explained, finally, to someone, anyone, that I'd *always* felt different and that was always bad.

But if I could accept that I'm different and *that's good*—that's what I needed.

She understood *perfectly* when I explained that I never understood the world except by feeling set apart and looking in on it.

"Is that how everyone feels?" I asked.

She told me that she sure never understood anyone that doesn't feel that way.

In my idea for a movie, a young art critic struggles to write a review of a series of performances.

The *artiste*, whom the reviewer is in love with, sneaks a very loud thrash band into a crowded apartment building to play one song at full volume, once a day for a month.

To achieve this the *artiste* has to remain totally attuned to the goings-on of the entire building, all 30-odd units.

At a moment's notice, the band has to be prepared to load in, set up, play the song, then break down and load out again, all without being caught.

Of course depending on the day of the week this has to happen at different times.

And the band are dolts, obnoxious and crude and lazy.

So the *artiste* has to deal with that.

But at least the song is short, being so fast.

The critic reviews the meticulous documentation of each day: what time they began to load in, which door, where they set up in the building, where the electricity came from, photos and time-stamped recordings of the same song each day.

In the most suspenseful part, the drummer holds his breath around a corner while an old lady fussing with a drain in the basement floor, inspects the foam ring of his hi-hat.

But most of the film is the critic writing the review.

My Diana would play the *artiste*.

CHAPTER 56 The Effort Invested into Being Myself

Same as Pops and his siblings literally couldn't *see* Grandfather's benders, all lying is simple once you've learned to lie to yourself.

Of course, Wise Reader, I could never lie to you.

My original mission to set the record straight *finito* and *sans qualification* re: my family and that *Objective* or Subjective Biography, etx. remained clear in my mind.

And that mission did feel urgent.

But like some dizzy butterfly bumping into myself, I trashed *My Diana* with my psycho *loneliness*.

She struggled to carry too much at once.

I passed her in the doorway, tried to catch a glimpse of her straight-on before she evaporated.

She told me she had to run.

I wilted like a squirrel skull.

I could see with such clarity now the sadness that so often preceded seeking The Act of Love back in my playboy phase.

Hours zipped past on the lookout for the exact right accident and how to live within it.

But now *My Diana*, how she *knew* how to be, even *that* could not compare to how she actually was: defect-less, effortless, sublime.

Back among The Barbarians I'd occasionally get weepy at Coming Attractions for corny movies that'd make me *barf with anger* if I ever actually saw the movie.

That sense of belonging had been replaced by this estranging *Realism* of Being Awake.

Like a hairy pig mad at a statue of a pig, nosing it, about to attack.

Below, in the muddy, flooded yard, *River's Edge* played out, with all their teeth and grime in their seams like rusted tubs.

The blimpish killer John aka Samson was the exception; Keanu, Crispin, and their friend Tony all looked a lot alike.

Mike, their friend with a job and a truck, looked less like them with shorter hair but still rocked the same jean jacket, and saunter, like a mild version of his friends.

They listened to light-hearted rock 'n' roll on an innocent field trip to see Jamie's corpse.

They all thought it was a joke.

Keanu stayed back in class instead of joining them.

Crispin, so overboard performative, got mad when Mike wanted to walk away and said, "You're all acting like it's a show."

John aka Samson pulled Crispin off of Mike.

He gets it, the murder that he himself committed, in a way that Crispin can't.

Crispin's identification with John aka Samson was *extreme*.

Little Timmy and his friend literally shot fish in a bucket.

Little Timmy's friend threatened Keanu with nunchucks.

"What am I going to do?" their mom asked when Keanu dared her to parent more aggressively.

Keanu organized a funeral for their little sister's doll.

"Nothing's gonna happen. He had his reasons," Crispin said re: John aka Samson and the murder.

John aka Samson's mother was dead, so some implications like Uncle Sigmund and recessed motives bubbled up.

"What makes John aka Samson more important than Jamie?" Ione asked. "Who do I call, the police?"

No one wanted to be the one to call the police.

John aka Samson took care of his aunt.

She called him Samson.

She had a statue of the scales of justice.

"It ain't that important," John aka Samson said.

"I'll be expecting beer for this. I'll do it myself," Crispin said re: burying Jamie.

John aka Samson wasn't interested in burying her.

Keanu couldn't tell Ione over the phone about the doll funeral.

I loved her like I don't want to be *myself* at all.

Not that I ever did much appreciate the limited technology of mirrors.

How was I supposed to *appear,* standing there, cradling my guts back in while they blobbed out over my arms?

Just nullifying pain can feel like a flip into ecstasy.

However intensely you *Start Life Over*, you bring *something* with you, if nothing more than the desire to *Start Life Over*.

There was a fly in the ice cube and rounded ice cubes can be so tricky to pull from a glass.

Buzzed with wakefulness, my fingertips numbed, I spun and called out, "Hello. Hello."

Cracked paint reflected light differently depending on each chip's angle in relation to the lamp.

Like cooling globs of whipped cream on burns, *My Diana.*

I opened the door.

She looked up and smiled.

She had *such* beautiful knees, how bone stretches skin thin, glowing.

I slammed the door.

All systems of ranking flattened; all propagandas outed as glaring artifice; *Weltanschauung* exploded; all symbols to simplify and decipher *Life on Earth* collapsed by the smell of her *weird* flesh.

I swung the door open, and she threw her arms around my neck, rested her head on my shoulder.

She smiled big, asked me what game I was playing.

"What game are you playing?" asked the totalitarian fire to the leaf-flesh and dung nuggets and heaps of kernels and deer marrow and brittle bone shard and brush dust and leaf-vein before the calcination of the forest floor.

"There's quicksand, and in this other clearing, not far from here, there's this great Tin Man statue made out of tank scraps that'd been mangled by bombs."

A forest fire does need the cracked bird skulls and sea-shells of its forest floor.

Frogs fenced in a marble pool chirped in a choir with a howling owl tall up in a tree.

The frog pool's shallow water was thick and green, their resonant frog throats big with vulnerable bubbles.

I'd never before *missed* someone standing beside me.

The effort I invested into being *myself* with *My Diana* clearly translated into *not enough* or too much.

In all my life of tabulated failures, my greatest failure, Halcyon Reader, would be any attempt to render her, however urgent the impulse.

Like how the slack legs of a drugged cat hang when you lower and drape it to the ground, attempting to force it to stand, I could not.

If she was with me and *mine*, The Family would accept me for who I am.

They'd think *if she likes him, he must be OK.*

My Diana's laughter came from the kitchen.

The Guangdong Chef was demonstrating how easily anteater scales slip off after boiling.

He insisted that she try and handed her his knife.

Stepping behind her, he put his arms around her, his hand folded over hers on the knife.

I watched from around a corner.

She could do the mingling, joke with all The Good Men and chums.

I'd hang back with our kids, suggest challenges with blocks, and lead hand hockey games on our knees with a rolled-up sock.

We'd glance to each other, stifling our giggles at the aristocratic pomp and ritual, how the *elite* speak to each other when feeling completely free, no codes necessary to mask their nostalgia for empire, The Golden Age of their *teeming womb of privilege* . . .

The Guangdong Chef was singing "It Had to Be You," a *stunning* impersonation of Frank Sinatra.

He looked into *My Diana*'s radiant eyes while singing.

I approached and poked her elbow.

She nodded at me, then looked back to him, not breaking her gaze again until he finished.

She applauded, and he bowed, smiling big.

She nudged me, and I clapped slow, careful not to roll my eyes too obvious.

"You've seen *Annie Hall*?" The Guangdong Chef asked her.

She nodded.

"And *Casablanca*," he said.

In a *terrible* Humphrey Bogart voice, he began to say, "*Of all the gin joints—*"

But I cut him off.

"And *The Roaring Twenties* and *I'll See You in My Dreams* and *Incendiary Blonde*," I said.

My Diana looked at me confused.

The Guangdong Chef tilted his head like a poodle or a teeny-bopper named Trendy.

"Don't forget that song is *also* in all those movies."

She shrugged.

"It's really *quite a cliché,* actually," I said.

The Guangdong Chef picked his knife back up and returned to his work in silence.

CHAPTER 57 A Made for ze Tube Movie

Attempting to incriminate Nxn in H2oG8, The CIA intended to forge the *appearance* that he and the agency were inseparable, so that if he tackled CIA involvement in 11/22/63, the agency could assert that Nxn himself was also involved.

Nxn's Casa Blanca got *crammed* with intel operatives and all of them had pushed hard to get there: Deen, Bieterfuld, Gather, Pops.

Nxn believed that they'd brought him to Dallas 11/22/63 to demonstrate their wheels-within-wheels.

One Prez assassinated in '63, another squeezed out in '74, why would it be any surprise to find the same players behind both?

Nxn's Chief Staff said re: H2oG8, "The FBI agents who are working the case, at this point, feel that's what it is. This is CIA."

And Nxn himself said, "The whole thing was so senseless and bungled that it almost looked like some kind of a setup."

Gather led The Plumbers at H2oG8.

He was also The CIA's man in charge of The Bay of Pigs Thing in '61.

In fact, three of the five H2oG8 Plumbers were veterans of that mission.

Former CIA Director Helms went on record saying that Gather was in Dallas and involved in the conspiracy that so-publicly chipped King Arthur's skull.

When a magazine reported this, Gather sued for slander and the magazine was found Not Guilty.

In the proceedings Gather testified that right after WWII he worked in Paris for Harryman, Grandfather's partner, reporting directly to him daily.

Another Plumber, Sturgis, had served in several branches of the military, and was undercover in Cuba during the revolution in '58.

He told Marita Lenz, "We killed King Arthur."

Lenz was a CIA operative from Germany who had an affair with Castro in '59, then was part of The CIA attempt to assassinate him in early '60.

Shaken by 11/22/63, she testified repeatedly that shortly before the assassination she was involved with CIA anti-Cuban militants Gather and Sturgis.

That very afternoon, 11/22/63, King Arthur's brother RKF went on record saying that he knew it was CIA and their anti-Castro Cubans.

A week later, Hovver, Head of The FBI, wrote a memo; its subject: Assassination of The Prez.

He wrote that the FBI was investigating a "misguided anti-Castro group in The CIA," and named Pops as responsible for this group.

Pops was summoned to Capital City 11/23/63 to answer for this group.

While in jail, Gather sent letters to Nxn saying that he needed $2,000,000 to keep his mouth shut.

You remember Divine: Pops's ex-partner.

He paid Gather $2,000,000.

Gather wrote a few novels re: the occult.

Deen officially switched teams.

He told the prosecution that Nxn was incriminated in the cover-up.

Spring '73: Deen and Wiekest became neighbors.

Remember Wiekest, he fell for The Townhouse Operation?

He was convinced of a conspiracy against him, and he

was put in charge of the H2OG8 investigation, and then he and Deen became chums.

The Director of The FBI concluded that Deen was central to "hatching the plot that would eventually drive Nxn from office."

But Deen continues to narrate the official version.

And Nxn *always* the villain, Tricky Dick, the sweaty-browed deceiver, hiding bugs in the tails of Red cats.

I've seen *a lot* of actors portray him in the last 14 years since he resigned, and it's never flattering.

Of course, he pioneered playing himself shabbily.

The first of his four debates against King Arthur, the first Prez debate ever broadcast on ze Tube, was the turning point in his campaign.

He stayed out barnstorming until only a few hours before.

And he wasn't totally bounced back from a stay in the hospital, looked sallow, ailing, gangly, and drained.

He refused makeup, and his stubble popped out prominently on ze black-and-white Tube.

His mother called him as soon as it ended, worried that he was sick.

King Arthur, on the other hand, was well rested, prepared, tan, assured, relaxed, and sanguine.

70,000,000 dimly sentient blobs watched this debate and the people that watched it on ze Tube all thought King Arthur won, but the smaller audience listening to the radio all thought that Nxn did.

Rich Little did Nxn on ABC Comedy Hour in '72.

Then Dan Aykroyd did him on *Saturday Night Live,* but he mostly impersonated Rich Little impersonating Nxn.

The '79 miniseries re: H2OG8 called *Blind Ambition* was based on Deen's version.

Martin Sheen played Deen, and Rip Torn played Nxn.

I'll watch Rip Torn in *anything*.

Have you seen *Coming Apart*?

Or that Norman Mailer movie *Maidstone:* they get in a real fight on set, and Rip Torn hits Norman Mailer in the head with a hammer, then Norman Mailer bites off part of Rip Torn's ear, and they yell at each other using each other's real names instead of the character's names.

Anyways re: Nxn portrayals, Altman's version in '84, *Secret Honor,* starred Philip Baker Hall.

It was interesting, more philosophical, a disgraced Nxn paces and pontificates, alone with Scotch and a gun.

Hall portrays him subtly, a little more sand in his throat than any of the other actors or even Nxn himself; brooding humility, self-pity, and blistered pride.

Plot-wise it has an interesting twist: Nxn staged H2oG8 *himself* to escape the clutches of "Bohemian Grove" and "The Committee of 100," whom he regretted becoming a willing tool for.

Hall was only 5'6" and Nxn was actually 5'11" and a half.

But it didn't matter cuz it was a monologue, so they made the desk and bookcases all 6" shorter, like how Junior does his photo shoots.

The H2oG8 break-in was brazen and bizarre and set up to *guarantee* failure and discovery.

Burglars in business suits that lived right by the scene of the crime; Cuban expats carrying documents in their pockets that led straight to The Prez's office; they didn't take anything.

They put tape over the lock *horizontally* so that a passing security guard could see it even with the door closed.

Vertically it would've been invisible.

But why tape at all when they were already inside?

The guard actually removed the tape, and The Plumbers put it back.

They carried IDs and a check signed by Gather along with his phone number.

They were registered at The H2oG8 Hotel, and carried

room keys that led investigators right back to not only The Prez's Office, but also The CIA.

And not just *any* CIA, but the exact same misguided anti-Castro posse led by Pops.

Nxn, who was looking into The Bay of Pigs Thing, now faced this burglary, supposedly carried out *in his name* by specifically the same group he was trying to learn about.

Not a bad intimidation tactic, eh?

In 3 acts:

1) The Crime
2) Incriminating Nxn
3) Using "Facts" to Squeeze Him From Office

CHAPTER 58 Keep Hold of the Exposed Piping

What would be the point of reporting Aaron AWOL?

I ducked achy down low under the shelf, wigwagging around in the dark pantry until my elbow bumped a door-knob and I pulled it open toward me.

I stepped thru the door and stood up tall, the smell musty sweet like the royal quilt gallery.

I stood atop the hidden staircase, feeling just as dusty and majestic as the barely tangible memories of having ever been a boy at all, all that energy invested in reigning in all that bustle and zip.

I stepped down a step and another: this place *did* exist.

And another step and another, my memories affirmed: *This* place.

Lowering into the bunker's depths, my perspective phased in increments.

Like the reptile hidden under human skin, like The Vice hides at dusk, I *did* hide here as a child.

Memories crash like: *integrate* or halt.

Like a stranger's sneeze on your wrist while you grip the cold handrail on a crowded bus—you remain yourself, *somehow.*

Like Grandfather's drinking or the bifurcation to guard against an innocent bone's *ping;* same as *business* and "Government" burrow deep into one another: the bunker.

I had not *dreamt* those memories, just kept them parallel.

Certain depths of self-awareness achieve an aspect of glamour, like eating a sandwich on the toilet, pondering your own ego and the pulsating paradox of individualism, how *everyone is exceptional.*

Feeling small and willing all at once to *break* my *self* open on display for each one of the matrix's innumerable *snarling* creatures, this foolish victory was *absolute*, exigent, crude, instinctive, and universal.

Disorder only needs the slimmest crack in *order* to prevail, but order requires *total* domination.

Perfect order had been restored *in* totality, *by* totality.

The staircase stank like musty whitefish and gun powder.

A mirror lit from below at the first turn of the stairs startled me.

Pulled along while standing still like on a moving side-walk thru an airport's neon tunnel, like how severe diamond sculptures jut out of an airport ceiling, reflecting and amplifying the twisted neon's effect ad infinitum in cubed and curling glass, I came up against variations of my *self* in the blank perfection of that hidden staircase.

Could even such dream tunnels as these ever be enough to actually *prepare* anyone for the shock of cutting across time?

Like when I resist sleep, and I babble, the *unhinged* logic of my dream world given voice.

This was *not* the time.

I raced back up the stairs to *My Diana*.

Clenched and prepped to shatter, I lay on my back, arms at my sides, steel spike in the center of my field of vision burrowing deep into the ceiling.

I relaxed into the rhythm of my deep breaths, calming the swirling vertigo, intentionally reversing foreground and background until they settled into balance.

I always found Hitchcock insecure and domineering, but vertigo he sure knew how to deal with.

In my mind, I mapped the ice castle outward from where I lay.

Keep hold of the exposed piping, it'll lead me down the hall.

The kitchen with the strange water heater, like a battery or heart set awk in the middle of the room . . .

Keep hold of the exposed piping . . .

But the map *exploded* into innumerable room-shards, expanding fractal, quaquaversal, hundreds of hundreds of ribbons uncoiling viral.

Like a sleeping limb tingles, rolling over itself like wind-blown dunes in darkness, I heard my *self* suck in air hard.

From the window, my minivan parked around back looked like itself but sculptural.

Dawdling the potholed gravel road tired me.

The remnants of a small fire had been rained on before burning itself clean of its evidence.

My sandals clumped with mud, I'd meandered too far out into the thawing prairie.

I came upon that knotty old tree that Grandfather exploited to calibrate our senses of scale.

The shallow slope was short, but a challenge nonetheless.

I leaned heavily uphill.

The thick trees screamed birds.

How O'Malley and The Greek used to do *Deliverance*, "Squeal, *squeal* like a pig."

And how they did *Evil Dead*—the forest floor *itself* possessed—"Queen of Spades, 4 of Hearts, 8 of Spades, 2 of Spades, Jack of Diamonds, Jack of Clubs—"

"Ash, you aren't gonna leave me here are you? Are you, Ash?"

A lifetime of feeling crowded had not prepared me to consider the number of years that had passed since the last time anyone had stood at that precise spot.

And below me, the four-story tall owl.

Moving thru each door, I locked it behind me, every room, the rooms inside rooms, and the halls in the rooms inside rooms.

I locked every lock on every door.

I moved thru every room backwards, toward the center of the house, locking every room that each room opened up into.

Finally, I felt under control: No keys.

CHAPTER 59 Infinity's Limits

I'll admit that some small but persistent part of me has always enjoyed living at least *a little bit*.

How it feels, from the inside, to be a *self* among selves, has *so little* in common with our perceptions of the other dimly sentient blobs.

That's the part I struggle with—being left alone with your own best explanations, like some unseen cat's meow spermy as a comet tail.

But I like the games.

And with a clank in the doorway, staring at me: Don Quixote.

Don Quixote!

He clattered off down the hall before my reflexes knew whether to chase him or hide.

The *staggering* perspective of that little bug's trek epic across a glass shower door's vast transparent landscape: those factors of infinity are old light or new?

Does a fair'nbalanced *Subjective* Biography need to know how to distinguish I can't *breathe* cuz I can't breathe from I can't breathe cuz I can't *breathe?*

As much as sleep deprivation had me weepy and nauseous, disrupting your biorhythms can also bring clarity if you muster the nerve to persevere.

Course not as sharp as anteater blood.

But eventually—it's an instinctual bloom of evolution—you *cannot help* but recognize *Life on Earth* as long waves of overlapping patterns.

That doesn't mean you learn to *control* anything, only that you learn to recognize which things to stay out of the way of.

I'd stripped my *self* of all that's practical.

The simplicity of some questions belittle the utter profundity of the unknowability of their answers.

Like two spinning sirens hollering at each other, both unable to hear the other over ourselves.

The name of the town she lived in one junior high summer, long ago, learning to smoke, became a sing-song melody to me, forcing me to breathe shallow.

That small town, between other places I'd never heard of or don't remember.

The full force of the infini-verse stampeding thru me, buzzing and ruptured—

You do just *know* all at once, right?

Like a bird lost in a subway tunnel.

Do *not* write your *notes to self* backwards on the mirror, that's trying too hard.

Like a critter chased to the corners of its prairie when the waist-high hickory smoke of a controlled burn creates a low ceiling exactly equal to the expansiveness of its entire conception of the infini-verse: me.

"Can you see the yin-yang in that head of broccoli?" she asked.

I struggled to see it, willed it so hard.

But from my perspective there was only the moon.

Simmered dust had seared and hardened on the big gas heater's pipes.

Silence corrected the margins of errors inherent to my personal asymmetries.

For the first time, I could distinguish the resonant hum of my own skull from a branch brushing and wapping against the window.

Do partially-blind people prefer dim and sparse spaces?

It's counter-intuitive that people with limited palettes prefer bland food and the calloused prefer casual touches.

But we bristle at reminders of our lack?

My name when *My Diana* said it, her tongue soft against her teeth, and the flash of her breath hanging in the room.

The scent of her delicate sweat dislodged and bandied about my sense of continuous *self*.

No way is there the exact number of eyes-to-eyelids in the world.

Like how streetlights equalize all the knife-shine and cardboard sprawl into a singular flat yellow, I thought *only* of *My Diana*.

Have you ever been locked in a room and then freed, Auspicious Reader?

The alleviation of shame can feel like sainting.

I swallowed hunger's caveman anxiety.

How *cheery* to imagine myself back in my condo, O'Malley spitting a chewed donut on The Greek, acting out the scene from *Animal House*.

When we were boys, Pops used to play a game with us based on a Red cosmonaut stress test: "3,127 times 534—quick!"

And you'd have to solve the equation in your head while layered tapes spit out endless integers sans sequence, their various inflections only adding to the stress.

That famous fork in the road quote, you know, re: the path less traveled, etx., you do *know* he was talking about his *mind* right?

He wasn't talking about a *literal* footpath thru woods.

I'm *so slow* to pick up on things.

When *I* was 19 my impulses and appetites had fantastic clarity.

Do 19-year-olds *ever* get tired?

And they're resilient enough to absorb the endless bolts of awareness?

The *Reality* is that *Life on Earth* requires being born again, and again, and again, and again and again, and again and again and again.

Like the efficiency of the rumor mill between predators: a deer on the western slope slowed by its hemorrhaging tumor, a leaking beehive making this tree-trunk a sticky feast: *My Diana.*

Like the thrill among microscopic parasites with their proportionally *vast* senses of humor when they topple a strutting bear with stomach cramps: *My Diana.*

Romantic Reader, I can tell you every speck of the back-story of Sophia Loren playing Ione's part in *River's Edge.*

Her overbearing mother couldn't quell the impulse to compete with her.

Her dad frankensteined shattered Christmas ornaments rather than spend 50 cents on a new one.

Her brother quit a series of liquor stores and gas stations.

Like *Pierrot Le Fou*, she'd sing to me from the other room while she dressed—*Don't it make my brown eyes, don't it make my brown eyes, don't it make my brown eyes blue*—while I smoked in bed shirtless, spooning jam from its jar.

Like *The Ruling Class*, we'd play hide and seek thru the topiary garden, crawling thru dirt in our white clothes.

We'd race tricycles down the ice castle's long halls and leaping, laughing, our ecstasy would freeze-frame mid-air.

It's hard to believe the species didn't *die off* given how awk the first time fucking with The Act of Love with some-one can be.

Back in my playboy phase, the most difficult part was always how *late* you were expected to stay up, waiting for everyone else to leave.

It's not *acting* like a cowboy that makes a cowboy, but the stamina to carry on the act.

CHAPTER 60 My Mean Old Man Routine

From an upstairs window I watched *River's Edge* play out in the flooded yard, in the perpetual dusk.

My mission to set the record straight *finito* and *sans qualification* re: my family and that *Objective* or Subjective Biography, etx. remained clear in my mind.

But I never won't watch it when it's on.

Crispin rolled Jamie down the hill and into the river.

He tidied up carelessly and his logic was equally untidy, yelling at John aka Samson, "It's people like you sending this country down the tubes."

Finally, Keanu called the police.

Dennis Hopper's, Feck's, red room.

Dennis Hopper, Feck, and John aka Samson compared murders, how it felt.

Dennis Hopper, Feck, said he blew her brains out cuz he loved her.

And he hadn't stepped foot out of his home in five years.

Little Timmy desecrates Missy's grave.

Missy being his little sister's doll.

However warped, Little Timmy did have *some sense* of justice: he rats on his brother Keanu.

Like The Dullis Bros.

It's all noir.

Big lights bolted to the top of Crispin's car, like sirens.

Crispin assumed Mike told the police cuz he's the square with a job.

Crispin *demands* that his friends follow his orders sans question: "You've let yourself get jerked around Little Girl."

Tony's dad blows out his own front window with a shotgun and that's pretty far-fetched.

Dennis Hopper, Feck, *knows* that his blowup doll is a blowup doll.

John aka Samson *knows* that he's insane.

Dennis Hopper's, Feck's, best line is: "There's my leg. I wonder if there's any beer in that can."

John aka Samson said, "I figure once you start fighting,

then you're always defending yourself."

His philosophy was: do shit, it's done, then you die.

Ione defends herself against Crispin's name-calling.

It's much tougher to see one corpse than the heaps piled up.

It would require the platonic form of *pizza itself*, the Jungian archetype of *cartoon itself,* to block out *this* corpse, Jamie, the corpse I always thought of when I thought *corpse.*

And *I get it* that Crispin's acting style creates tension between the actor and the role he's playing, calling the whole dramatic cathartic *thing* into question, but it's *so goddam* cloying, watching him grasp haphazardly for *meaning.*

"Hello." I hoped to startle them out of their collective stupor.

Like a catcher tumbling into the stands to chase a foul ball at a Congressional hearing, cigarette dangling, I broke into *River's Edge.*

Down the steps and out the door, I called again: "Hello. Hello."

John aka Samson turned his dull eyes to me, while his face remained straight ahead.

His nose tilted up and cheeks puckered. Dennis Hopper, Feck, crushed a beer can and dropped it with a clang.

I moved in a wide-stepped circle to the middle of all of them, my hands behind my back, looking at the ground, like Patton, if not Napoleon himself, addressing his squadron.

No mistake who's in charge here.

I clapped my hands loudly and Crispin hissed at me.

Let them rush me all at once.

I looked him in the eye.

He sneered at his toes.

Ione shook her head at me, squinting.

She mouthed the words, *Come on,* dramatically, but didn't articulate them.

She looked *so young* in so much makeup, and said,

229

"Come on. Don't."

"Don't what?" I said.

"Don't call the police. Don't tell on us."

She sounded like a child.

I pointed with my thumbs back behind me to the drive-way.

"Now?" John aka Samson asked.

"Yes," I said. "Now."

They all stood up and grabbed their jackets and warm six-packs.

"OK?" I said.

"We're going," Keanu responded.

"OK," I said.

I waited, watched them pack and begin to shuffle off.

"I'm gonna have to call the cops if you guys don't move along," I said when they dawdled.

"Alright," Crispin said. "Can you at least give us a couple minutes head start before you call the cops?"

An odd request considering how far we were from the nearest town, but I remained firm.

"No," I said. "You don't understand. If you leave *right now* then I'm not going to call the cops."

"Oh."

"I'm going to call the cops if you *don't* leave."

"Oh, I get it. I thought before you meant that you were going to call the cops—"

"Yeh, I get it," I said. "I understand what you thought I meant, but no. That's not what I meant."

"Right. You *will* call the cops—"

"Yes. If you don't go."

"Oh, OK. I got it," he said.

Denim and flannels, glass pipes and warm beer in each dimly sentient blob's hands, they sauntered off.

I *get it*, Trusted Reader, if *River's Edge*, my *favourite* movie, appearing to me when I'm in hiding—run away or locked up, I don't know—if you take that as *symbolism* or surreal mumbo-jumbo proving the *unreliability* of My Report.

It saddens me that My Report is necessary at all.

But by accepting the mission, I'm obligated by history and circumstance to register everything *exactly* as it happened.

Romance, Guns, Shrewd Artfulness: You'd be reasonable to assume that My Report *should be* X-rated!

But I can only hope that *Realism* proves to be fantastical enough for you, Reliable Reader.

So I *agree* it's certainly unusual that *River's Edge* was quite literally playing out around me.

But you find that hard to believe?

How do you explain the 3,600 year old life-size crystal skulls found in South America that required a powered cutter to manufacture?

Or the giant stone balls of Costa Rica found in the 30s, made of granite not found in the region and crafted too perfectly for any simple explanation?

Or the Chinese characters on Central American figures from 3,000 years ago?

Or the ancient Chinese seals scattered all over 18th-century Ireland?

Or the ancient stone forts across Europa 60 in Scotland alone melted and made glassy by heat that no conventional fire could produce?

Or the ancient computer dated 100 BCE found on the island of Antikythera off Crete in 1900, made of differential gears not invented until the 16th century?

Or the ancient Iraqi battery of 220 BCE?

Or the 13 mystical sites covering a 450-mile radius that when seen from space form a Maltese Cross, the emblem of the Crusader Knights?

Or coins the *exact* same size and weight found *thousands* of miles apart, remnants of *cultures* that existed thousands of years apart?

Or the Babylonian tablets that explained the phases of Venus, the four moons of Jupiter, and the seven satellites of

Saturn, none of which are visible sans modern telescopes?

Or the pyramids?

Working 24 hours a day, seven days a week, it'd take 23 years even if you somehow placed a stone every 4 minutes and 39 seconds.

Did you know that the builders of the pyramids invented the inch: 1/5,000,000 the distance of the North Pole to the South Pole?

Or the 16th-century Turkish map of Antarctica, based on a map predating Alexander The Great, that accurately depicts a region that'd been covered with ice for 4,000 years?

Or the 16th-century Turkish map of The Amazon basin in South America, based on a map predating Alexander The Great, that accurately depicts a region not surveyed until the invention of aircraft in The 20th Century?

Or *My Diana,* her smell and her smile?

So *River's Edge* appeared before me at Hyacinthignatzi, big woop.

On the porch, I tried to lean my forearm above my head like Aaron had leaned that night we arrived and felt awk doing so.

I slackened, crashing from the rush of sending *River's Edge* walking off into the trees.

I lugged my *self* up the steps, slurped down a watery mudslide and poured another.

Pops, when I was a boy, bundled a litter of newborn kittens in a pillowcase, filled it with stones and sank it in the creek.

I regretted my posturing bluff, the ridiculous *mean old man* routine.

I could've cohabited with *River's Edge*, why not?

I should've ordered pizzas, told them to make themselves at home and shown them one of my tapes, maybe The Steelers and The Immaculate Reception.

But where could I order pizzas from?

CHAPTER 61 Excuse Me While I Get a Little Castaneda Here

There's no greater *serenity* than the well-balanced symmetry of one's sense organs.

I achieve equilibrium by stripping my one good ear of any signal.

The conscious reversal of foreground and background emancipates me from the blinding glare of that steel spike in the middle of my field of vision.

My *Life on Earth*, one long *game* of corrective perspective.

But I didn't get it too bad.

Not like My Little Brother, his visitors casually opening a window to politely deal with the stench from the grunt of his struggling breath.

We become accustomed to the normalized levels we set for each of our five senses.

And stifling our intuitions—the resonances buried deeper than the distinctions we make *between* our five senses—we each live within the parameters of this established network of subjectivity at the expense of blocking out the faint hunches of what lies beyond our own personal borders.

So-called *Religious Rites*, in practice, are grounded in so-called *Science*.

They shift your subjective state.

And science does testify to the observer's effect on the observed.

Assume I'm a kook if you have to, Discerning Reader, and go find yourself a book with a wide-chested man in a billowy shirt on the cover instead of this hermit wizard's *Report*.

The 3D material world is the result of the intersections of the psychic, emotional, spiritual, and material worlds: the manifestation of the sum of all desires, conscious and unconscious.

The Family does *everything it can* to make sure that as few of The Barbarians as possible ever cultivate a sense of vision to recognize this.

And that when they do, their ability to communicate this vision is limited.

You know that *so much* of what you know can't be taught. But once it's *seen—it's all one thing—*it can't be *unseen.*

The *world* requires *conscious* construction.

And seeing with symbolic awareness complements the physical world, it doesn't negate it.

You recognize its *depth* and complexity instead of its surfaces and superficiality.

And as a work of conscious construction, *world* exists solely in your Weltanschauung.

When you're out trolling for The Act of Love, you can only see potential partners or not.

If it wasn't The Family crafting Weltanschauung, *someone* would be doing it.

Cursing *us* only implicates *you.*

CHAPTER 62 A Made for ze Tube Movie 2

As ambassador to The UN, Pops *acted* steadfastly loyal to Nxn.

All Nxn's tantrums granted eternal life on tape, he never, not *once,* said anything against Pops.

At one point he even yelled, "Eliminate *everyone* except Pops. Pops will do anything for our cause."

After Nxn's re-*eleccion*, when Pops asked to be made The Head of The Party, Nxn even let Pops keep his seat in cabinet meetings, same as when he served as ambassador.

Pops remained *uniquely* well-informed re: who-knew-what.

The Smoking Gun Tape, popularly thought to damn Nxn, distorted the context of some of its most famous comments.

Pops himself selected tiny parts to make it look like Nxn ordered the block against The FBI, omitting that it was Deen's suggestion.

Then Pops pressed that disclosure *must* come from The Prez himself.

And it was Pops that gave Nxn the word when it was finally time to resign.

Defying The Family's "no writing anything down" policy, Pops's diary entry the day that Nxn resigned read: "Suspense mounting again. Deep down inside I think maybe it should work this time. I have that inner feeling that it will finally abort."

Couldcard was the *quintessential* Good Man: Yale, Top-Secret Security Clearance, and secretly worked at La Casa Blanca for years.

After working at The Pentagon, *someone* at La Casa Blanca recommended him for the job at *The Washington Post.*

Then he brought down The Prez.

The Washington Post is SkullnBones, its owner even helped finance Pops's earliest business ventures.

And in '77, Bernstein himself wrote about The CIA's *extraordinary* penetration of its newsrooms.

The Deputy Director of The CIA from '50-'65 eventually *killed himself,* but he was The CIA's *premier* orchestrator of "black operations" and often bragged of his "Mighty Wurlitzer," a wondrous propaganda instrument that he built and played aka The Media.

He was the *maestro* of Bernays's timeless pied piper score.

And his best friend was the publisher of *Newsweek*.

When *Newsweek* was purchased by *The Washington Post*, its publisher was notified that The CIA would occasionally be using the magazine as needed.

Hayg, an alum of The Bay of Pigs Thing, chose Jowarsky to be the H2OG8 Prosecutor and probably recommended Couldcard to *The Washington Post*.

Couldcard tied The Plumbers to Nxn.

Bieterfuld had the tapes.

Couldcard and Deen pointed to him.

Then The CIA Deputy Director points out The Smoking Gun excerpt.

Couldcard admitted at least one significant distortion compared to how he reported the story: no Deep Throat.

That just made the better story.

Couldcard's new book, *Veil: Secret Wars of The CIA, '81-'87,* politely eschews any meaningful mention of Pops.

H2OG8 Prosecutor Jowarsky was a close chum of L-BJ and TX legal counsel for powerful Oil Men and Cotton Kings.

A prosecutor in the post-WWII War Crimes Tribunals, he

refused to participate in Neurenburg.

Somehow his Top Secret Clearance was never revoked.

He also made a point to publicly deny the existence of any conspiracy re: 11/22/63.

Pops got bellicose with The H20G8 Committee's top investigator Bellino, who was most likely to recognize a plot.

Pops *demanded* that Bellino be investigated, trumping up a case that Bellino had attempted to hire three private dicks to plant bugs and eavesdrop on Party senators.

He *demanded* that Bellino be removed from The Committee.

Bellino accused Pops of slander and defamation.

And after 10 weeks defending himself against Pops's attacks, he eventually cleared all charges.

Jowarsky's H20G8 inquiry never looked at Pops.

When someone brought him up, they made it clear they weren't interested in him.

The FBI started to investigate the H20G8 funding trail, which threatened to lead back to Pops.

And The CIA interfered.

The CIA's Deputy Director testified that Nxn's highest aides told him that it was Nxn's wish that The CIA tell The FBI not to pursue any investigation beyond burglary.

All the investigators *claimed* to be interested in the money trail.

But all of them stopped as soon as they got close to TX Money.

Early '74, Congress looked into anti-trust violations by people on multiple oil boards and *everyone* on the investigators' list had two chums in common: Pops and GDM.

You know, Honorable Reader, that Nxn was pardoned *before* he was ever charged with anything.

This insulated him against charges later, but it also branded him forever to the blotch of H2oG8.

Within a month of Nxn's resignation, Pops became The Homelan's official envoy to China: a year of leisurely bike rides, resplendent BBQs, and no messy investigations or political discombobulation.

Fxord offered Pops that job *before* he even pardoned Nxn.

CHAPTER 63 Science Fiction

Doctor Harold Urey, winner of The Nobel Prize for Chemistry, said "I'm terribly puzzled by the rocks from the Moon and in particular of their titanium content."

Moon rocks contain processed metals, including brass and mica, and the elements Uranium 236 and Neptunium 237 that have never been found to occur naturally.

Isaac Asimov, the renowned and prolific author and professor of biochemistry at Boston University, said: "We cannot help but come to the conclusion that the moon by rights ought not to be there. The fact that it is, is one of the strokes of luck almost too good to accept... Small planets, such as Earth, with weak gravitational fields, might well lack satellites... In general then, when a planet does have satellites, those satellites are much smaller than the planet itself. Therefore, even if the Earth has a satellite, there would be every reason to suspect... that at best it would be a tiny world, perhaps 30 miles in diameter. But that is not so. Earth not only has a satellite, but it is a giant satellite, 2160 miles in diameter. How is it then, that tiny Earth has one? Amazing."

Irwin Shapiro from The Harvard-Smithsonian Center for Astrophysics said: "The best possible explanation for the Moon is observational error."

He also noted: "The Moon is bigger than it should be, apparently older than it should be and much lighter in mass than it should be. It occupies an unlikely orbit and is so extraordinary that all existing explanations for its presence are fraught with difficulties and none of them could be considered remotely watertight."

In their book *Who Built the Moon?*, Christopher Knight and Alan Butler wrote: "The Moon has astonishing synchronicity with the Sun. When the Sun is at its lowest and weakest in mid-winter, the Moon is at its highest and brightest, and the reverse occurs in mid-summer. Both set at the same point on the horizon at the equinoxes and at the opposite point at the solstices. What are the chances that the Moon would naturally find an orbit so perfect that it would cover the Sun at an eclipse and appear from Earth to be the same size? What are the chances that the alignments would be so perfect at the equinoxes and solstices?"

The Apollo 12 mission to the Moon in November '69 set up seismometers and then intentionally crashed the Lunar Module causing an impact equivalent to one ton of TNT.

The shockwaves built up for eight minutes and NASA scientists reported that the Moon rang like a bell.

Geophysicist and oceanographer Maurice Ewing, said, "As for the meaning of it, I'd rather not make an interpretation right now, but it is as though someone had struck a bell, say, in the belfry of a church, a single blow, and found that the reverberation from it continued for 30 minutes."

Ken Johnson, supervisor of the Data and Photo Control department during the Apollo missions, said, "The Moon not only rang like a bell, but the whole Moon wobbled in such a precise way that it was almost as though it had gigantic hydraulic damper struts inside it."

Dr. Gordon MacDonald of NASA said, "It would seem that the moon is more like a hollow than a homogenous sphere."

He surmised that the data must've been wrong.

But it wasn't.

Carl Sagan, everyone's *favourite*, noted, "A natural satellite cannot be a hollow object."

And Dr. Sean C Solomon of MIT said, "The Lunar Orbiter experiments had vastly improved knowledge of the moon's gravitational field and indicated the frightening possibility that the Moon might be hollow."

Farouk El-Baz of NASA said, "If water vapour is coming from the Moon's interior, this is serious. It means that there is a drastic distinction between the different phases of the lunar interior—that the interior is quite different from what we have seen on the surface."

Dr. D.L. Anderson, professor of geophysics and director of The Caltech Seismological Laboratory said, "The Moon is made inside out. Its inner and outer compositions should be the other way around."

Dr. Robin Brett of NASA said simply, "It seems much easier to explain the nonexistence of the moon than its existence."

But the moon was as *real* as anything's *ever* been real to me.

CHAPTER 64 A Gap in Logic

I ambled far out into the prairie to where—running low thru the brush—train tracks extended from thick trees only to come to an abrupt end out in the open.

Weepy and nauseous with sleep deprivation, I set pen to page, unsure where to begin.

You remember writing letters, Amiable Reader, the *clarity,* and that perfect sense of being set in relief against a world of flattened backgrounds?

Whatever hard *bolt* of aching need motivates the writer, it's an act of giving *bereft* of generosity.

Love, more than anything, must be the spontaneous awareness of the lack inherent to all language.

I had no instinct and no cultivated sense of how to *embody* this acute tuning.

But I walked out into the prairie cuz I wanted her to know exactly where I sat as I wrote the letter; the better I could render the act of my writing, the more *complete* and subtle her reading of it would be.

Something like: *I'm on the big log green with lichens, behind the small blue tree, off the path to the right when you're walking away from the house.*

She *needed* to know that there was once a man that could not *help* but write this letter.

Out there in the prairie wet down and yellow with late fall, chocolate smeared with spit on the back of my wrist, I'd deliver the means with which she could blackmail me.

She supposes either of us can remain unchanged in the face of this *totalitarian* wallop and bliss?

I could only submit.

With my thinking clarified and heart slashed open, my pen began to move.

Fuck it, Magnanimous Reader.

What *is* love—I ask you—if not itself a gap in logic?

I found a mothballed suit and couldn't zip the pants all the way, but the coat hung low.

I showered and washed my hair twice.

I used one of those rough crumpled sponges that scrape skin.

I found rich soap in a linen closet.

I baby powdered all my waist-down folds.

I slicked my hair straight back.

I'm all neck and a shallow swoop of chin, but I shaved up, then down, then up again.

I'd forgotten what a good shave felt like, with good razors and cooling aftershave.

I'd let my nose hairs go, so I had plenty to pluck.

I tweezed each ear hair and trimmed the corners of my eyebrows.

I scraped my tongue.

I trimmed my pubic hair, not shaved, but neated it up, above and under.

I trimmed and filed my fingernails, pushed back the cuticles.

I lathered on *a lot* of lotion.

I patted the sagging bags under my eyes lightly with two fingertips.

And with the letter folded in my coat pocket.

All I could do was wait.

I think I got feeling problems.

I don't really *feel* I have thinking problems, except when the feeling problems are on my mind.

All I could do was wait.

It felt good to be clean.

Yep, crisp.

All I could do was wait.

After a while I took my pants off cuz they pinched.

I didn't *decide* to do this, but eventually I became aware

244

of my *self* walking in circles, in my boxers with a suit coat hanging long off my shoulders, six antacid tablets in my mouth, mumbling, "*It's Teddy. That's Teddy. The same goddam Teddy*" over and over like a mantra in time with my stride.

You've picked up by now, Benevolent Reader, that I very much do like to *feel* rational.

But it'd been a long time since I'd given up attempting to rationalize my feelings.

The limitations of *any* model reveal themselves as soon as that model is made to stand beside the mysterious and watery poisoned orb itself.

Some terms exist only in pairs so that each word can be most easily defined by the other's absence.

My Diana and me, we were like that, I think.

I held the door open and called her name, my sweaty claw clutching the letter in my pocket like a vice.

I launched loud into reading:

Duh, unga-bunga,
Duh, unga-bunga. Duh, unga-bunga. Duh, unga-bunga.
Duh, unga-bunga. Duh, unga-bunga. Duh, unga-bunga.
Duh, unga-bunga. Duh, unga-bunga. Duh, unga-bunga.
Duh, unga-bunga. Duh, unga-bunga. Duh, unga-bunga.
Duh, unga-bunga. Duh, unga-bunga. Duh, unga-bunga.
Duh, unga-bunga. Duh, unga-bunga. Duh, unga-bunga.
Duh, unga-bunga. Duh, unga-bunga. Duh, unga-bunga.
Duh, unga-bunga. Duh, unga-bunga. Duh, unga-bunga.
Duh, unga-bunga. Duh, unga-bunga. Duh, unga-bunga.
Duh, unga-bunga.
Duh, unga-bunga. Duh, unga-bunga. Duh, unga-bunga.
Duh, unga-bunga. Duh, unga-bunga. Duh, unga-bunga.
Duh, unga-bunga. Duh, unga-bunga. Duh, unga-bunga.

Duh, unga-bunga. Duh, unga-bunga. Duh, unga-bunga.
Duh, unga-bunga. Duh, unga-bunga. Duh, unga-bunga.
Duh, unga-bunga. Duh, unga-bunga. Duh, unga-bunga.
Duh, unga-bunga. Duh, unga-bunga. Duh, unga-bunga.
Duh, unga-bunga. Duh, unga-bunga. Duh, unga-bunga.
Duh, unga-bunga. Duh, unga-bunga. Duh, unga-bunga.
Duh, unga-bunga.

Duh, unga-bunga. Duh, unga-bunga. Duh, unga-bunga.
Duh, unga-bunga. Duh, unga-bunga. Duh, unga-bunga.
Duh, unga-bunga. Duh, unga-bunga. Duh, unga-bunga.
Duh, unga-bunga. Duh, unga-bunga. Duh, unga-bunga.
Duh, unga-bunga. Duh, unga-bunga. Duh, unga-bunga.
Duh, unga-bunga. Duh, unga-bunga. Duh, unga-bunga.
Duh, unga-bunga. Duh, unga-bunga. Duh, unga-bunga.
Duh, unga-bunga. Duh, unga-bunga. Duh, unga-bunga.
Duh, unga-bunga. Duh, unga-bunga. Duh, unga-bunga.
Duh, unga-bunga.

Duh, unga-bunga. Duh, unga-bunga. Duh, unga-bunga.
Duh, unga-bunga. Duh, unga-bunga. Duh, unga-bunga.
Duh, unga-bunga. Duh, unga-bunga. Duh, unga-bunga.
Duh, unga-bunga. Duh, unga-bunga. Duh, unga-bunga.
Duh, unga-bunga. Duh, unga-bunga. Duh, unga-bunga.
Duh, unga-bunga. Duh, unga-bunga. Duh, unga-bunga.
Duh, unga-bunga. Duh, unga-bunga. Duh, unga-bunga.
Duh, unga-bunga. Duh, unga-bunga. Duh, unga-bunga.
Duh, unga-bunga. Duh, unga-bunga. Duh, unga-bunga.
Duh, unga-bunga.

Duh, unga-bunga. Duh, unga-bunga. Duh, unga-bunga.
Duh, unga-bunga. Duh, unga-bunga. Duh, unga-bunga.
Duh, unga-bunga. Duh, unga-bunga. Duh, unga-bunga.
Duh, unga-bunga. Duh, unga-bunga. Duh, unga-bunga.
Duh, unga-bunga. Duh, unga-bunga. Duh, unga-bunga.
Duh, unga-bunga. Duh, unga-bunga. Duh, unga-bunga.
Duh, unga-bunga. Duh, unga-bunga. Duh, unga-bunga.
Duh, unga-bunga. Duh, unga-bunga. Duh, unga-bunga.
Duh, unga-bunga. Duh, unga-bunga. Duh, unga-bunga.
Duh, unga-bunga.

Duh, unga-bunga. Duh, unga-bunga. Duh, unga-bunga.

Duh, unga-bunga. Duh, unga-bunga. Duh, unga-bunga.
Duh, unga-bunga. Duh, unga-bunga. Duh, unga-bunga.
Duh, unga-bunga. Duh, unga-bunga. Duh, unga-bunga.
Duh, unga-bunga. Duh, unga-bunga. Duh, unga-bunga.
Duh, unga-bunga. Duh, unga-bunga. Duh, unga-bunga.
Duh, unga-bunga. Duh, unga-bunga. Duh, unga-bunga.
Duh, unga-bunga. Duh, unga-bunga. Duh, unga-bunga.
Duh, unga-bunga. Duh, unga-bunga. Duh, unga-bunga.
Duh, unga-bunga.

Duh, unga-bunga. Duh, unga-bunga. Duh, unga-bunga.
Duh, unga-bunga. Duh, unga-bunga. Duh, unga-bunga.
Duh, unga-bunga. Duh, unga-bunga. Duh, unga-bunga.
Duh, unga-bunga. Duh, unga-bunga. Duh, unga-bunga.
Duh, unga-bunga. Duh, unga-bunga. Duh, unga-bunga.
Duh, unga-bunga. Duh, unga-bunga. Duh, unga-bunga.
Duh, unga-bunga. Duh, unga-bunga. Duh, unga-bunga.
Duh, unga-bunga. Duh, unga-bunga. Duh, unga-bunga.
Duh, unga-bunga. Duh, unga-bunga. Duh, unga-bunga.
Duh, unga-bunga.

Duh, unga-bunga. Duh, unga-bunga. Duh, unga-bunga.
Duh, unga-bunga. Duh, unga-bunga. Duh, unga-bunga.
Duh, unga-bunga. Duh, unga-bunga. Duh, unga-bunga.
Duh, unga-bunga. Duh, unga-bunga. Duh, unga-bunga.
Duh, unga-bunga. Duh, unga bunga. Duh, unga-bunga
Duh, unga-bunga. Duh, unga-bunga. Duh, unga-bunga.
Duh, unga-bunga. Duh, unga-bunga. Duh, unga-bunga.
Duh, unga-bunga. Duh, unga-bunga. Duh, unga-bunga.
Duh, unga-bunga. Duh, unga-bunga. Duh, unga-bunga.
Duh, unga-bunga.

Duh, unga-bunga. Duh, unga-bunga. Duh, unga-bunga.
Duh, unga-bunga. Duh, unga-bunga. Duh, unga-bunga.
Duh, unga-bunga. Duh, unga-bunga. Duh, unga-bunga.
Duh, unga-bunga. Duh, unga-bunga. Duh, unga-bunga.
Duh, unga-bunga. Duh, unga-bunga. Duh, unga-bunga.
Duh, unga-bunga. Duh, unga-bunga. Duh, unga-bunga.
Duh, unga-bunga. Duh, unga-bunga. Duh, unga-bunga.
Duh, unga-bunga. Duh, unga-bunga. Duh, unga-bunga.
Duh, unga-bunga. Duh, unga-bunga. Duh, unga-bunga.

Duh, unga-bunga.
  Duh, unga-bunga. Duh, unga-bunga. Duh, unga-bunga.
Duh, unga-bunga. Duh, unga-bunga. Duh, unga-bunga.
Duh, unga-bunga. Duh, unga-bunga. Duh, unga-bunga.
Duh, unga-bunga. Duh, unga-bunga. Duh, unga-bunga.
Duh, unga-bunga. Duh, unga-bunga. Duh, unga-bunga.
Duh, unga-bunga. Duh, unga-bunga. Duh, unga-bunga.
Duh, unga-bunga. Duh, unga-bunga. Duh, unga-bunga.
Duh, unga-bunga. Duh, unga-bunga. Duh, unga-bunga.
Duh, unga-bunga.
  Duh, unga-bunga. Duh, unga-bunga. Duh, unga-bunga.
Duh, unga-bunga. Duh, unga-bunga. Duh, unga-bunga.
Duh, unga-bunga. Duh, unga-bunga. Duh, unga-bunga.
Duh, unga-bunga. Duh, unga-bunga. Duh, unga-bunga.
Duh, unga-bunga. Duh, unga-bunga. Duh, unga-bunga.
Duh, unga-bunga. Duh, unga-bunga. Duh, unga-bunga.
Duh, unga-bunga. Duh, unga-bunga. Duh, unga-bunga.
Duh, unga-bunga. Duh, unga-bunga. Duh, unga-bunga.
Duh, unga-bunga. Duh, unga-bunga. Duh, unga-bunga.
Duh, unga-bunga.
  Duh, unga-bunga. Duh, unga-bunga. Duh, unga-bunga.
Duh, unga-bunga. Duh, unga-bunga. Duh, unga-bunga.
Duh, unga-bunga. Duh, unga-bunga. Duh, unga-bunga.
Duh, unga-bunga. Duh, unga-bunga. Duh, unga-bunga.
Duh, unga-bunga. Duh, unga-bunga. Duh, unga-bunga.
Duh, unga-bunga. Duh, unga-bunga. Duh, unga-bunga.
Duh, unga-bunga. Duh, unga-bunga. Duh, unga-bunga.
Duh, unga-bunga. Duh, unga-bunga. Duh, unga-bunga.
Duh, unga-bunga.
  Duh, unga-bunga. Duh, unga-bunga. Duh, unga-bunga.
Duh, unga-bunga. Duh, unga-bunga. Duh, unga-bunga.
Duh, unga-bunga. Duh, unga-bunga. Duh, unga-bunga.
Duh, unga-bunga. Duh, unga-bunga. Duh, unga-bunga.
Duh, unga-bunga. Duh, unga-bunga. Duh, unga-bunga.
Duh, unga-bunga. Duh, unga-bunga. Duh, unga-bunga.
Duh, unga-bunga. Duh, unga-bunga. Duh, unga-bunga.

Duh, unga-bunga. Duh, unga-bunga. Duh, unga-bunga. Duh, unga-bunga. Duh, unga-bunga. Duh, unga-bunga. Duh, unga-bunga.

Duh, unga-bunga. Duh, unga-bunga.

Duh, unga-bunga. Duh, unga-bunga.

Duh, unga-bunga. Duh, unga-bunga.

Duh, unga-bunga. Duh, unga-bunga. Duh, unga-bunga. Duh, unga-bunga. Duh, unga-bunga. Duh, unga-bunga. Duh, unga-bunga. Duh, unga-bunga. Duh, unga-bunga. Duh, unga-bunga. Duh, unga-bunga. Duh, unga-bunga. Duh, unga-bunga. Duh, unga-bunga. Duh, unga-bunga.

Duh, unga-bunga. Duh, unga-bunga. Duh, unga-bunga.
Duh, unga-bunga. Duh, unga-bunga. Duh, unga-bunga.
Duh, unga-bunga. Duh, unga-bunga. Duh, unga-bunga.
Duh, unga-bunga. Duh, unga-bunga. Duh, unga-bunga.
Duh, unga-bunga.
   Duh, unga-bunga. Duh, unga-bunga. Duh, unga-bunga.
Duh, unga-bunga. Duh, unga-bunga. Duh, unga-bunga.
Duh, unga-bunga. Duh, unga-bunga. Duh, unga-bunga.
Duh, unga-bunga. Duh, unga-bunga. Duh, unga-bunga.
Duh, unga-bunga. Duh, unga-bunga. Duh, unga-bunga.
Duh, unga-bunga. Duh, unga-bunga. Duh, unga-bunga.
Duh, unga-bunga. Duh, unga-bunga. Duh, unga-bunga.
Duh, unga-bunga. Duh, unga-bunga. Duh, unga-bunga.
Duh, unga-bunga. Duh, unga-bunga. Duh, unga-bunga.
Duh, unga-bunga.
   Duh, unga-bunga,
   Duh, unga-bunga

   A choir of frogs chirped, like how birds in a prairie cry a
warning in chorus, "Alligator!"
   In slo-mo my stomach capsized.
   I did not blink.
   I put on a grin same as the smile My Mother George
Washington hoists around.
   Thinking I should breathe, I stepped backward toward
the door while extending my hand outward, steeled my
nerves in anticipation of that ping of bone that occurs when
we touch.
   The backs of my hands looked old; my knuckles vain,
foolish, childish, rash, self-centered, self-important, and
moronic.
   A deep yawp flooded my skull to its asymmetric capacity.
   And she did not take my hand.
   When I stepped slow back to close the door, I felt her
soften.

My imbecile grin.

Animals do die of *natural causes*.
They *eat each other alive*.

CHAPTER 65 Re: Everything

Memory warps *Present Circumstances*.
And Present Circumstances warp *Memory*.
Present Circumstances warp *Future*.
And Future warps *Present Circumstances*.
That's all Saint Orwell, and everyone knows it.
And note the quaquaversal expansions, Trusted Thinker:
Memory warps Future.
Future warps Memory.
Memory warps Memory.
Present Circumstances warp Present Circumstances.
Future warps Future.

And yet still no *possible* answer, where *am I* in the endless and ever-shifting halls of my family's ice castle—on a
mountain in small woods surrounded by vast prairie on
"Government"-restricted land on a peninsula?

And who *is* this ever-shifting Pops, *My Father,* his
strange reptilian blood rushing thru my veins, his name
slowly pooling in my balls?

Blame Darwin, that *Marxist* of genealogy.
His *re-creation* of *creation* kicked all the arbiters of
moral and ethical superiority off-balance.
God *doesn't* stick his big holy nose in human affairs to
protect his loyalists: he can't even match the exact number
of eyelids to eyeballs.

Darwin suffered *deep* depression.
He was *constantly* sick and achy cuz he felt so alienated,
so alone, and so fated to never *not be* alone.

My five senses, however asymmetrical, and my memories
conspire to create this profound illusion of subjectivity,
its perseverance primary to how I interpret my *Present*

Circumstances.

Could the revelation of any secret *explain* or quell that *blind spot* that stands in the center of each of our fields of vision, exactly where we each expect our *self* should stand?

There are as many interdependent universes as there are dimly sentient blobs to witness them, and this blind spot is the only unanimous commonality.

What secret could explain *duration*'s expanse when we suffer or its quickening thru joy; how we envy our friends at the expense of our own vitality; or how we tell tiny lies without noticing while resenting that same treatment by others?

Crowley was The 20th Century's mechanistic materialist occultist.

Expanding Nietzsche's obit of God and anticipating Barthes' obit of the author, he claimed the primacy of the magickal practitioner's *experience* in granting rites their powers.

Rituals *objectively* allow you to enter a *heightened* subjective state.

Expand that personal experience to the cultural scale, and it's apparent how ideology *shapes* culture and society.

And oil enables it all.

Society is shaped to disguise this, but every *possible* possibility can only exist given the condition of oil's free-flow: refrigeration; your commute and your workday's chiseled schedule; the pretense of democracy ennobling each individual's rich and complex interiority; the nuclear family; all the triggering microchips and plastic toothbrushes.

Donald Duck called Daffy Duck a racial slur first time they met.

And during WWII Bugs Bunny fought Hitler in "Herr Meets Hare" and The Japanese in "Bugs Bunny Nips the Nips."

MoMA in NY was conceptualized and helmed for generations by The Ruckafellas.

In '50 The CIA established and funded The Congress for Cultural Freedom (CCF), an anti-communist advocacy group that eventually became active in 35 countries.

In '52 The CCF sponsored "The Festival of 20th Century Masterpieces" and its agenda was clear: "On display will be masterpieces that could not have been created nor whose exhibition would be allowed by such totalitarian regimes as Nazi Germany or present day Red Russia and her satellites."

This meant, primarily, Abstract Expressionism.

Ruckafella purchased over 2,500 pieces of Abstract Expressionist art, displaying many pieces in his banks' lobbies.

This patronage, along with the help of Bonesman Luce's *Life* magazine, shifted the artist's social role.

Not long before that, artistes were commonly Marxists scraping by financially and aligning themselves with progressive social movements.

But they became cynical loners in multimillion-dollar Tribeca lofts, producing work for their wealthy patrons instead of to inspire hope in their communities as the guardians of liberal ideals.

In '55 Guy Debord defined psycho-geography as "the study of the precise laws and specific effects of the geographical environment, consciously organized or not, on the emotions and behavior of individuals."

Oil creates the consensus trance.

And accrued momentum—cultural and personal—sustains it.

Uncle Sigmund wrote about the compulsive impulse to

re-live trauma to *conquer* it: always ending up in the same bullying dynamics, perpetually swinging between credit and debt, etx.

It's *impossible* to anticipate exactly how the same trauma will play out across a sampling of individuals.

Surviving The Vice, for example, motivates some people to fuck with The Act of Love indiscriminately to prove what a big deal the trauma *wasn't;* and other people freeze upon any touch.

Uncle Sigmund's nephew Bernays aimed to guide this tension, like plumbing and gutters: a soft landing from the ubiquitous trauma of being a dimly sentient blob at all crushed among the throngs of others' rich and complex interiors.

Everyday brutality and systemized global resource wars on ze Tube lessen the shock.

Of course, any mass of dimly sentient blobs *produces* its leader.

The leader is *symptomatic,* the symbol they've all sub-consciously chosen together.

And The Barbarians can't *identify* with this leader, only project upon and *worship* him.

Repressive tolerance, that subtlest of controls, means that The Barbarians have the *privilege* to criticize this leader and to criticize all those who protect their privilege to *criticize* him.

Hitler's *belief* in the occult, *not* his disbelief, inspired him to outlaw its lighter practices like tea leaf and palm reading.

Stunts and cut-rate astrologers always irritate serious occultists.

We brought all *his guys* to The Homelan to help start The CIA, not to charge them with *war crimes.*

And personally, any glimpse of any *God* that I've ever
gotten has happened in the simplest tricks of the light:
the glaring sheen of grease in a pan set on a tablecloth in
sunshine; my brother's long arm swinging upwards to break
the shine of a lake seen from its far shore; the icy glimmer
of chilled shrimp skin; sweat coalescing on a bottle; a profile
silhouetted by the moon, low and huge.

There's *The Father*: your antenna.

And The *Son:* that engine pumping blood.

And some *Holy Spirit:* the balanced dualities and near-
symmetries of your five senses that your piloting ghost
depends on to execute its will, while constantly *grinding*
thru your memories to churn out your biases.

And The Family attacks at *every one* of these levels of
being.

They clutter your receptors with constant noise, polluting
that quantity of sky dished within your skull.

They tear thru your heart's thick meat with weaponized
cutesiness, nostalgia, and pride.

And crowd *the world* lousy with pizza and cartoons.

Part 3
11/8/88

CHAPTER 66 Tomb Construction

The back wall came up chest-high on me.

The two side walls stood equally tall toward the back but diminished in blocks down to knee-high at the front.

A single row of soup cans marked the would-be front wall's position.

The mannered actions with which we *extend* ourselves out into the *world* are not counted among our senses: speech is not hearing, *being looked at* is not seeing, being handled is not touching.

The infini-verse, that charged *ping* of bone thru the troubled scrim of *wordage*, and The Family, all *inevitable* and also all *impossible*.

It stings to *feel* like you understand completely, but to *know* that you only understand a little bit.

I'd no longer need to question light sources, old or new, and how they bounce.

Everlasting non-existence literally couldn't *be* that bad.

Balancing my weight on the hard corner edges of a large Tupperware, I topped off the back wall.

Completing the tedious top rows required the careful re-setting of my balance after each step down to grab a couple more soup cans.

The mud had hardened, but I was reticent to invest any more of my rationed water.

The back wall complete, I finished one side wall before I was forced to scrape excess mud and water it down with what little spit and piss I could muster to complete the last two walls.

Poe's best movies, *The Tell-Tale Heart* and *The Raven,*

both grapple with that moment *right before* you crack up.

I always loved Vincent Price.

Of course, I understood how my behavior *appeared:* I hadn't just moved back in with my parents; I was building a tomb inside a bunker inside a mountain under an ice castle in small woods surrounded by vast prairie on "Government"-restricted land on a peninsula.

But for the first time in my life, I had purpose and *meaning*: I'd set the record straight re: that best-selling, so-called *Objective biography* that claims that I—*me*—am My Mother George Washington's *favourite.*

And for the first time in my life I knew how to go about achieving such an ambition.

Same as that momentary floating sensation I'd learned to summon to spare my *self* the perpetual conical glare of that steel spike in the center of my field of vision: I would reverse foreground and background.

A long *game* of corrective perspective.

A *long* game of corrective perspective.

Philosophical questions are *only* answerable in private, *unanswerable* in any public way.

Silence would annul my mushy ear.

I'd restrict the depth to which that steel spike in the center of my field of vision could expand outward.

I couldn't quite touch the parallel walls with my arms extended and fingers fanned out fully.

This was no Champagne Unit.

I'd finish construction within a couple days.

Sitting down, I was careful not to set my weight against any wall.

And though its cover image of a classic hermit wizard with a long white beard and pointy hat carrying a lantern epitomized my *Present Circumstances*, I couldn't get into *Mysterious Stranger*.

I found the fairy tale tone cloying, too *morally,* and the paper chalky.

Planning interested me more: life confined, compressed, sans light, and liberated of all that *open-endedness.*

No flimsy closet door.

Standing and feeling like a tub had been filled chest high around me was my goal for the next day.

I don't know if you've seen the movie *Inherit the Wind,* Fervent Reader.

It's about how God didn't create the sky until the second day, so who could say how long that first day lasted?

Why her, of all the innumerable dimly sentient blobs, *how* exactly *she* triggered in *me* everything that she did?

Like distinguishing between languages you don't speak, I've moved thru a million nights, my stare fixed on the glow of a curtain's edge, how its seam, all blur and cotton in moonlight, brightens with sunlight.

And in this same way, many nights have moved thru me, until I wake each morning wondering where I am.

Who I am.

CHAPTER 67 The Family Jewels and Church

Christmas '74: CIA Mind Control experiments became headline news when *NYT* published Seymour Hersh's cover story on "The Family Jewels," a 693-page report on global CIA actions.

It detailed LSD experiments on unsuspecting citizens, dental fillings made into antennas, weaponized shellfish toxins, assassination attempts on foreign leaders, and Dullis's 20-year program of reading people's mail.

Doesn't even matter which Dullis Bro.

Schlesinger, in only his fifth month as Director of The CIA, ordered "The Family Jewels" report in response to press allegations of CIA involvement in H2oG8.

Kissinger called the report the tip of the iceberg.

And once The Barbarians learned how The CIA *really* operated, public pressure for answers re: 11/22/63 intensified.

March '75: *Life* magazine finally premiered Z'puda's classic film to wide acclaim.

They'd bought the rights *years* earlier but decided to keep it under wraps while emotions ran high.

Z'puda hadn't bothered to bring his camera along that day.

His assistant insisted he go back and get it.

And immediately after filming King Arthur's very public skull chipping, Z'puda ran into a newspaper man and told him about the film.

The newspaper man told a Secret Service guy that he knew.

More than 11 years had passed, and the public still *loved* it!

It was up there with *The Godfather* movies, *Jaws, The Rocky Horror Picture Show, Dog Day Afternoon*, and *One Flew Over the Cuckoo's Nest*.

Not to mention *Z'puda* is a cool name like Han Solo or Apollo Creed.

I wish, Resolute Reader, that you could see O'Malley and The Greek do Pacino and Cazale in *Dog Day Afternoon.*

It's perfect, *so* funny.

Their *Godfather Part II*—"I know it was you, Fredo. You broke my heart. You broke my heart," and the kiss on the mouth—that was *also* great.

But oddly, they switch actors.

They do *Dog Day Afternoon:* O'Malley as Pacino and The Greek as Cazale.

But it's vice-versa for *The Godfather II.*

Anyways, The Z'puda film was *huge.*

And its release, if not a direct result of The Family Jewels, was at least inspired by the same collective feeling.

But within a few years everything cooled down, and returned to light-hearted cat-and-mouse, spy-versus-spy disinformation.

You ever see *Hopscotch*?

The camaraderie between Walter Matthau and The KGB is cute and toothless fluff enough to *un-qualifiably* qualify as disinformation.

Prez Fxord commissioned The Ruckafella Group to investigate the procedures of The Homelan's spy sector: domestic spying on dissident groups; why King Arthur's head snapped *backwards* in Z'puda's film; what those Bay of Pigs Thing operatives were doing at H2oG8.

Surprise surprise, Ruckafella's commission found no evidence of conspiracy re: 11/22/63.

The entire investigation was established to preempt the more serious congressional probe: The Church Report.

In '75 and '76 The Congressional Church Committee revealed a *remarkable* array of domestic dirty-tricks: The FBI and CIA sent anonymous letters to get politically suspect workers fired; break-ins; disinformation campaigns; The FBI bugged MLK's hotel room and mailed him a recording of him fucking with The Act of Love extra-maritally, threatened to leak it unless he killed himself.

Frank Sinatra introduced King Arthur to a young woman named Exner.

She testified to The Church Committee that Sinatra also introduced her to the Chicago mob boss Giancana.

She had affairs with all three of them—Sinatra, King Arthur, and Giancana—and claimed to have relayed messages between her lovers, including King Arthur's directive to Giancana to assassinate Castro.

The Church Committee unearthed quite a number of CIA plots to kill foreign leaders.

And it found these *unbecoming* to the national image, a transgression against the implied gentlemen's agreement between leaders.

So Fxord issued an executive order banning state-sanctioned assassination attempts on political leaders for political purposes accomplished thru surprise attack.

He used 11/22/63 as an example.

As part of the massive re-shuffling effort to re-empower the Intel Community after all those public embarrassments, Fxord's men Chainy and Rummy fired The Director of The CIA.

And they appointed Pops in his place to reign in the leaks.

CHAPTER 68 Baph and The Champagne Fountain

Junior had joined The National Guard with no flight experience, no officer training, and a score of 25% on his pilot aptitude test.

At flight training in GA, he was the single Guardsmen among 200 Air Force pilots.

People called his previous TX unit "The Champagne Unit" thanks to its high-society roster.

Baph was The Champagne Unit's very popular leader.

He was charismatic, sharp, an exceptional pilot, and already honorably discharged by the time he moved to Houston to join The National Guard.

He didn't *go to Yale*.

And he didn't even come from money, but he was "Sheep-dipped."

That's when The Air Force loans a pilot to The CIA, *officially* making the pilot a civilian.

His military records get transferred to a clandestine department within The Air Force and his routine promotion and retirement points continue to accrue, but this part of his record remains beyond the reach of The Freedom of Information Act.

Baph's first good deed was big: The odds of *two* suspensions happening at the same time in the same National Guard unit are *outlandishly* far-fetched, but Baph got suspended the same time that Junior got suspended, giving the impression that a suspension is more routine than it actually is.

Baph said he can thank The Family and The Kingdom for *everything* he's ever had.

He said he'd still be scrubbing aircraft toilets if Pops hadn't intervened.

He even oddly went on record once re: how he'd never speak on record.

He said: "There's all sorts of civilian participation (in The CIA.) The people who are called on by their 'Government' and serve—I don't think you're going to find them talking about it."

In '75, a short, pudgy, balding, goateed, cigar-smoking young man named Ghaith Pharaon became the first Kingdom national to buy controlling interest in a domestic bank in The Homelan, the ailing Detroit Bank, more a foot in the door than a meaningful purchase in its own right.

His father was The King's closest advisor; The King's personal physician, appointed ambassador of *all* Europa.

He sat beside The King so they could whisper.

But even with his father's breath on The King's ear, The Royal Family never fully accepted Ghaith cuz his father was born in Syria.

Ghaith wasn't *ethnically* of The Kingdom.

Educated across Europa, then Stanford and Harvard Business Schools, equally at home in Damascus, Karachi, Paris, and Miami, Ghaith had no *real* allegiance to The Kingdom.

He was an invention of BCCI—Bank of Credit and Commerce International—a one-stop financial hub for *everyone* from dictators to drug lords.

It financed MI6, Israeli Mossad, and Kingdom intel; Iranian, North Korean, Chinese, and Pakistani militaries.

It laundered hundreds of millions of dollars for The CIA to bypass congressional approval for cover-ops.

Everyone feared the leak of BCCI's secrets.

Ghaith was the front for anything that BCCI wanted to buy.

BCCI, trying to cozy up to The Kingdom, loaned Ghaith $300,000,000 against phony assets and manipulated bank shares.

But BCCI didn't know that Ghaith had fallen out of favor with The King when he tried to extort a commission for an under the table oil deal between The Kingdom and Spain.

Shortly after Pops's takeover at The CIA, Fxord announced a *major* reorganization, increasing the agency's power to do controversial operations, and The Director's authority over the larger intel community.

Pops formed his Team B to directly politicize intel to lean The Homelan into a more hardline stance against The Reds.

Its members included Chainy and Rummy and Wolfie and they explained to *Newsweek* that The CIA's analysis had been flawed cuz it was based too much on *hard data*.

As Director of The CIA, Pops requested a copy of a report re: Jack Ruby's visit to mob leader Trafficante, who would later admit to a House Panel that he participated in a CIA-directed operation to assassinate Castro.

Trafficante had been recruited by Rossellini.

Rossellini testified about Castro in April '76, while Pops was Director of The CIA, and he was called to testify again, this time re: 11/22/63.

But before that could happen, his decomposing body was found inside a 55-gallon steel drum floating in Dumfoundling Bay, his legs sawed off.

Another of Trafficante's associates was gunned down before testifying on this matter.

Frank Church of The Church Committee said: "There is no question in my mind, but that concealment is the new order of the day."

Pops personally monitored *all* media references to The CIA.

And he personally looked over *every single* secret file re: 11/22/63—Ozzy, GDM, Trafficante—however insignificant it appeared to be.

In his 355 days holding the position, Pops testified to Congress 51 times, including denying any CIA involvement in feeding propaganda to The Media, and pressing The Justice Dept. to prosecute Woodward.

Remember, Undeviating Reader, Grandfather's drinking taught everyone how to keep secrets real good.

My Mother George Washington was suicidal that whole year.

I can't say why *that* year.

No one ever mentions that singular lapse in her power.

My cousin with schizophrenia suffered terrifying violent fits.

Pops's uncle died a slow and agonizing death in The Philippines.

Junior was arrested for a DUI.

And Pops's *job* was keeper of secrets.

Pops is a master illusionist, flimflamming *calculated* distractions, purposeful murkiness, and fuzzy warpings of unexceptional details so that *any* fact can slither away into obfuscation.

He *epitomized* The Family's essential paradox: serving shadowy forces while *craving* constant attention.

He taught us all to live double-lives, setting people up to speak freely then sitting around the corner of an open door to listen.

And he *loved* to repeat that line chiseled into The Scottish Parliament: "Let us flourish by telling the truth."

As Head of The CIA, besides scrubbing operations and cooking intel, Pops also enlisted The Kingdom to finance missions that Congress barred, in effect *privatizing* The Homelan's covert ops.

In March '76 Baph launched an aircraft brokerage and received a call from Salem bin Laden—aka "The King's private contractor"—to buy a plane.

On short notice Baph flew himself to The Kingdom and stayed three weeks with bin Laden.

The oldest of 54 children, bin Laden was the 30-year-old heir to the *vast* construction and engineering empire that modernized The Kingdom, building roads, schools, hospitals and hotels.

Bin Laden was a gregarious, Westernized, English-speaking, cocktail-loving, international playboy.

He loved to play the piano and sing at parties.

And he invested $1,000,000 in Junior's first business.

While there, Baph also befriended Khalid bin Mahfouz, the 25-year-old heir to The National Commercial Bank of The Kingdom.

This was the *only* bank in The Kingdom not nationalized in '74, and the bank where The Royal Family kept their money.

Both bin Laden and bin Mahfouz were tight with King Fahd.

And by July '76, bin Laden signed Baph on as his business representative in The Homelan.

Bin Mahfouz soon hired him too.

They paid Baph on commission: 5% personal interest in every purchase that he made with their money.

Their names never appear.

When Ghaith and BCCI eventually came under scrutiny, bin Mahfouz was implicated.

He paid $225,000,000 to get the charges dropped, and his bank was barred from *ever* doing business in The Homelan again.

Meaning: this ultimate international crime bank, funded at least in part by The Royal Family's bank, bought controlling interests in domestic Homelan banks.

Chairman of The Foreign Relations Subcommittee on Terrorism, Narcotics, and International Operations, John Kerry, led The Senate investigation.

Himself a Bonesman, he'd received significant campaign

support from BCCI, so no *serious* investigation took place.

Investigators never mentioned bin Mahfouz's connection to Baph and Baph's connection to The Family.

In fact, The Treasury Department official responsible for scrutinizing BCCI's dealings was Pops's cousin.

Eventually Ghaith was charged in absentia for embezzling hundreds of millions from BCCI.

He returned to The Kingdom and they refused to extradite him.

No one knew if he was stealing on his own behalf or for others, and *everyone* feared what he might reveal if extradited.

BCCI now focuses on developing a global surveillance system.

And Ghaith last popped up in The News when he filled a fountain in a Paris nightclub with champagne.

So as Head of The Homelan's intel community, Pops engineered a private foreign policy, deepening the codependent Brutal Friendship with The Kingdom.

This perfect transnational quid pro quo secured a steady oil-stream for The Homelan and also created an infrastructure for covert intel operations, evading Congressional oversight, using The Kingdom as surrogate funders.

Pops placed Baph as his key intermediary to The Kingdom, a reward for taking care of Junior's fumbling National Guard service.

Baph represented The Family's interests.

Bin Laden and bin Mahfouz represented the interests of The Royal Family.

The TX-Kingdom partnership orchestrated by Pops—an off-the-books international intel operation—grew to control a sprawling hidden empire.

CHAPTER 69 Hoisting Soup Cans Down into The Bunker

I'd bundled eight cans of soup at a time in my arms.

Stacking them was simple but picking them up was tricky.

The strain hit my lower back, my thighs, and my calves by the time I knew that I'd need to repeat the movement 100 more times.

My sense of *Spirit* never included anything so *formal* as penance, but it did instinctually account for karma.

People weren't born pure and gradually corrupted by the world.

A curse hibernated in my DNA.

Dazed with fatigue, I lugged each stack of cans down the many stairs and then lugged my *self* back up them.

I sought immediate relief from what: *my privilege?*

The thin-blooded fates of King Charles II and Darwin?

Stacking the last cans at the bottom of the steps, my skin burned like a hair-shirt in the cool bunker air.

My focus was a *beam.*

If I didn't immediately execute Step 2, hoisting the cans across the bunker, I'd learn to live with a giant stack of soup cans.

Even back among The Barbarians, every one day of living required one day of recuperation and repair.

My body clenched, but I pressed on.

My materials were simple, and the ends might *appear* simple, but its labor and construction were not.

My cans all in position, I passed out, drenched in sweat and dusty on the concrete floor, happy as a pig scratching itself against a tree.

The combined forces of exhaustion and hunger weakened me so that I struggled hard to stand up.

I lingered in that in-between state equal parts wakefulness and sleep.

The few steps to the nearest toilet were an epic trek.

I'd open my eyes to *My Diana* inspecting me from the door.

But I understood and accepted by then that she would vaporize if I ever attempted to look at her straight on.

A phantom of my periphery.

Lying on the floor, I was not only planning but practicing.

Maybe the fifth day I had enough energy to masturbate, but I certainly wasn't the one doing most of the work in the fantasy.

Maybe day seven I lost touch with the dreamy side of that languid state, a conscious man in a series of mellow stretches in a bunker, among hundreds of soup cans.

I say day seven, but who knows how long that first day lasted.

I'd have an easier time orienting myself within a rectangle than a square.

But in the end, I intuited the tomb's dimensions while standing inside four lines drawn out in cans on the floor.

It felt right, bigger than a coffin, the size of a wide closet, in the middle of the bunker's big room, closer to the kitchen than the command center.

I considered building it around a sink, or a sink and toilet, but intuitively I knew that all my corporeal functions and needs had to be equalized: sleeping, food storage, waste, there should be no hierarchical distinctions.

CHAPTER 70 GDM's Swan Song

GDM resurfaced, and a Dutch Tube journalist, Oltman, began to steer GDM exactly the same as GDM had steered Ozzy.

Oltman came from a rich family with a history in colonial Indonesia.

He was the same Yale class as Bukkles.

He had no *apparent* ties to Dallas, but he'd begun hanging out there in those conservative circles around the same time whichever Dullis was forced out of King Arthur's court cuz of The Bay of Pigs Thing and GDM had been approached by Moste to suggest he should meet Ozzy.

In '64 Oltman randomly met Ozzy's mother on a plane.

She confided that *she* suspected a conspiracy.

By '76 GDM had started work on his autobiography, emphasizing his time with Ozzy.

He sent the manuscript to Oltman.

And after "The Family Jewels" scandal and the controversy with the intel community, *Reader's Digest* began its own investigation into 11/22/63.

It had long ties to Hoover and The CIA.

Ruckafella's brother was on its board.

And it was less interested in uncovering *new information* than in investigating *why* new information continued to emerge.

The magazine had actually been approached with the suggestion for the story by Epstein, a CIA officer who'd purportedly left the agency, but continued to work as a media consultant, arranging interviews and ghostwriting.

So *Reader's Digest* commissioned a new book project by Epstein to beat The House Select Committee on Assassinations—aka HSCA—to the punch, attempting to influence its conclusions.

Sept '76 HSCA got a staff of 170 lawyers, investigators, and researchers.

But Epstein and *Reader's Digest* got to *every* witness before HSCA did.

GDM wrote Pops a letter.

Desperate and harassed, he saw Pops as someone he could trust with the power to help him.

The letter was written in a knowing tone, like *'We both know what's going on here.'*

With his response, Pops strategically established a record of topics that GDM had not brought up in his own letter, giving future researchers alternative explanations for GDM's disquiet: his daughter's death, the stress of harassment by the press.

GDM's wife, a known intel officer, had him committed.

He suffered depression, heard voices, saw visions.

He thought his tormentors were everyone *except* The CIA.

Later, his wife said that a doctor had arrived mysteriously and given GDM injections.

The doctor disappeared, and GDM had a nervous breakdown.

GDM came clean to Oltman, the Dutch Tube journalist.

GDM said: "Willem, I have to tell the story as it *really* was. But don't betray me . . . you are the only journalist I will trust. Don't incriminate me in 11/22/63. I don't want to go to jail. How could we do it in such a way that I don't go to jail?"

Oltman asked him: "Well, first tell me, did you do it or didn't you do it?"

GDM replied: "Yes, I am responsible. I feel responsible for the behavior of Ozzy . . . cuz I guided him. I instructed him to set it up."

GDM *begged* Oltman to get him out of the country.

They flew to Amsterdam, and GDM began providing *fragments* of a scenario in which TX oilmen, in league with intel operatives, plotted to kill King Arthur.

They spent a few days at Oltman's Amsterdam home, GDM editing the manuscript of his autobiography.

One day Oltman suggested they go out to lunch.

Oltman told GDM that a Red man would be joining them.

GDM excused himself and never returned.

He knew that Oltman had betrayed him, making him *appear* as a Red agent himself.

If they could all three be seen eating lunch, a spy could photograph it, and use it as proof.

In March '77 GDM went to Palm Beach to stay with his daughter.

He requested that Savage drive his car to Florida.

Savage had helped Pops with the Zappatoes platform parked 54 miles north of Cuba.

And he worked at Sun Oil with the Red that Crytin had recommended to translate Ozzy's wife on 11/22/63.

The HSCA sent someone to interview GDM.

But *Reader's Digest* got there first.

They agreed to pay him $1,000/day, for four days of interviews.

GDM spent the whole first day talking about his life up until meeting Ozzy.

The next morning they talked again.

He returned home for a light lunch.

His daughter told him that an HSCA man had come by.

He nodded OK.

And a little later that afternoon, the maid found him in a pool of blood, a 20-gauge shotgun blast to his mouth.

Investigators proclaimed suicide.

March 20, '77, *The Dallas Morning News* headline read: "Mental Ills of Ozzy Confidant Told."

And with his claims discredited, his suicide soon after surprised no one.

CHAPTER 71 Inter-dimensional Border Patrol

A perceptual gap is the *beating heart* of The Family's success.

There's the *appearance* of genial Pops and pious Junior.

And then, in actuality, there's the secrecy, intimidation, and dark arts of psy-ops.

Those on the receiving end of the weapons usually don't even realize they're being targeted.

It's a sleight of hand, *magick* to achieve and maintain Political *Realism.*

Equally illusion and *not*-illusion, we each pass thru and smash our lumpy biocomputer against that grandest collaboration: the sum of all intent aka the matrix.

So The Family attacks that fundamental level of being most difficult to even prove the *existence* of: Spirit.

And it's all simple programming, micro and macro: that *ping* of bone from a stranger's touch is the same bifurcation as that keen anticipation of WWIII that saturates every second-guessed action.

Psy-Ops 101 is the exact opposite of Guerrilla Warfare 101.

As *Lawrence of Arabia,* Peter O'Toole strategically attacked supply lines.

That's psy-ops: you attack your opponent's point of strength, put them on the defensive about their strong points.

What's casually and broadly referred to as "CIA Mind Control" is actually very many, very specific things.

Remember Ozzy hung out at The Cafe Bluebird in Japan.

That's an example of how The Family organizes triggers.

Even the most dimly sentient of blobs has as many

neurons embedded in the coral reefs in their skull as there are stars in the galaxy, each linked to any of the others in innumerable combinations.

The Family intentionally links specific subconscious memories to particular subconscious triggers.

You've seen *The Manchurian Candidate.*

The Act of Love is commonly weaponized cuz it truly is strange how we grapple and push against each other at all, that rush of expectation that precedes the thrusts, the deep luck and acumen of procuring an appropriate partner.

Maybe in Eden it was all games like a sunny day at the beach with chilled pickles.

But The Family *creates* desires in The Barbarians, like releasing a persistent fly to buzz around that beach.

Surface and the shock of each surface in the infinitude of troubled surfaces, negotiating the borders of body, language, nation, spirit—the borders that differentiate *self* from other, body from spirit—it's in these border negotiations where The Family intercedes.

Manipulating *perceptions,* all five of your senses and your memory*:* that's witchcraft and that's spycraft.

Consider the corpse, that unknowable but substantive *being* stranded at a border.

The corpse in my favourite movie, *River's Edge*, that's *the corpse* I think of when I think of a corpse.

We see her whole naked body.

She's on her back, arms spread open, her fingers bent clenched, but not closed.

Her mouth hangs open, frowning and shocked.

She's bone pale, barely pink at her lips, purple bruises across her neck, and mud smeared at her eye socket.

Her eyes wide open, bluishness under a film of white.

Her name is Jamie.

Is her name *still* Jamie?

Her name *was* Jamie.

Jamie was the name of the sum of her actions, shorthand for the kinetic energy that she embodied, her tastes and biases?

Or Jamie is the name of the body sprawled at the river's edge?

Each Barbarian shrivels as scanty as his controlling desire and blooms to be as great as his dominant aspiration.

You think The Family doesn't know that?

A dimly sentient blob has 100 times more information on its brain than a rabbit.

Does that make 101 rabbits smarter than a dimly sentient blob?

It flatters The Barbarians to call them *animals*; animals may not have the critical faculties of the average dimly sentient blob, but at least they tune their instincts to their environments.

The Barbarians are more accurately *brain-washed animals* cuz we control the environments that determine their instincts.

The "psychic driving" techniques of CIA Mind Control—tape loops played 16 hours a day repeating the desired new attitude—certainly don't differ much from our anemic Media.

Thus The Barbarian's contemporary crisis: historical, social, socioeconomic, political, moral, and cultural forces all *intentionally* thrown all out of whack, and bifurcated by our border patrols.

Even The Barbarian's simplest day-to-day tasks—the basic upkeep of *Life on Earth*—mutually amplify each other to create negative synergy: sluggish from long work hours means the dishes pile up stinky means you don't want to cook means you eat a bad breakfast that makes you even more sluggish.

1+1=3.

These borders that The Family patrol are *inter-dimensional*: psychic, emotional, spiritual, and material, each cinching when a thread is pulled elsewhere.

The Family is an interconnected component of the totality of multidimensional *Reality*, same as every dimly sentient blob, a manifestation in the field while simultaneously an agent able to affect change within the field.

The Family is *symptomatic* of The Barbarian's alienation in contemporary society; not the *cause* of this alienation, but the *effect*.

How to cope with technological potential, material evolution accelerating beyond the imaginative capacities of psychic evolution?

The Barbarians: *victims* of their own projections.

It's not that everything exists simultaneously *within* the totality of these different dimensions.

It's that these border crossings, moving thru the boundaries of the interpenetrating fields, manifests material form.

Likable Reader, *you know?*

CHAPTER 72 The Simplest Simple Weapon

The Abstract Expressionists were overwhelmingly men, former Marxists turned jaded Marxists; individualistic, autonomous, despairing, anxious, and dreading atomic annihilation.

They believed that they had to present pessimism.

They somberly refused to paint frivolous and superficial *reality* or viscera.

The brutality of their art was a scream of rage.

Nothing should be finished, or refined, or inauthentic.

Crudeness, power, and destruction: the only forthright reactions left.

Nihilism was the only language left, aesthetically and ethically, to respond honestly to the horrors of their dehumanized political reality.

Modern conditions couldn't be represented or described.

To attempt to do so was beneath the *artiste* and tantamount to accepting it.

Still, The CIA glommed on to Abstract Expressionism for its purported anti-communism.

The CCF exported enormously expensive exhibitions of The Abstract Expressionists throughout Europa.

France especially became a target, to demonstrate The Homelan's cultural dominance.

When one CCF show in Barcelona included paintings so large that the museum's doors had to be sawed off to move them in, *La Libre Belgique* wrote: "This strength, displayed in the frenzy of a total freedom, seems a really dangerous tide. Our own abstract painters seem pygmies before the disturbing power of these unchained giants."

Take the debunking of UFOs, for example: if mass hysteria set in, that's a collective psychological event and such an event could threaten The Homelan's defense capabilities and The Reds could march right on in.

So The Family *has to* define the acceptable borders of discourse.

Curiosity *beyond* those borders makes you a *kook*.

Questioning the official story makes you paranoid.

Numerals symbolize quantities, and the letters of the alphabet symbolize the potential sounds you might make with your mouth.

The Founding Fathers were *all* unabashed occultists.

Behold, Ardent Reader, the raw mechanics of the images on your currency; the architecture of Capital City.

Behold the immaculate graphic design of the swastika.

Behold *your name* symbolizing the sum of your aware-ness in *Present Circumstances,* held in place by the tension of your memories.

In '70 Brzezinski of The TriC imagined a society "that is shaped culturally, psychologically, socially, and economical-ly by the impact of technology and electronics—particularly the area of computers and communication."

Control how the population *thinks* by controlling what they see and hear: orchestrated conflicts, desperate and spreading starvation, destitution, and plague, all seduce and distract.

It's simple trauma bonding.

The Family rears the youth on principles and theories that *of course we know* to be false and destructive.

Attack emotions and perceptions to destroy *spirit*, roboti-cizing The Barbarians *sans The Barbarians' knowledge* that any change had occurred.

Uncle Sigmund believed that *loving your neighbor as yourself* runs counter to instinct, and the more *other* that neighbors are made to *appear*, the more instinctual and natural it seems that they are not worthy of love, giving The Barbarians permission to unleash their hidden and prohibited lusts for cruelty, intolerance, and murder in the name of God and Country.

Murder is wrong, but abstract genocide is just unfortunate and necessary cuz it's too big to understand.

History commonly misattributes Stalin as having said, "One death is a tragedy. A million deaths is just a statistic."

But he may as well have said it.

Like in the movie *Catch-22*, Alan Arkin says, "They're trying to kill me," and all of his wacky friends in his platoon say, "They aren't just shooting at you. They're shooting at everyone."

And Alan Arkin says, "That doesn't mean that they aren't shooting at me."

I was trying to remember who *I am,* who I was *before* they programmed me.

I was planning a coup: Overthrowing the *self* like Uncle Sigmund's disciple Jung prescribed.

A good coup is a Family *tradition!*

'33: Grandfather conspired to recruit that FDR stumper Smedley to install a fascist dictatorship in The Homelan.

'53: Mossadegh in Iran was overthrown after GaDoyla's son-in-law sat by his bedside for *80 hours.*

Feb '63: Iraq's Qasim was killed in a Ba'ath party coup led by a young thug Saddam that The CIA supported and trained in Beirut.

The planned coup against Papa Doc in Haiti gave GDM reason to interact with high-ranking officials, including L-BJ's military advisor, in Capital City months before 11/22/63.

That most *spectacular* spectacle, 11/22/63.

And Ummer, my parents' companion that afternoon, orchestrated the coup in Indonesia that brought Suharto to power to ease The CIA's link with the nation's largest mine, Freeport.

Why not indulge in a small coup of my own, extending to the furthest borders I had access to: my *self*?

The Family patrols the inter-dimensional borders of every Barbarian man, woman, child, alpaca, shrew, platypus, lamprey, prairie rat, genome, coral reef, algae, iceberg, nightshade, bay, dental hygienist, octogenarian, crawfish, trout, pilchard, periwinkle, mealy redpoll, black-gloved wallaby, snotty-nosed giraffe, pygmy hippo, and bug—all interconnected manifestations of the field while simultaneously agents able to affect change within the field.

I am *symptomatic* of the alienation born of the endless battle: cause *versus* effect.

Same as they destabilize a region to make sure that no other power rises, *so many channels* is in itself the disinformation that keeps the dull and uncurious in a lulling stupor and scrambling those who do seek answers with layers of mazes of disinformation.

In pre-literate cultures, reading was a secret power that only hermit wizards with long white beards and pointy hats possessed.

Widespread literacy totally transformed how The Barbarians processed *Life on Earth*.

The Honest Abe-Douglas debates were *day-long* events, standing in a hot field sans shelter from the sun: one man had 90 minutes to speak, then the other had 60 minutes for rebuttal and only cuz literacy was the primary model of understanding could such a public feat be possible.

The collective leap or tipping point of ze Tube colonized The Barbarians' entire mode of thinking: juxtaposed images compressed all values and emotions.

Structurally, everything gets weighted the same: weather, sports, genocide, celebrity abs, individual corruption, systemic bias.

The biases are structural, content secondary.

It's the simplest simple weapon: low consciousness appeals to everyone, and that's why it spreads.

Of course, the most widely disseminated *propaganda* among The Barbarians is that *we* don't use propaganda; the *other side* does!

Biologically programmed to stare at potential dangers, The Barbarians will surrender *anything* to not feel afraid.

The Media, exhausted and warped as it may *appear*, does *exactly* the job it's designed to do.

The networks filter and frame in contrast to one another to boost ratings as if political ideology were a binary and superficial choice, Pepsi versus Coke.

Systematically it's not just that The CFR owns *The Wall Street Journal* and these Good Men all take turns pushing hard and dry into the same gagged 13-year-olds.

Physiologically, the more Tube you let infest you, the tougher it is to distinguish it from reality.

Exaggeration and repetition are the tools, the weapons.

Imperialism isn't *policed* by the media.

Imperialism *is* the media.

Every Reporter and Tube personality a Manchurian candidate, none of them able to comprehend the scale of the actual project.

Violent programming keeps us on edge.

And when that fundamental uncertainty in common gets weaponized, intimacy itself is weaponized, and fucking with The Act of Love becomes the nuclear arsenal.

CHAPTER 73 It's Teddy. That's Teddy. The Same Goddam Teddy

Like living in a submarine, I'd rolled over and gotten right to work stacking cans, light on my feet and hummingbird buzzing.

And then I turned, and only a step away, staring at me: *My Diana*

I wiped my brow with my bandana, sighed, and steadied my gaze just right so that she wouldn't evaporate.

She looked curious, like maybe she'd once known me, a bug to stomp.

I nodded hello.

I gestured to the walls with a shrug, flopping my hands at my sides.

I pivoted and dropped four cans in place.

"Duh, unga-bunga?" I asked, bending to dip the plastic knife in the thin mud.

She took a short step toward me, her toe to the lowest row of cans symbolizing the front wall's eventual position.

She leaned close to a side wall, looking it up and down.

I set the next can in position and glanced at her sideways.

She shook her head and sighed.

She stepped back and paced in a circle, then set her feet and squared her shoulders.

I shrugged.

"Duh, unga-bunga," I said, splendidly and rapturously *enthralled* by her *thoughtful* analysis.

"Duh, unga-bunga."

She shrugged.

"Duh, unga-bunga," I continued, wowed by such *very keen* insight she offered.

She snorted.

I shrugged.

It popped out as simple as I needed it to: "Duh, unga-bunga."

I glanced up at her but couldn't keep looking.

She stepped away as I set the next can in position.

She stopped in the door, set one hand to the frame and turned her head, but didn't turn all the way around.

She asked me if I'd like a beer.

"Duh, unga-bunga?" I said.

I thought a second.

I wish it was just that a furrowed brow flattered her, or she looked good flushed.

But I *liked* seeing her troubled.

It made me feel important.

"Duh, unga-bunga," I said. "Duh, unga-bunga."

She nodded and stepped out the door.

I called after her, "Duh, unga-bunga . . ."

She stopped, turning an to ear me, but didn't pivot.

"Duh, unga-bunga."

I inhaled deep.

This was important.

I had to explain it right.

I didn't want her coming back.

"Duh, unga-bunga? Duh, unga-bunga."

I made her promise me, OK?

I didn't want to see her again.

Don't come around here.

She nodded, her hand set to the doorframe.

I couldn't look at her.

"You won't see me again," she said and stepped out the door.

Hungry and focused, I doubled my speed.

And by the time I paused again, both side walls equaled the back wall's height, chest-high.

If a 10-by-6-foot cell with no change of clothes, living on bread and water, was good enough for Saint John of the Cross, then that was *good enough for me* to correct that *insane* and puerile so-called *Objective* biography.

The further away from The Family I ran, the more I resembled them.

Pops, Junior, Future-Gov Brother, King Brother: which

of them do you expect would *not* build himself a pharaoh's tomb?

Before finishing the other walls to the ceiling, I began work on the front wall.

My hands raw with blisters, broken open and bleeding.

My only option was to push thru the pain, and, after not very long, my system streamlined by repetition, working on one wall instead of two parallel, I'd completed the front wall knee-high.

I stopped to move all the soup cans to inside the four walls and re-stack them.

The steps over the short wall were tall and the frequent bending and lifting made the task more aerobic.

Vacuum-seal Tupperware to shit in and only a couple day's food supply: adapting to live on less and less each day would solve both those problems.

If we were pharaohs, My Little Brother would still reign as the demigod.

Locked away his entire life, though mirrors were forbidden, he'd enjoy getting spiffed up in a suit under his birdcage, with cufflinks and a handkerchief in his breast pocket and a big knot in his tie.

His irrepressible tears, struck by a visiting woman's beauty—he hated to *let her down,* simply *appearing* as he did.

And *everyone's* tears hot and sudden, how it *exhausted* other people simply to be near him and not let on how it affected them.

But he never *had* to grow up.

He'd never have to cope with how *Life on Earth corrupts* you in exactly the same measures that it *exhausts* you, and still *somehow* you have to learn to live with yourself.

Like The Pope toiling to comprehend the view from his telescope.

My Little Brother never had to make the choice, never had to live like me, keeping your distance from The Family while still reaping the benefits, facing the shame and ridicule from both sides, until your personhood is negated and it's implicit, even if no one acknowledges it, but everyone *knows* it's simpler, the simplest of all options, you become a ghost.

He never had to *grow up* and either integrate body and mind or suffer their split.

He never had to endure the nagging appetites, and learn how to keep moving, however little is expected of you, keep moving thru each day, the tasks growing more and more important to your sense of personhood even as they diminish to the *bare minimum* of personhood: groceries, laundry, what else can you find to do?

James Dean would've gotten fat and taken on some dud roles had *he* lived long enough to do so.

All Sal Mineo's good offers dried up long before he was stabbed to death.

CHAPTER 74 Being Your Own Man

Every glass and pot and pan in the bunker I filled with water and moved inside my tomb.

I covered them all with old newspapers so that dust wouldn't settle on their surfaces.

And suddenly crowded with supplies, I had no choice but to finish the walls to get the cans off the ground.

Plunging ahead with adrenaline, after not long at all, the last wall also stood chest high.

I modified my pattern, circling around all four walls, setting the next layer down and then the next and soon the walls were all chin-high, and finally, for the first time in a long time, maybe ever, like *never* before, peace washed over me.

Finally.

I chugged a jar of water before realizing I had to begin whittling away at my appetites.

Water required conserving, and finally, I felt submerged, swaddled, cocooned.

It's not inconceivable to imagine that Tsar Nicholas II of Russia—the wealthiest head of state in all of history and the wealthiest saint of The Russian Orthodox Church—and Tolstoy, the anarchist, would've had occasion to meet.

Historical contemporaries and the most influential men in their country, they were undoubtedly aware of each other.

Tolstoy came to see ascetic morality as the only spiritual path to holiness for rich kids like The Buddha and St. Francis.

Matthew 19:24—"It is easier for a camel to go thru the eye of a needle, than for a rich man to enter the kingdom of God."

There's a movie of Tolstoy's 80th birthday party, his wife picking flowers, his daughter sitting in a carriage, his students and closest aides and confidantes around.

Nothing really *happens* in the movie, but it being 1908, just seeing people talk and move made for a good movie.

In '73, after Yale, Junior showed up to Harvard Business School in cowboy boots and a flight jacket, spitting tobacco, but he never did register with The Air Force Reserve Unit like he was supposed to.

Out of 108 students in his class, Junior finished in the bottom 10%.

Still, upon graduation, he had 53 interviews at Fortune 500 companies.

But he didn't land a job.

He remained unemployed for several months until Harvard invested in his first oil company in '77.

After Harvard, Junior met his wife at a BBQ, and within three months they married.

He'd become a West TX *landman*, The CIA itself investing in his company.

After their guard duty together, Junior *denied* any relationship with Baph, but by '78 Baph already *loved* to tell everyone that Junior would be Prez someday.

And if Baph, on record, invested $50,000 and that represents 5% of the total investment, that means that his investors—primarily bin Laden—invested $1,000,000 in Junior's first business.

Junior put $1,400,000 into wells that geological data *proved* were bust.

Then he ran for TX Congress in '78, his campaign funded by The Family's Christmas list: Ford Motor Company; Taft; The Prez of CBS who headed the propaganda project *Radio Liberty*, etx.

CHAPTER 75 My New Day-to-Day

A familiar voice murmured my name, and I stood up, groggy, unsure how long I'd been sleeping sitting up, my head on my knees.

Standing, the wall came up to the tip of my nose.

And directly across from me, one soup can's width away, Aaron stood with the wall up to the tip of his nose.

We looked each other in the eye.

He wore an armored 17th-century Spanish helmet.

And he'd grown pointed little wisps of hair above his lip and on his chin.

"Duh, unga-bunga," I said, surprised see him.

"Sir."

"Duh, unga-bunga?"

"Sir?"

"Duh, unga-bunga. Duh, unga-bunga?"

"Oh," his eyes glanced away, and he sighed, "Nowhere in particular."

"Duh, unga-bunga? Duh, unga-bunga."

"Sir?"

He raised his eyebrows, made glancing eye contact, then looked away again.

"Oh," his drawl softened. "You know, it certainly didn't seem from *my perspective* that I'd disappeared."

Good point, it wouldn't seem that way from his perspective, would it?

"Duh, unga-bunga?"

I assume he shrugged but I couldn't see below the tip of his nose.

"Oh," he answered, "Around."

"*Duh, unga-bunga?*" I said, vexed by his cavalier attitude. "Duh, unga-*bunga*?"

"Honestly, Sir," he said with a sigh. "You are not the authority that I report to."

"Duh, unga-bunga?"

"After you challenged my skills, I began to wonder if I hadn't let myself get a little rusty. So I've been on a sort of professional vision quest within the house."

"Duh, unga-bunga?"

"Consider it a retreat, to hone the skill-sets necessary for my work, Sir."

"Duh, unga-bunga." I waved at him to stop talking and shook my head.

"I have remained on constant patrol while doing so, Sir."

I turned from him and paced the small circle that my four walls allowed.

"Duh, unga-bunga?" I asked him, stopping again to stand eye to eye.

He raised his eyebrows in surprise. "And, Sir?"

I waved my hands high over my head so he could see my exaggerated gesture of exasperation.

"Sir?"

"Duh, unga-bunga."

"Yes, Sir," he said.

We looked each other in the eye another moment and said nothing.

He stepped back a step and inspected the wall between us.

He stepped to each side and inspected each corner.

He ducked lower than I could see him and ran a finger clicking across the cans.

His head popped up again back into the original position at which I still stood.

He nodded and glanced to the ceiling.

"So, uh . . ." he said, looking at me, "You're good?"

"Duh, unga-bunga," I said. "Duh, unga-bunga."

He nodded. "Good, good."

"Duh, unga-bunga?" I asked.

"Oh yeh, yeh fine."

"Duh, unga-bunga," I said.

We looked at each other another moment, quiet as frozen waterfalls.

"Can I get you anything?" he asked.

"Duh, unga-bunga." I said, "Duh, unga-bunga."

"You sure?"

"Duh, unga-bunga."

"OK," he said.

"Duh, unga-bunga," I said.

"Yeh sure," he said. "So . . . "

"Duh, unga-bunga," I said.

"OK," he said. "Well, I guess I uh . . . " He shook his head. "I'll be around," he continued. "I'll check in, see if you need anything."

"Duh, unga-bunga," I said.

"OK then."

When he stepped away, I could see for the first time that head to toe he was dressed as Don Quixote.

"Duh, unga-bunga," I called after him.

"Yes, Sir?"

"Duh, unga-bunga?

"Around *here*, Sir?"

"Duh, unga-bunga."

"No, Sir. No young woman around. Of course not."

Zonked, smarting and blistered, I drank three sips of water, and I pissed little dribbles.

I inspected the sealed Tupperware with sniffs, and it passed the test.

I did not have occasion to try out my defecation strategy that day.

I ate one can of soup and invested most of the day concentrating on my hunger.

In my past life such hunger would've made me cranky.

But at home in my tomb, this hunger finally enabled me to *really see* the minute feathering in every brick's grain, the texture in every mug chipped at its lip, and really hear the scrunch of every plastic bag and every fan blade's creak.

Finally I could truly recognize the singe of any permanent marker's bouquet.

I thought of all ze Tubes at The Club, all lined up in a long row, muted and flickering, and the steam rooms we never used.

I wanted to feel exactly the same as I already felt, and always did, but without that constant nagging doubt that it was not an OK way to feel.

I thought of my deep need to see my reflection in hotel mirrors and cooking simply for *My Diana* like she was Sophia Loren.

The Family would've appreciated my smile as I said goodbye.

I thought of *My Diana* and me at the apex of The Necropolis at noon, the edge of a cloud's shadow on my toe, alone with the unseen *whoever* that keeps the graves clean and the gravestones left leaning against their pedestals after cracking off, in the perfect sunlight.

Upon hearing muttering curses, I stood up, the wall to the tip of my nose.

And Aaron, still dressed as Don Quixote, glanced at me.

He said nothing and gave me the *Thumbs Up,* implying with a gesture that he meant it as a question.

I responded *Thumbs Up.*

He approached and carefully handed me an anteater steak over the wall.

We were careful to balance the plate during handoff, the blood broth tempting its edges.

"Your *favourite,* Sir."

He held out a fork and knife, but I picked up the steak and bit at it.

Gnawing, with a deep breath and grunt, that Barbarian that I took notice of among his friends—all of them in face paint at The Other Greek Place, they came to The Game with us—the one so desperate for the approval of his friends, his face *appeared.*

I imagined each bite of steak a thick cut of his shaky leg.

I imagined him conscious and aware that I chomped away at him, the look of deep confusion and despair as he watched me eat him.

Swallowing, I said: "Duh, unga-bunga?"

Aaron nodded.

"Duh, unga-bunga."

He nodded. "Well, good day, Sir," he said and spun away, clanging.

"Duh, unga-bunga."

"Yes, Sir?"

"Duh, unga-bunga?" I looked him up and down.

"Halloween, Sir."

"Duh, unga-bunga?"

"Well, Sir, it's Halloween *season*. And I like to celebrate when I can."

I didn't recall that from previous years, but our eccentricities certainly flourished at Hyacinthignatzi, so I didn't argue the point.

I bent and picked up the Tupperware filled *almost* to the brim with cold piss, its top not totally secured, and I lifted it awk over the wall.

"Duh, unga-bunga?"

He grimaced as he tried to grip it with his fingertips and sighed when he finally needed to press his palms against it.

A German boy locked in a closet until the age of 14 couldn't see any further than three feet, the distance of the closet's far wall.

And what's that story I was trying to remember about some Native people, how their sight normalized in reciprocity to the particular Great Plains they inhabited for countless generations, and then one of them stepped out of a forest into a clearing overlooking an ocean cliff, and toppled in spiritual awe?

I traced geometric patterns across the cans.

I assumed that each time Aaron checked in on me, a day had passed.

I thought of how some people think that just cuz they speak first it means they have something better to say.

I thought of how the *heart* is the true source of intel and how grief is a *mental construct*.

And how comparing pains becomes competitive hyperbole.

My interactions with Aaron required less and less talk as they became ritualized.

He'd hand me a steak.

I'd hand him back an empty soup can or two.

He'd hand me washed Tupperware.

I'd hand him back a piece of old newspaper with thin shit smeared into it.

When I asked, he always answered the same: hadn't seen her.

I wished I could adjust the lighting in some minor way, anything.

Silent except for the clang of his armor, Aaron inspected the back and side walls, now all reaching the ceiling.

"I see you're proceeding."

I paused my work and stood, hands on my hips, and nodded.

He lowered his eyes and nodded, twisting his little mustache. "And when do you expect to complete it?"

"Duh, unga-bunga," I said. "Duh, unga-bunga."

He nodded as if he'd been thru all that before and it made sense according to his experience.

"So . . .?"

"Duh, unga-bunga." I sighed, hands on hips, looking over the work I had left to do. "Duh, unga-bunga."

He nodded. "And you're completing all four walls to the ceiling?"

I nodded. "Duh, unga-bunga."

He nodded. "I see."

We stood quiet a moment. I bent down to mix up more mud.

"*So...* " he said, and I continued my light splashing.

"Sir," he said.

I sighed and stood up straight again. "*Duh*, unga-bunga?"

"You're leaving a window on the front here, I presume. Have you figured out exactly how you plan to do that yet?"

"Duh, unga-bunga."

"Well, I did work as a mason as a teenager," he said.

"Duh, unga-bunga," I said, unsurprised.

"Well, Sir," Aaron said, "I only bring it up to offer my help in strategizing this window. I know it can be tricky leaving an opening on a canned soup wall."

I looked at him.

"Actually, you may have built this up a little tall already. The bottom of the window will come up to your nose. So we may want to get a plan together. Don't add one more layer here until I figure out exactly how we should do this. OK, Sir?"

"Duh, unga-bunga," I said.

"Right, so it's time we develop a plan."

"Duh, unga-bunga."

His expression remained flat, and he said nothing.

We looked each other in the eye a moment.

I bent to return to my mud mixture.

He stepped away from the wall.

Clunking armor slowly paced the room, until finally, he spoke.

"No window?"

I sang out, not pausing my work, "*Duh, unga-bunga.*"

"I see."

He paced another minute, and neither of us spoke.

"You're aware, Sir, that your father's *eleccion* is now only a few days away?"

I continued splashing mud water to coyly mask my surprise.

"And, Sir, you are aware, as part of the *Eleccion Night* activities, your family will begin converging here in 72 hours?"

I could not help but stop splashing in the shallow mud mix.

"The decorators have begun to arrive."

I bolted upright. "Duh, unga-bung—"

"No, Sir. No young woman. But the tables have been delivered, and catering. Of course, the *actual* party is in Capital City. But early evening The Family has decided to convene here."

I scored the ratio of my own acts that I'd choose to keep on record if given the opportunity to review.

"There will be media and such," Aaron said.

"Duh, unga-bunga."

"You don't expect. . ." he called out, then paused.

He approached the wall, his nose right up to it, and continued in a lower voice. "You said you don't expect to be done before this time tomorrow?"

I sighed and paused, looked back up at the tops of the two walls still incomplete.

"Duh, unga-bunga," I said.

He nodded, stepped back away from the wall.

"OK then," he said, pausing at the door. "You don't need anything?"

I considered his offer this time in a way that I hadn't considered it before.

"Duh, unga-bunga."

He knuckled lightly on the doorframe. "Well, OK," he said, "I'll see you tomorrow then."

I thought of the scaffolding of cathedrals under construction, how generations inherited and carried on the work of building this space to inspire wonder, to *feel* real within, and the immanence of how light blown thru glass makes a story real.

I wanted to know how it *feels* to believe.

The scaffolding of a cathedral being cleaned, like My Little Brother's erector set exoskeleton, not enough to block out his stunned tremors at the mere mention of *friends*, always quick to compliment any new person's *noble* face.

CHAPTER 76 Houston and The Philippines

In '77—my last year self-conscious and *cool* at Yale, fix-ated on Cy Franklin—as soon as The Peanut Farmer became Prez, Pops got axed as Director of The CIA.

He moved to Houston, bringing Rover with him, to be a consultant at First International Bankshares Dallas—aka FIB—TX's largest bank holding company.

And when asked, ever since, Pops has said that he couldn't exactly *recall* his duties there.

And neither could the man that hired him.

FIB reached *deep* into the netherworlds of intel and intrigue.

A law passed in '70 had made it possible for banks to ex-pand rapidly into giant holding companies, so FIB handled *massive* transfers of funds for The Kingdom.

The Peanut Farmer lacked foreign affairs experience, which put him at the mercy of The TriC.

You remember The TriC, Ruckafella's private interna-tional policy group.

The Peanut Farmer appointed a Pollyanna CIA director, creating bitter internal resistance.

The second in charge pledged *total* disloyalty to his new boss.

Many CIA vets were disgruntled, Pops most of all.

And FIB's Houston location allowed Pops to set up his "Government" in exile.

At the end of WWII, the Japanese hid the gold they'd plundered from all over Asia in a mine in The Philippines.

The Homelan's forces, under MacArthur, found it and kept it secret.

Estimated to be worth somewhere between $45,000,000,000 and hundreds of billions, knowledge of its existence would've created *mayhem* in the international gold market.

The Philippines had become The Homelan's possession after The Spanish-Homelan War in 1898: After a long talk with God, Prez McKinley concluded that we should keep The Philippines and *Christianize* The Filipinos.

When reminded that The Filipinos were already Roman Catholics, he thoughtfully answered, "*Exactly.*"

Twain, a vocal opponent, suggested that the stars and stripes be replaced with a skull and crossbones.

I should've been re-reading Twain's *Mysterious Stranger*, never stepping foot off a Japanese bullet train, tunnels cutting thru mountains, living on canned iced-coffee and hard-boiled egg sandwiches on soft white bread.

I'd chew fruity gum all day, my breath fresh like a teenage girl.

Instead of being trapped in a soup can tomb with a tired alligator.

Before becoming Prez, Family chum Taft, descendent of the SkullnBones' founder, served as the civilian Gov of The Philippines.

Stimson, a Bonesman who served in five presidential administrations, also held the position.

And before MacArthur commanded our troops in The Philippines, he had vast holdings in its largest gold mine.

Quasha, a Homelan national and powerful lawyer, headed The Party's large ex-pat community there.

And he was also The Grand Master of The Freemasons.

And tight with The Philippines' leader, Marcos.

In exchange for helping Marcos get all of his own money out of the country, Marcos put Quasha in charge of "Alien Property Administration," *meaning* this vast Japanese Gold was put under his control.

This loot went a *long* way in financing covert operations, off-the-books intel work, weapons trafficking, and coups.

Thru the '50s and '60s, so long as Marcos held strong against The Reds and turned a blind eye to the inconceivably *massive* international money machine being run out of his country, The Homelan protected him.

We winked and assisted him in looting his own country, basically turning The Filipino "Government" into a laundry for his own stash.

Marcos recently delivered $10,000,000 cash to The Actor's last campaign.

And Quasha just bought Junior's oil company, placing Junior on its board.

CHAPTER 77 Worlds Collide

The laughter from the other side of the wall had to summon me a few times before I stood up, certain that the crack-up I'd been anticipating had finally overtaken me.

"*Yoo-hoo!* Anybody home?" a familiar voice called out, breathy and gasping thru chuckles.

Stunned, I stood nose-to-nose with O'Malley and The Greek.

"Well fuck me," The Greek said, his lips pursed, tone hushed.

That was his favourite gag, pretending to think seriously about something.

"I'll be a goddam son of a bitch," he said.

O'Malley's raspy laughter resonated into turbo-speed panting before it became a full-on coughing fit.

"It's true," The Greek said. "You really have built a fucking canned soup room without a door."

"Duh, unga-bunga?" I said.

"*How am I?*" The Greek responded.

He slapped O'Malley's arm. "He asks me how *I'm* doing?"

O'Malley's coughing laughter doubled in density and he bent over choking.

"How am I?" The Greek shook his head. "Well, I've been dragged away from my otherwise peaceful and tranquil, I dare say *ideal* afternoon, to a fucking bunker under a quaquaversal maze in an ice castle in the middle of nowhere to have a drink with my old chum here, who *for some reason* has built a goddam little canned soup *coffin* around himself."

"Duh, unga-bunga." I smiled and swallowed a lump hard. My eyes wet.

O'Malley brought his nose up to the wall, shaking, obviously standing on his tiptoes.

"How you doing in there? How you doing?" he said.

"Duh, unga-bunga," I said. "Duh, unga-bunga?"

"Never been better," O'Malley said. "I love it. I fucking love it. It's brilliant."

I shrugged. "Duh, unga-bunga?"

"Oh yeh," he said. "This is great."

The Greek shook his head.

"Get you a drink?" O'Malley said, and I said, "Duh, unga-bunga."

He stepped away from the wall.

That Mike, the bartender from The Other Greek Place, standing back by a cooler in the middle of the room waved hello.

"How you doing?" he called out.

"Duh, unga-bunga."

"Good, good," he said, cracking open a can of beer.

"Duh, unga-bunga?" I asked.

"Oh." That Mike looked at me, startled. "She's good, starting school. Got me up *early* every morning. I can't complain," he said. "We're good."

"What the fuck?" The Greek said, staring at me with his red eyes intense, his nose pressed up to the wall. "What the *fuck* are you *doing* in there?"

I shrugged.

"No," he said. "Tell me. I want to know."

"Duh, unga-bunga."

"You *don't know?*" He raised his voice.

O'Malley handed me a plastic cup of mudslide over the wall.

"Here you go."

"Duh, unga-bunga."

Days since I'd had a drink, I immediately *slackened*.

"I want to know. I *need* to know what the fuck you are doing," The Greek said. "I know you've always been a little *out there* . . . "

And I joked, now I'm in here: "Duh, unga-bunga."

The Greek called me some names I'd rather not repeat.

O'Malley handed him a beer. "Hey, hey, let's all calm down here, yeh? We came to have a *nice* visit. No reason to *attack* anyone."

"Attack?" The Greek shouted.

"Yeh," O'Malley responded. "Let's calm down and have a

nice visit."

We all stood silent, sipping our drinks.

"Hey," O'Malley said. "I got an idea. Let's put on a little music, eh? What kind of party is this without music?"

The Greek sighed and shook his head.

He stepped away from the wall and paced.

"Duh, unga-bunga," I said.

I turned around and sat down, my back against the front wall, my knees raised up to my forehead.

I heard a record start, my *old favourite* from my cool years long ago, Cy Franklin.

I downed the drink, stood back up and turned around.

"Duh, unga-bunga?" I said, shaking my plastic cup above the wall.

"There you go," O'Malley said.

He grabbed my cup quick, took a few steps, and poured me another.

I asked about games I'd missed and everyone struggled to differentiate one game from another.

There were few surprises how the season was turning out, and we all agreed, none of the teams could rival the *old teams* on The Classic Sports Channel, *still* the best game in town even if everyone already knows that Joe Montana is going to hit a leaping Dwight Clark deep in the end zone with 58 seconds left to get to The Super Bowl.

They tried to fill me in on a little gossip around The Club: so-and-so's wife split, and so-and-so's sick.

But I didn't really know who they were talking about.

I asked about Diana Herself, if anyone knew if her barber son had taken her to Florida yet.

But none of them had seen her.

That Mike lingering awk in the background, not saying much, dropped his can of beer and it spilled all over the floor.

He slowly bent to pick up the can, but then made no move toward a towel or anything to wipe it up.

He just kind of *symbolically* rubbed it in with his toe and continued listening to our conversation like nothing had happened.

"Duh, unga-bunga?"

"What?" That Mike said, shrugging. *"That?"* He nudged toward the small beer puddle.

"Duh, unga-bunga."

"You serious?" he asked, seeming seriously surprised.

"Duh, unga-bunga?"

He shuffled in place and shook his head, muttering.

He wiped his nose quick with his thumb and cocked his head.

"Duh, unga-bunga?" I said.

"You're really a piece of work," he said, stepping up toward the wall. "You know that?"

"Duh, unga-bunga?" I said.

"What do *you care* if I spill beer out here in your fucking bunker?"

"Duh, unga-bunga?" I said. "Duh, unga-bunga."

"Rude?" like he was exasperated. "Hate to break it to you, but there's a stench down here like *shit and piss*, not to mention, you do happen to have a *wall* between yourself and that spilled beer, right?"

"Duh, unga-bunga?" I said.

"So?"

"Duh, unga-bunga."

His eyes widened, and I couldn't see them behind the wall, but I know his nostrils flared too.

"Come on, That Mike." The Greek slapped him on the shoulder. "Let's just clean up the beer, OK? I'll help you find a towel."

That Mike held his glare, then shook his head and exhaled.

"OK?" The Greek said.

"Yeh, yeh, OK." That Mike paced a little.

"Where's the kitchen? You got a towel?" The Greek

looked at me.

I nodded. "Duh, unga-bunga."

"OK," The Greek said. "OK, kitchen, let's go."

He threw his arm over That Mike's shoulder and they stepped away.

"Duh, unga-bunga."

The Greek nodded, and That Mike rolled his eyes and they stepped off into the back room.

The record ended and neither me nor O'Malley said anything.

He sauntered to flip it over.

Cy Franklin up loud again, O'Malley approached the wall and summoned me close, "Psst," so we could whisper.

"Duh, unga-bunga?"

"I can help you get out of there."

"Duh, unga-bunga?"

"You wouldn't have nothing to be ashamed of. It's not too late."

"Duh, unga-bunga."

"Oh come on, before the guys get back. What do you say? It's no big deal."

"Duh, unga-*bunga*."

"I know. Of course, you knew what you were doing. Just sometimes, all of us lose our heads a little bit, you know? Nothing to be ashamed of."

"Duh, unga-bunga?"

"No one. That's what I'm saying."

"Duh, unga-bunga?"

"What?"

"Duh, unga-bunga?"

"No, no. Course not. You got to do what you feel is right."

"Duh, unga-bunga."

"Hey, it's OK. We just came here to see you off. Aaron said if we wanted to see you, this was our last chance."

I shrugged and stepped away from the wall, turning my back on O'Malley.

309

"Hey, what?" He raised his voice. "We're having a party here, OK? Relax. I'll pour you another drink. Give me your cup."

I downed the end of my mudslide in one swallow and handed the cup back over the wall.

"I'm just saying," O'Malley grumbled, grabbing my cup over the wall, "All I *meant* was, if you *did* need help, you know your old pals are here to help you. OK?"

"Duh, unga-bunga."

"No one's telling anyone what to do."

"Duh, unga-bunga."

"No one's trying to tell you what to do. Just, if you *want* help, we're here for you. OK, buddy?"

"Duh, unga-bunga," I muttered.

"OK?" He raised his eyebrows, and his fixed stare on me.

You know, Compassionate Reader, under most churches there's another church?

And *that's* the church that the church leaders think of as the *real* church?

I'd stumbled upon my unexpected utopia.

How could I expect my Barbarian chums to understand?

Years I'd dared to be as *useless* as I could be.

Looking back at all the little knots and the gross aggregate of all the stitched particulars, no one *ever* ends up where they intended.

So the monster repents.

That was it: My *Life on Earth*, my sense of self-determination moving thru the mysterious and poisoned watery matrix, spent and depleted.

It certainly *did* seem that there should've been *so* much more.

But the hours got sucked up, poo-pooing possible hobbies with arms crossed and thoughtful nods, cynically considering the likelihood of returns on passive investments, the mechanics of how each game got discreetly rigged.

And that was it, *enough*.

Fulfilled, roly-poly, and doltish, I was upbeat to finally be *alone* with the big naked lady who holds up the tree from which the world blooms.

CHAPTER 78 Pizza

O'Malley hunched back at the cooler pouring me a drink when The Greek and That Mike crashed back into the bunker with a third guy.

He looked familiar from *somewhere*.

Their arms were all full.

"Hey, *pizza!*" That Mike called out.

"Duh, unga-bunga?" I pressed up against the wall, my voice hopping up an octave.

"Hey, hey!" O'Malley called out and stepped to grab a box from The Greek.

"That's right," The Greek said. "Your last meal or whatever. You think we're not going to take care of you?"

The smell made me dizzy.

Tears filled my eyes, and I felt ready to tear thru the wall.

"And," The Greek said, opening a box and waving it in front of me at the top of the wall, "as a special treat, for this most special occasion, allow me to introduce our delivery guy."

The delivery guy stepped up to the wall and bowed.

He looked old to be delivering pizzas, with a full head of gray hair, and his glasses down at the tip of his nose.

He looked like any quiet old man with a careful walk, too weak to balance more than a single pizza.

"*Cy Franklin*," The Greek shouted, and the delivery guy bowed again.

It was really him!

Under the Chee-to dust smeared neon into his T shirt which hung low over his ill-fitting camouflage pants, under 30 extra pounds, *it really was really him.*

When I was a kid at Yale blowing off SkullnBones while Junior strut around trying not to trip over his cowboy boots, Cy Franklin wrote the *only* songs that spoke to me directly, angry and pointed, poetic and passionate, politically righteous *and* erotic; his voice, so many tried to copy his style, but *no one* could make it sound like *anything* but a lousy impersonation.

His singing was *all* his.

And he bounced all over the stage, wiggling and writhing and falling to the floor, standing on his head, leaping from stacks of speakers, all with guitar in hand, never missing a note, like a man *possessed* and protected.

He'd make feedback walls scream and howl, then come crashing down with the slightest gesture.

Big rooms, giant sound systems were all under his command.

Thousands of people followed him *everywhere,* but righteous with passion and anger as his songs were, he was always quiet, mysterious in interviews, never letting on *anything* re: his personal life.

And here he stood, before me, pizzas in hand.

"Duh, unga-bunga."

I lifted my hand awk above the wall to shake his hand.

"Duh, unga-bunga."

He handed two pizzas to The Greek and shook my hand.

"Thanks a lot," he said. "That's real nice of you."

"Duh, unga-bunga."

"Ah, you're too kind," he said with a big smile.

He looked around to the other guys and made a gesture at me. "You guys weren't kidding," he said.

"Duh, unga-bunga?" I asked.

"Oh, they said you built a wall of canned soup around yourself, and you're not coming out."

I shrugged.

The Greek said, "Hey, hey, it's not like that."

"Let's eat some pizza," O'Malley said.

"These guys told me," Cy Franklin said, "they said you're my biggest fan, always, since you were a kid."

"Duh, unga-bunga," I said.

He smiled big and nodded at the other guys again.

O'Malley approached the wall with a paper plate. "Sausage and peppers, and a pepperoni piece, good?"

I grabbed the plate over the wall. "Duh, unga-bunga."

I lifted the too hot piece to my mouth, symbolically blew on it, and took a bite.

I balanced it with my tongue, my mouth slightly open.

Everyone was balancing their plates and dealing with their first bites.

"Duh, unga-bunga."

"What?"

"Duh, unga-bunga."

"What're we going to do?" The Greek said. "You son of a bitch, you stepped into some limo and *disappeared*."

They all laughed, snorting thru mouthfuls of hot pizza.

"Duh, unga-bunga," I said, then the heat of the pizza must've confounded cause and effect cuz hot tears came rolling big down my cheeks.

Sucking air in hard to cool the hot cheese, it tasted *so good*.

"Oh no," The Greek said, everyone chuckling. "It's OK, pal."

I was crying, but laughing too, and took another bite.

"Good," O'Malley said. "It's good to see you."

The mouthful of hot cheese and the tears muted me.

I folded the rest of the first slice into my mouth and with the second slice finally sniffled back the tears.

I couldn't believe they'd gone thru all the trouble of finding Mr. Franklin and finding him a pizza delivery costume.

"Duh, unga-bunga," I said. "Duh, unga-bunga."

"Call me Cy," he said.

"Duh, unga-bunga," I smiled, so appreciative that he went along with my chums' joke, dressing up as a delivery guy, though it *was* Halloween season.

He tore at a long piece of cheese stretching from his mouth to his plate.

"Mmm," he said. "What do you mean?"

"Duh, unga-bunga," I said.

The Greek stood behind him, waving at me to shut up.

"Duh, unga-bunga," I repeated myself.

"What?" Cy stepped closer to the wall. "What *do you mean?*"

"Duh, unga-bunga."

"Who's *dressing up?*" he said, his voice hushed and raspy like from one of his classic dramatic intros.

I took a bite.

"Duh, unga-bunga?" I said, complimenting the pizza.

O'Malley said, "Hey, we need some napkins."

I grabbed crumpled newspaper and handed it over the wall and said, "Duh, unga-bunga."

"That your toilet paper?" That Mike said with a sneer.

O'Malley said, "It's weird about pizza, you know? How many pieces of fucking pizza you going to eat in your life, and still *every single one*, it's always fucking great."

"This is *my job*, man," Cy said.

"Duh, unga-bunga?" I said.

He looked at The Greek, his nostrils widened, and he smiled.

I told him what I always loved about his songs was the *social conscience*.

It was like activist music, and it was so *inspiring*.

"Duh, unga-bunga," I said.

He laughed and pointed a finger at me, looked to the other guys. "This guy," he said.

"Duh, unga-bunga?" I said, confused.

"I don't visit sick punks in the hospital or chain myself to trees or cut ribbons at new Planned Parenthoods. I deliver pizzas."

"Duh, unga-bunga," I said.

"Yeh, oh."

"Duh, unga-bunga."

"Yeh," he said. "What do you think? I got *rich* playing music?"

"Hey, let's all be cool," The Greek said, putting a hand to Cy's shoulder. "You want another piece of pizza?"

"No, I'm good, thanks," Cy said. "You don't think I get enough fucking pizza, 50 hours a week?" His voice sharpened.

"Duh, unga-bunga," I said.

"Yeh, yeh," he said, stepping away from the wall, turning

315

his back to me.

"He doesn't mean anything by it," O'Malley said. "He's real excited and happy to meet you, Cy, for real."

"Duh, unga-bunga." I said.

Cy shook his head and sighed. "We had a lot of idealistic ideals, you know?"

He stepped across the room, his back turned to us, and put his hands on his hips.

"Duh, unga-bunga," I said, half-swallowing my words.

He chuckled. "Yeh, sure. That's why I'm delivering pizzas at 50 years old."

"Duh, unga-bunga," I said.

O'Malley and The Greek stepped to him.

That Mike got out of the way, shrugged, and started on another piece of pizza.

I finished my plate and *really* wanted more.

I stared at the open boxes, but O'Malley and The Greek both stood with Cy at the back wall talking quietly, and I felt bad interrupting.

O'Malley and The Greek both sighed and dug into their pockets, emptying their money clips.

They combined the stack and handed it to Cy.

"It's *humiliating*, you know?" he blurted.

O'Malley and The Greek both shrugged.

Cy crossed his arms.

O'Malley and The Greek both pulled the last bills from their wallets and handed all of it to Cy, both shaking their wallets upside down to demonstrate their emptiness.

Cy stood tall and slapped them each on the shoulders.

He crossed the room back toward me with a big smile.

"Listen," he said. "Did I ever tell you about the time I came off stage. We were playing the legendary Hammond Theater. Thousands of people. The show was *bananas*, thousands of kids freaking out. I come off stage all sweaty and kind of dazed, you know? I mean, my performances back then could get *pretty intense*, you know? I was a bit of a *wild man,* so I never *really* remember what happened..."

After a while I felt comfortable gesturing to the pizza and

The Greek brought me a plate, handed it to me over the wall while Cy kept talking.

The pizza was good, cold now but still good.

Feigned wakefulness must be the most common state of *being* among the dimly sentient blobs.

And tight quarters usually diminished the effects of the steel spike in the center of my field of vision.

But persevering Cy's monologue, feigning wakefulness, the spike returned *hard*, a swirling whirlpool of Cy's past glories: admonishing teenage skinheads for eating ice cream cones in public, slam dunking himself thru a basketball hoop mid-song.

He *loquaciously* pontificated re: the innumerable stabs in his back he'd survived.

He yacked and jabbered, tabulating names we'd recognize from ze Tube.

I now know the nuanced metaphysical findings of his experiments in saving his seed in a jar so that its mold literally *creates a new world,* an ecosystem that otherwise would *not* exist.

And just cuz its biology and social structures existed beyond the limitations of his understanding, that didn't make it any less *real*.

I thought of how Christianity's gory corpse hung on a cross—stripped and beaten, bleeding and splayed on display—perfectly represents the endurance a singular moment can demand.

Eventually, right before you *really* learn to live with it, numbering your disappointments probably begins to make sense.

Watching O'Malley and The Greek squirm and sigh, I thought how weird, how quick you forget how to feel at home with people.

Admittedly, isolation had *stranged* me a little.

But undeniably, Cy was uncommonly voluble.

That Mike slept sitting up far against the back wall.

O'Malley and The Greek both sat behind Cy on the floor, silent, drinking, looking down.

I stood with my nose poking out above the wall, nodding and occasionally saying, "Oh," and "Wow" and "Oh, really? Wow."

Cy prattled uninterrupted for *hours* re: people more famous than him whose phone numbers he has, famous people's preferred destinations for exotic holidays.

None of these illustrious people he was so *delighted* to know shared his social consciousness or righteous anger or poetic sensibilities.

Hours his voice droned unaccompanied by the time O'Malley and The Greek got up and stretched and said, "What do you say, Cy? It's almost midnight, and we all got a long drive back."

Cy thanked us all profusely, said he didn't know the last time he'd enjoyed himself so much.

That Mike woke and creaked upright.

O'Malley and The Greek, we all clutched hands a moment over the wall, looked each other in the eye.

And I recognized in their bloodshot eyes that they wanted to say something poignant.

"Duh, unga-bunga," I said.

They nodded, and both looked away.

That Mike started waving his arms, coming toward us.

"Hey," he shouted.

"Duh, unga-bunga?" I said.

"Come on, let's go." O'Malley put his arm around The Greek and tried to spin him around.

"No, no," The Greek said.

"You're not going to *tell him*?" That Mike shouted. "This is insane."

"Duh, unga-bunga?" I said.

"No, come on," O'Malley said, pulling The Greek.

"Goddamnit," The Greek said. "That Mike is right."

Cy shrugged and reached his hand over the wall, leaning

between those two to shake my hand once more.

"Real good to meet you, pal," Cy said.

"Duh, unga-bunga," I replied.

"You gotta tell him," That Mike said. "We can't go."

"Duh, unga-bunga?" I asked.

O'Malley shook his head.

The Greek pulled hard back against O'Malley and said, "We gotta tell you something."

"We been using the credit card," O'Malley said.

I'd expected that, and it was really no problem, so I said, "Duh, unga-bunga."

"That's not it," The Greek said.

"Goddamnit." O'Malley was pulling him hard, and all at once their struggle *escalated*.

They scuffled, spanking at each other's foreheads, yanking each other's ears, stomping on each other's feet.

Falling backwards into That Mike, he pushed them both aside.

"You fucking fruitcake—" That Mike staring, came straight at me.

"Hey." O'Malley popped up tall and pushed The Greek down.

He lunged at That Mike, grabbed him by the shoulder.

That Mike spun and looked at him, then turned straight back toward me.

"There is no fucking *wall*," he said.

Shaking his head, Cy waved from the bottom step. "I'll show myself out."

No wonder I'd always felt that Cy Franklin sang only for me, that no one else understood me like he did.

Maybe all along I'd been identifying with the latent blowhard subtext.

The bunker felt especially hushed after so much activity, my senses quieting back into symmetry.

And I could finally get to work, *finally* live out that destiny that'd give my wretched *Life on Earth meaning,* My

Report, correcting the melodramatic and irksome claims of that best-selling so-called *Objective* or Subjective Biography, etx.

No wall?

CHAPTER 79 The Art of War

After first rejecting him, all that CIA money laundered thru MoMA eventually supported Warhol big time.

His widowed mom joined him in NY in '51.

And he put her to work, often using her handwriting to accompany his illustrations and making her the subject and star of one of his films.

But a year before she died, after 20 years in NY, she moved back to Pittsburgh, angered that Andy's financial help to the rest of the world was less generous than he could afford.

In The Philippines in The '50s, we strung up the dead to *appear* like a local vampire legend.

In Vietnam in '54 our astrologers predicted the deaths of their leaders.

And we staged the second coming of Christ in Cuba and cast Castro as The Anti-christ.

To jimmy Vietnam open to Homelan intervention, an actual event wasn't even necessary, just its *appearance*.

Witnesses at The Gulf of Tonkin at the time of the sup-posed Incident saw nothing.

France had to abandon its colony after WWII, the country formally split in two at the Geneva Convention.

Why did WWII take three years to defeat both The Germans and The Japanese, but Vietnam took almost 20 years to lose?

It wasn't a blunder.

It all happened exactly as planned.

It wasn't fought to be *won*.

Twelve high-ranking officers all interviewed separately confirmed that the rules of engagement *prevented* victory and it would've been won quickly without the imposed restraints.

A single torpedo sunk The Lusitania.

Its hull loaded with munitions, it made a massive explosion.

Earlier that very same day—*before* the attack—The Homelan ambassador to The UK was talking to The UK King and The UK King happened to ask what effect the sinking of The Lusitania might have on Homelan public opinion.

Homelan Courts officially acknowledged Pearl Harbor's fraudulence, but the trial results were classified.

The fleet was only in Hawaii to provoke the Japanese.

The Korean War was created to empower The UN and demonstrate that congressional approval was no longer required for The Homelan to enter a war.

MKUltra, The CIA's Mind Control program, was named after the abbreviation of the German word for "Mind Control."

Its precursor was named "Operation Bluebird" not unlike the cafe Ozzy frequented while stationed in Japan.

Former CIA Director Helms—who you remember, Astute Reader, was responsible for Gather's slander lawsuit—ordered the destruction of all evidence of The MKUltra program's existence.

And money itself is of course imaginary.

Belief alone sustains it ever since Nxn took the dollar off the gold standard in '71.

The Barbarians aren't *supposed* to understand the language or mechanics of how money works: *symbolic* numbers, not backed by *anything* of tangible value, loaned with interest.

Inflation is manipulated up and down by those who control the flow and this is the magick of converting debt into money.

Honest Abe printed money to gain independence from The British in Canada and The French in Mexico.

And then—*Bang*.

In June '63 King Arthur became the only other Prez to again try to print interest-free money thru The Homelan treasury instead of The Federal Reserve.

And then—11/22/63.

The Federal Reserve, a private corporation that is *not federal* and has *no reserves*, was established in '13.

The Homelan had already been a private company posing as a republic—a corporate instrument of international bankers that literally *own* The Barbarians, everything they own, and everything they might potentially do—ever since The Act of 1871.

The Act of 1871 *appeared* to be only about Capital City, but just change some capitalization and shift the "for" to an "of" and you get an *entirely* different document, a corporate constitution.

The Homelan itself, as a sovereign entity, is a private corporation, an artificial entity created with the power to exercise the functions of a corporation.

The Federal Reserve is *why*, not *how*.

It altered the country's mission so that it no longer served the interests of The Barbarians, but its own financial interests, eventually going so far as creating The Great Depression to consolidate power.

I should've just run away to Japan, traveled by high-speed train, free of the desire to ever determine any destination, days and weeks looking out over clusters of shelled roofs zipping by.

I'd reread *Mysterious Stranger*, scorch thru hours staring at the classic hermit wizard with a long white beard and pointy hat on its cover and never learn one word of Japanese.

A whole year of burping up fish and apple juice.

I'd embarrass all the poor shop assistants, in broken English, gesturing with their hands: "No sizes, too wide."

CHAPTER 80 The Elephant Man

There's that mythology re: his death, My Little Brother.
But I was there.

I know.

I *saw* it.

Have you ever *watched* a person die, Sympathetic
Reader?

The exact moment, the last breath and grip unclench?
The spirit un-attach itself?

Unlatch itself from its anchoring pith and core?

The bifurcation and transformation when a dimly sentient blob becomes a corpse?

My Little Brother's big head, a mysterious and watery
poisoned orb, was too big for him to hold up.

All he ever wanted to do was sleep lying down one time.

Being weepy and nauseous from sleep deprivation was his
total experience of *Life on Earth*, never allowed to remove
that big birdcage from his face.

Like the exoskeletons of extinct jellyfish, nature decided
he *was not needed* and weeded him out.

It was a natural cause.

His full body retainer, like a cathedral being cleaned, like
The Death Star under construction, never killed his easy
smile.

He *always* asked me to help him lie down.

Afterward I lied to myself and everyone else, but I did
know.

I *did* understand exactly what it meant to help him take
the birdcage off his face.

I did know how that big head of his would droop when I
walked out and closed the door behind me, never looking
back to *see* the corpse.

CHAPTER 81 The Iran-Contra Thing

Baph was a principal investor in Main Bank of Houston, which was established to create a *public* joint-banking venture between TX and The Kingdom to distract attention away from BCCI and FIB.

Main Bank was a *pip-squeak* by comparison, but by *appearing* to make The Kingdom's geopolitical agenda public—the funding of our covert ops and the related money laundering—it downplayed the scale of the reality.

By the time Pops became Vice Prez in '80, the Baph-fronted and Kingdom-funded cover for The Homelan's intel activities involved supplying BCCI with airplanes in what eventually got named The Iran-Contra Thing.

Baph had already fronted quite a number of The Kingdom's aviation purchases by the time he bought Houston Gulf Airport on behalf of bin Laden in '77.

He bragged that the airport had no Customs.

Baph then set up Skyway Aircraft Leasing Ltd. in The Cayman Islands, and became its sole director.

Contracted by Pops, he set up this quasi-private aircraft firm for CIA-sponsored activities funded by The Kingdom.

Meaning that Baph—The Family's business-front—was the channel thru which bin Laden came to own a CIA-connected airline.

And Pops denied knowing Baph, only exchanging brief winks if they ever bumped into each other.

Today Baph's airport has the contract to refuel Air Force 1 and other military planes, marking the fuel up by 60%.

CHAPTER 82 The Last Mud Had Hardened

I bolted awake, anxious to get to work.

The last mud had hardened over the course of the day *wasted* with visitors.

Mixing new mud meant locking myself away with even less drinking water, but I wasn't about to wait for Aaron.

I scraped the mud with the knife, hard and fast as a tuck-pointer.

"Hello," said a familiar voice from the other side of the wall.

I stopped scraping, closed my eyes, and sighed.

I swallowed hard.

"Duh, unga-bunga?" I said.

"There are caterers, decorators, media all over the place. Your father's advance team let me in when I told them you're my *boyfriend*."

"Duh, unga-bunga."

"Just being funny."

I dropped the knife and stepped to the wall, my nose barely poking over it even standing up on my tiptoes.

"Duh, unga-bunga," I said.

Diana Herself sighed and turned her back to me.

She must've been sitting with her back to the front wall, waiting for me to stir.

Shorter than the wall, she had to step back a few steps so we could see each other.

She looked good, her makeup thicker on one side of her face and all smidged lower on the other to compensate.

It's Diana. That's Diana. Same goddam Diana, I tried to convince myself.

"Relatively speaking," she said, gesturing to the wall, "I'd say *I* dealt with things pretty well."

I rolled my eyes.

"What the fuck are you doing?"

I shrugged and sighed.

"Really, *what?*" she asked.

"Duh, unga-bunga . . ." I said. "Duh, unga-bunga . . ."

She spun away from me.

Her shoulders lifted and dropped again.

"Duh, unga-bunga."

"You do, do you?" She turned back to me, tears in her eyes, and her cheeks bright red. "You weren't too worried about me when you decided to build a fucking canned soup wall around yourself."

"*Duh, unga-bunga.*"

My pleading tone stunned me.

I cleared my throat. "Duh, unga-bunga."

"This is *my* fault?"

"Duh, unga-bunga."

She turned away from me again, shaking her head. "So, what are you doing?"

"Duh, unga-bunga," I said, aware that I sounded like a whiny little kid. "Duh, unga-bunga?"

She said no thanks, and I helped myself to a slice of pepperoni.

I had learned that there is nothing to learn.

And there's no way for anyone to teach this to anyone else.

You cannot know it except thru executing your every necessary action.

At 100 years old, Abraham fathered Isaac.

And around 5 years old, Isaac finds his loony 105-year-old dad standing over him with a dagger raised high over his head.

When you can't *help* but think of how *every single little* decision you ever made—the stupefying majority of them unconscious—all *literally* changed the course of your life in itty-bitty ways that it's impossible to anticipate or tabulate, all you can do is sit backwards and trace how *everything* delivered you to *exactly* this intersection of time and space.

And sip down a couple mudslides.

And stare at a flimsy closet door.

Time often passed for me in that way it passes when

you've asked something and sit awaiting an answer.

The experience of time passing comes to be the only thing that fills the passing of time.

Would the symmetrical sense organs of the *average* Barbarian be suddenly *flooded* in books and dreams if the pizza and cartoons were removed?

Like those Native people whose perspectives had evolved in The Great Plains, stepping out from the forest into a clearing overlooking an ocean cliff, the *big problem* is that you have to *continue* from there.

Things—the *stuff* of *Life on Earth:* weather, sports, genocide, celebrity abs, love as above so below love—all *equal* as incidents to measure intervals between.

Diana Herself scraped a chair along the floor to the middle of the room, far enough back from the wall that we could see each other's eyes.

She rested her elbows on her knees and lowered her head.

She looked at her feet a long while.

I didn't say anything.

She cleared her throat.

I liked just looking at her.

She tapped her foot, stopped, sat up and threw her head back with a long, low sigh.

"Did I ever tell you . . . ?"

She chuckled to herself.

"Of course, I never told you. I've never told anyone. What I mean to say . . ."

She moved her hands to the top of her thighs and leaned the chair back on its back legs.

"I'm going to tell you a story."

"Duh, unga-bunga," I said.

She looked at me and pinched her lips into a grimacing smirk.

"*Ooooooooh* well," she moaned. "This thing happened. It was a long time ago. It's not like an everyday thing or something, but I guess I think about it. Things remind me

329

sometimes . . . "

She paused, but I never said anything.

"I don't ever *want* to think about it. Sometimes it's funny how stupid it is. Then other things can happen to remind me, and the very same memory is not funny at all."

She smiled again, her eyes glassy.

She stepped up close to the wall and threw her hands up to its top.

We looked each other in the eye.

She took a deep breath.

She sat down again, her back against the wall, below me.

I couldn't see her, but I kept my nose to the top of the wall.

"You can hear me?" she asked.

"Duh, unga-bunga."

I didn't know if she did it intentionally, but we were in the same positions as that monologue scene in that new movie *Paris, Texas.*

I was the young wife, and she was the Harry Dean Stanton.

"Eighth grade. The boys were a little younger, seventh grade. He was very cute, very popular."

"Duh, unga-bunga."

"He was tiny, but always the first one to have a stylish new hairstyle like in the movies, or the first to know how to fold his pants a certain way or wear his collar up."

"Duh, unga-bunga."

"And we all thought he was the *coolest*. He had an older brother and an older sister. The sister was a cheerleader, and they were both a lot older, like five years or more. The older sister treated him like a little doll, dressing him up and doing his hair with mousse. And the older brother was a high school sports star, very dim-witted. And this little guy was my boyfriend."

"Duh, unga-bunga."

"And everyone knew he was too cute for me. I knew it

330

better than anyone. I was a lopsided little—"

I cut her off, "Duh, unga-bunga."

"No, no," she continued. "I was. And I *hated* myself. It's taken me a long time . . ."

Her voice drifted off.

"Well, so anyways, I was going with this little guy really just cuz I knew how to wear my bangs. I knew what new bracelets to wear. I was always the first with things the same way he was. And at an early age it made sense to me, like common sense, that *popularity*, whatever that meant within the confines of a junior high—and its top of the pyramid meant having popular friends at other nearby junior highs—it was all a matter of willingness. *I knew* I was lopsided. But I didn't let that stop me. I wasn't going to go *hide* in some corner. I wore the same tights Sophia Loren wore. I wore my hair wild. I didn't let *shame* stop me. It inspired me. My lopsided face made me try *doubly* hard and that was all that anyone cared about. Popularity meant that the other kids could all see that you committed to doing *whatever it took* to prove that you *wanted* to be popular. Make sense?"

I cleared my throat.

"So *wanting* to be popular did not *guarantee* that it happens. But if you were going to have any shot at it, the essential first step was to clearly demonstrate that it was important to you."

"Duh, unga-bunga."

"So I didn't have much money, but I was willing to play dumb, and I went overboard. I had a case of trendiness *psychosis*."

"Duh, unga-bunga—"

"No," she said. "I was *unstoppable*. So I was half of this conspicuously mismatched couple. And like I said, his older brother and sister told him about things, and *taught* him things, like how older kids dated."

She got quiet a moment.

My stare fixed on the seam where the wall met the bunker's ceiling.

"He lived across the street from this other school, not

the one we went to. And there was a baseball diamond and bleachers and a football field, basketball nets in the parking lot, and a big playground, all rubber and chains in wood chips. Of course, we rarely hung out just the two of us, if ever. We were always in big groups at the mall or splitting one beer between all of us in someone's basement. And a lot of the time we went to that park across the street from his house. His parents were laid-back and open to having a group of kids around without breathing down their necks.

"A couple harsh lights hung high above the park. So hanging out there late at night, this extreme lighting came down from straight above. Everything was in intense shadows, like noir. Everything was either blinding bright or pitch black. And this was how we'd hang out in a big group.

"Mostly we just dared each other, comparing who had the nerve to be most like the others. Cuz you know, we all always believed, and this is probably first and foremost what set us *popular* kids apart from everyone else—we were *so* insecure, *so* unsure of ourselves, so *completely* looking to others to show us how to be. We actually *hated* our friends. We hated everyone, but we hated each other most of all cuz we all believed that the others knew everything, and the group kept continuously resetting the bar of conformity just out of reach, daring each other to reach for it all the time.

"So one night, this group of us are all hanging out in the park and time comes, as it always did those nights, to splinter off into our couples and all walk off into dark corners so we could all lick at each other's mouths and grope each other. And as much as I look back at those people with venom, we should actually *appreciate* each other for the gift of this awkward struggle we all went thru together, learning how to touch each other.

"So my boyfriend and me head toward the baseball diamond. It was dark. I wanted to sit on the bleachers, I remember, but he keeps insisting that we head to the outfield. He says the outfield is so dark, we can stand there in the middle of it and no one would see us.

"His friend, his stupid little friend we all always mocked

332

cuz he'd never even gotten to second base, he was walking along behind us. And I kept asking my boyfriend, 'Uh, what's he doing? He following us?' And he said I'm being crazy, he's just heading back to the house to wait for all of us.

"And my boyfriend looks back at him and gestures to his friend to get out of there. And his friend looks confused. My boyfriend shrugs. I remember it all very clearly. It was over 20 years ago, but I still see it all. I don't know if his friend thought that we couldn't see him cuz it was dark. I don't know. But all at once my boyfriend was pressing his face hard against mine, panting, and breathing on my neck. It was awkward at first, but pretty soon I submitted and was kissing him back.

"It's funny, all those frustrated starts before you lose your virginity. You turn each other on and then linger there, for hours or whatever. Second base was going up my shirt. Third base was going down my pants. After a while us girls did learn how to touch the boys back, jerk them off, squeeze their little dicks real hard until they chafed and eventually, not a year later, putting them in your mouth and they'd explode immediately. But that year, we girls were still just objects to be acted upon. We *permitted* things, as much or as little as we did, but we did not *do* anything.

"And out in that outfield in the dark, my boyfriend doesn't go down my pants. Fingering was often awkward and painful standing up in tight jeans. I was always happy when it didn't happen. And that night, he was happy to keep feeling me up. My bra was undone under my shirt and hung tangled from my shoulders. His hands kept kneading my tits while we kissed each other's necks and nibbled on each other's ears.

"He pulled away a second, turned his head, and then quickly got back to kissing me. He started kissing me more intensely, with more self-conscious effort and intensity than ever before. He was grunting, not letting me turn my mouth away from his to take a quick breath. I felt his hands slip out from under my shirt. And two cold hands quickly replace them. Shocked, I opened my eyes. His eyes were open too, and when he saw me open my eyes, he quickly closed his and pressed his mouth to mine even more intensely.

"I leaned and turned my head. I could see, *ridiculously*, his friend bent down behind him, his hands up under my boyfriend's arms, and up my shirt. Naturally, I pulled away a little, twisted. That was just a reflex.

"Then my boyfriend gave up the front. He really thought until that moment that I wouldn't *notice* these other hands weren't his? He really thought the park was dark enough that he could hide his stupid friend behind his back? So he dropped the cover story and pressed my head hard between his hands, and kept kissing me hard on the mouth. I was *grunting*, closing my mouth, trying to turn away. But he held my head still, kissing me.

"It wasn't worth the struggle. Easier to just go with it. I kept Frenching him, grossly, for a long time, like way longer than people linger on second base after losing their virginity. A long time we stood there, the three of us in the park, two of us making out, and the other one bending low behind my boyfriend, squeezing and squeezing and squeezing. I was bruised and sore for days.

"I remember the lights of passing cars hitting us. And when they did, I could see the porch. And my boyfriend's parents pointing at us and laughing. We stood there, the three of us, a long time. I let it keep happening. I kept looking back at the porch. And they kept laughing. They kept laughing and laughing."

Like systematized murder and oppression, The Act of Love is a thing that you can't even *imagine* doing only one way perfectly.

You know *Reality* doesn't interest me, but *Realism* sure does.

Like a toddler daring to withstand the breath of a puppy

its own size—

Like a scientist decoding the sticky chemistry of fruit sugar on his lunch break—

Like all the unnamed animals who could never be properly sainted without names—

Like how anything becomes *noir* when pressed thru harsh enough filters, erasing all the grays—

Like how every *Holy Man* is essentially non-denominational—

Like the first caveman to ever stumble upon a flower—

Stiff and goopy with the force of *The Old Gods* pushing thru me, forces ancient and amoral convulsed and punctured—

Like cognitive shattering—

To *feel* like you potentially hold the power to repair or confirm someone's sense of bifurcated self according to your touch—

CHAPTER 83 Game Over

I gestured for Diana Herself to grab my hand.

"Duh, unga-bunga," I said.

I'd need to hit the space between the top of the wall and the ceiling perfectly perpendicular.

She pulled my one hand hard.

I put my foot to the wall to scale it, all my weight pressed against it.

I attempted to throw my torso up over the top of the wall, extending my neck to get my head up in there.

But straightening my legs, I lost my balance sideways against the wall and began to slip, cans scraping against my knees like shards of chipped skull.

I howled, and Diana Herself grunted when I set my feet back up against the middle of the wall and pressed them flat to lift myself up and I felt only the littlest give and slip before I understood, I was moving *thru* the wall, not over it, and the cans came tumbling and rolling out from under me, my chin landing hard on one, many on my forearms, and conking my noggin.

Diana Herself's grip slipped, and she flew backwards across the room, landing hard on her ass.

The bottom half of the wall jut up into my lower back, enough of the lower rows remaining stacked that I couldn't see my feet.

My masonry skills impressed me; the side walls wavered but remained erect.

A thousand distinct bruises throbbed into being.

Diana Herself spit.

It stung to shake my head.

"Duh, unga-bunga?" I asked her.

"Yeh, I'm fine," she said. "Let me help you."

I heard her step toward me but couldn't roll over to see her.

"I'll move some cans so you can scoot out, OK?"

"Duh, unga-bunga."

I felt the support under my legs shift.

She pulled my shorts high up along my thighs back down toward my knees.

I scooted, and she guided me.

"It's OK. Come on."

It got tricky around my elbows, but I kept twisting, the cans under me jagged up into my back.

Out up to my shoulders, I lifted myself up on my elbows and turned to her.

"OK," Diana Herself said. "You OK?"

"Duh, unga-bunga," I said, thru grit teeth straining.

"Almost there," she said.

I felt like a baby coming out feet first.

She didn't say anything.

I moved my head thru the wall, eyes clenched shut against sweat and dust, dented metal and mud.

"Duh, unga-bunga?" I said, cleaning my eyes with the back of my arm.

And standing at my feet, looking down on me, there she stood, with My Mother George Washington.

And Roddy.

And Aaron, back in uniform.

But he hadn't shaved his little Don Quixote mustache.

"Well," My Mother George Washington addressed the room with a sigh and a sneer. "There he is, my *favourite* son."

Roddy snorted and looked to her. "There he is, your *favourite* son."

I sniffed hard to catch a whiff of maybe *My Diana* was there too.

But no.

Diana Herself kicked a soup can rolling across the floor and brushed the dust from her dress.

Aaron put his arm around her, and she leaned her head to his shoulder.

She looked down at me and shook her head.

"We're done here," she said to Aaron.

Aaron gave her a soft peck on the cheek and sighed.

They spun around, her weight leaned into his.

He took his hand in hers, and they moseyed toward the elevator.

I remember as a young man being uneasy re: what kind of man I'd become, knowing that I'd never be an astronaut landing on the moon or a basketball coach, let alone a film-maker or Prez.

I needed to insist to *My Diana* that *it's my right* to remember what I remember in the way that I remember it, how one cloud gets set against another by forces that super-sede either cloud's desires or expectations.

Like the prayer beads on a banker's wrist, like the middle-aged firefighter pondering his waistline's profile in the mir-ror, *My Diana* was my *Realism,* whatever the reality.

My Mother George Washington tottered over to the eleva-tor, Roddy following close behind.

They all four stepped in and the elevator closed.

Game Over.

I was ready to understand and to be understood.

Ready to cooperate.

Who had the energy to resist?

My coup—my own personal *central intelligence agency*—had aimed to assimilate my subconscious into my conscious awareness.

But I'd been thwarted.

I'd broken *every* plan I'd ever made, but still, I did *not* see this coming: I was done with becoming my *self.*

I'd *Start Life Over* as exactly the man they always wanted me to be.

They could absorb me quietly.

Done fighting.

Myself out of my box.
Game Over.

And after not too long, the familiar miles of excom-
munication ahead of me, macro- and micro-, smiling and
scabbed, I stood up in that bunker like a demolition film in
reverse.

CHAPTER 84 *Eleccion '80*

When Pops ran for Prez in '80, I tagged along as a full-time volunteer.

This was right before I got married.

My self-conscious and cool phase and my obsession with Cy Franklin all left behind at Yale, it was assumed I'd end up Gov of Colorado or something.

Of course, Pops lost The Party nomination to The Actor.

When Pops debated The Actor, he sat on stage fidgeting and staring straight ahead as if into oblivion.

The Actor *pummeled* him in a thundering triumph.

Pops got out of the state early.

The Actor is *very* popular.

He's an actor, so, you know, he knows how to act.

He *clobbered* Pops in the primaries.

He called Pops a member of The TriC and The CFR and pledged to *never ever* offer him a position in his administration.

Everyone expected The Actor to tap ex-Prez Fxord for the hotly contested Vice Prez post.

Then late one night, unannounced and sans prepared statement, The Actor *dashed* into The Party convention and shocked *everyone* by naming Pops his running mate.

And *never again* did he utter a slander against The TriC or The CFR.

You know how actors motivate their performances with The Method Technique?

That's a funny use of that word *technique* cuz *technique* is a toolset independent from emotional investment.

The Actor was the first Prez to whole-heartedly embrace the idea of The Prez as a role.

He was always chopping wood and riding horses for the camera.

Pops is admittedly a little stiff for the role.

The Barbarians want someone that jogs and blows sax.

After the CIA-sponsored coup toppled Mossadegh—a democratically elected prime minister—in favor of the dictatorial Shah, it became immediately evident that The Shah needed protection from his own people.

So The CIA trained a new Iranian police force, going so far as to instruct a secret unit on torture techniques for dissenters.

The Shah was incompetent, fabulously corrupt, and gratuitously brutal.

And after years of oppressive rule, finally at the end of '78, mass protests erupted.

The Shah's troops massacred hundreds of demonstrators.

Still, The Peanut Farmer maintained his support for The Shah and dozens of specialists—CIA, diplomats, military— flew to our embassy to help him.

In early '79, The Shah was overthrown, and Ayatollah Khomeini came to power.

This provoked another oil crisis for The Homelan.

The new regime resumed exports of oil but inconsistently and at a lower volume.

The Kingdom and other nations largely made up the difference, resulting in only a 4% drop, but the psychological damage had been done.

Panic made prices skyrocket.

Brzezinski of The TriC convinced The Peanut Farmer to allow The Shah into The Homelan to receive medical treatment, and his sanctuary here drew angry crowds to our embassy in Tehran, demanding that The Shah be returned to face punishment.

The embassy was stormed, 52 employees taken hostage.

Ayatollah Khomeini put a contract out on The Shah's family, and one nephew was assassinated in Paris.

The Shah's son laid low at Baph's place.

The Ruckafellas used the takeover of our embassy as a

pretext to prevent Iranian revolutionaries from withdrawing petrodollars from Chase Manhattan Bank in London, where The Shah kept most of his assets.

The hostage crisis then provided justification for The Peanut Farmer's administration—under pressure from The Ruckafellas—to seize all of Iran's assets.

Perhaps the first use of international intel in a domestic *eleccion* came when Pops set it up so that the 52 hostages be held until after the *eleccion*.

The Party promised to deliver arms and spare parts to Iran in exchange for the hostages.

The combination of oil prices and international media attention on the hostages cost The Peanut Farmer the extension of his reign.

The hostages were released the day The Actor was inaugurated.

The Actor's inauguration was grand: Johnny Carson and Bob Hope cracking jokes, Charlton Heston and Jimmy Stewart earnestly bowing, and Frank Sinatra singing the national anthem.

Shortly after The Actor took office, he decontrolled oil prices, a move that made the oil industry $2,000,000,000.

And a month later, 23 oil executives gifted $270,000 to redecorate The Presidential Living Quarters.

3/30/81: Ten weeks into his first term, The Actor was shot.

The assassin had a six-shooter, but every recording of the incident clearly divulges seven shots.

If the bullet had hit a quarter-inch different, Pops would've been Prez seven years earlier.

Coincidentally, the assassin's father and Pops had been chums for years and years.

He ran Vanderbilt Energy Corp. and donated truckloads of money to Pops's campaign.

I was actually supposed to have his other son—the assassin's brother—over for dinner the same night as the assassination attempt.

We cancelled.

There was also a little-known assassination attempt on The Peanut Farmer.

In the spring of '79 he planned to go on ze Tube and announce sweeping changes, curtailing The CIA.

Then—*no joke*—Raymond Lee Harvey and Oswaldo Ortiz attacked him.

He cancelled the aforementioned sweeping changes.

Years later, the only person imprisoned as a result of The Iran-Contra Thing would be a peace activist in Indiana holding a street sign hostage in protest.

CHAPTER 85 The Party

I showered long, savoring the sensation of my skin thinning in the heat and the mingling scents of sweet rose and spicy soaps.

Everyone else in The Family wears makeup daily to cover the brittle alabaster transparency that comes with The Bloodline.

This day I indulged.

I basked in the drawn-out process of donning the suit that'd been laid out for me, buttoning buttons and combing threads.

The coat hung long on my wrists cuz it hung loose on my shoulders.

I hadn't tightened a belt so tight since my Yale days.

Glib at the heights of politeness and self-aware with monitoring, I was ready to be *whoever*.

I dipped into the periphery of the crowd gathered in a big living room.

I approached no one and kept my eyes down.

And no one let on that they recognized me.

Banks of cameras and microphones all pointed at one wall, and, on the opposite wall, lit dramatically from below, a strange sculpture in corrective perspective style redefined the space's shape and scale: a Queen Bee, larger than her hive.

The spread was traditional and simple: caviar and shrimp, blood pudding and baby toes.

Once upon a time, only The Barbarians ate cheese, unable to afford meats or game for protein.

Now Future-Gov Brother, two-handing it, spit chewed globs and cracker dust as he laughed and chatted.

Le 24-Hour-News Channel's Personality sweat on ze big screen Tube, manic with *eleccion* caffeine.

My ex across the room was the *real* mysterious stranger, the personification of a blind spot in the middle of my

344

memories.

Was she funny?

Kind?

Reliable? Surprising? A good friend? Demanding?

I was immune, but the room was charmed: She gave the impression that at any moment she might break out in a dance or act cute scowling coy in a sombrero.

Our bond had come to be no more than normalizing that loneliness of being fully dressed side-by-side after the first nakedness together.

My ex, who occupied the *center* of my *Life on Earth* for years, may as well have been anyone.

Imagine a lion's smile when a butterfly tickles its nose. *My Diana.*

Transformative and total, but not *comprehendible.*

With his flight jacket on over his suit and his suit pants tucked into his cowboy boots, Junior had assembled a small audience to gawk at the smoothness of Geronimo's skull.

His dead-eyed wife interrupted him to wipe blood from his chin.

My sons slashed waist-high thru the swarm, their noses high, feigning erudite and doctorish comportments.

They each extended a pinky pinching the stems of their wine glasses of sparkling grape juice.

My ex's bimbo husband followed a step behind them, not to keep watch, but more like no one cared to be audience to his pontifications re: his abs.

I was dull pondering the tanning bed rust of Future-Gov Brother's complexion when he spotted me, winked, and pointed at me from across the room.

Moving thru the social gauntlet of congrats and back slaps, it took Future-Gov Brother a long time to make his way over to me.

I slouched when he stuck his finger in the face of a young woman caterer, demonstrating for *everyone* how he would *not tolerate* a miniature hot dog with a lukewarm middle wrapped in a miniature bun that hadn't properly browned.

He spit his chewed food into her palm, and she stood holding it while he scolded her.

He stopped to dance a quick twist with some Good Man's drunk wife, rolling his eyes to me to signify such niceties were *beyond his control*.

His swinging butt sent a vase crashing from a table, and he scolded a nearby little girl for being clumsy.

He winked and blew me a kiss when the little girl began to cry and plead against her mother's soft spankings.

Have I mentioned that he and My Mother George Washington had a long-running joke of *pretending* to kiss on the lips *just a little bit* too long?

The chatter, reflecting back on itself, aggregated into a dense shriek.

"*I'd like to buy the world a Coke.*"

"*Have a Pepsi Day.*"

Then *finally*, here he came, Future-Gov Brother, right at me, arms spread open wide.

We agreed, neither of us could *believe* it, the day we'd all waited so long for was finally here.

I downed a beer from a waiter's passing tray in one long swallow before requesting that he procure me a mudslide.

Future-Gov Brother chuckled that he was happy that they'd found me.

I'd missed the rehearsal, but he was about to slip off for *the big entrance* if I wanted to join them.

The crowd swarmed me into its collective unconscious.

"Yeh, sounds like you've been thru quite a bit," he said.

I shrugged.

"Seriously," he said, looking suddenly serious. "What's your problem? Why is *everything* meaningless to you?"

I shrugged. "Duh, unga-bunga," I said.

"When are you going to *grow up?*"

I grabbed another beer from another passing waiter, unsure where to begin my explanation that I was finally ready to cooperate with The Family.

"No, *really,*" he said, his hand set against my chest. "What's your problem?"

I looked him in the eye, smelled his sour breath and sharp cologne.

"Duh, unga-bunga," I articulated more forcefully.

I scanned the room, plenty of lifelong chums.

No one is *My Diana* except *My Diana.*

I smiled big and intentional to explain it was just a fundamental crisis of meaning, I guess: "Duh, unga-bunga."

He shook his head, eyes closed and smirking, same as our farting contests as boys. "What does *that* mean?"

I wiggled my toes, cramped in closed shoes.

Thru waves of pressing flesh, faces emerged, warped large and leaning in close, chewing and laughing open-mouthed.

"Seriously, though," Future-Gov Brother said. "Seriously, why are you *such* a fuck-up?"

I stepped back.

He kept his hand pressed to my chest and I swatted it away.

"Don't swipe at me," he said with a sneer.

"Duh, unga-bunga," I said.

We remained still, looking each other in the eye.

He took a long deep breath, then cracked a smile.

He lifted his hands to my throat for a playful chokehold.

"You sure can drive us all so crazy, Little Brother," he said. "I should do The Family a favor," he said, tightening his grip.

We both smiled, nose-to-nose.

As little boys together, we were both *all potential,* nurtured the same, more-or-less, and gifted the same, more-or-less.

We never thought enough of each other to bother feeling competitive.

We both took it for granted that the other would grow up to be a No-Mind, fundamentally misunderstanding and squandering his *Life on Earth*.

He pulled me to him and hugged me tight.

His breath, hard from his nose, tickled my neck.

"I'm just fucking with you, Chuck," he said.

He released me a little.

We stood nose-to-nose, smiling again, or wincing.

Across the room, over his shoulder, she *appeared*.

My Diana and me locked eyes, straight-on.

But it wasn't her.

In the breathy tone commonly used to fake a yelling-voice quietly, from deep down in my gut where all the shamed ghosts of our thin-blooded ancestors nested, my breath hard thru my nose like a bull, my eyes burning salty, I growled slow, resonating low in my throat.

"*Chuuuuuuuuuuuuuck Noooooooooorrrrrrrissssss!!*"

Future-Gov Brother snorted and shook his head, glancing at me sideways.

"You're still trouble," he said, pointing at me.

"Look out," he called out loudly, looking around the room for an audience. "He always *was* trouble and he *still is!*"

I extended my hand.

"Duh, unga-bunga?" I said.

He nodded, his eyes softened and self-satisfied. "Yes, friends."

He put his hand in mine.

I squeezed it hard.

His breath paused.

Seizing *total control* over his hand, I bent, pulling it up toward my mouth and I bit down hard across his palm, my teeth in between his thumb and index finger, clamped like a vice grip, deep as an alligator bite.

He *howled*.

Yanking his hand away only made my teeth set further into it, reaffirming my *total* control.

He slapped and punched the back of my head hard with his other hand.

But the stun of his blows only made my jaw clench tighter.

My vision echoed, him pulsating.

A small crowd pulled at my waist from behind.

Salty blood tickled my chin.

A total clamp.

A hand in teeth.

A head echoing a crowd.

I could *not* release my bite, the impulse deep, beyond my control.

Did we agree, Trusted Reader, that inbreeding is a *Natural Cause* of death?

Locked into our singular fates so *total* and complete, *Life on Earth* itself is a *Natural Cause* of death.

My Little Brother couldn't hold his big *watery* head up straight.

His steady smile, pinched in and kept erect within his metal exoskeleton, everyone else thought that his perfect vacant gaze was his only power of speech.

But I knew.

He said to me, "Do you think if mother could see me with such lovely friends, perhaps she could love me as I am?"

He said, "Can they *cure* me?"

He was truly speechless catching his own reflection in the window that fateful night.

Sometimes I can forget what I *expect* to see and see what I *actually* see.

I can't force it, but I'm thankful when it happens.

And if that's ever happened to you before, Mystic Reader, you know exactly what I mean.

My Little Brother said, "I wish I could sleep like normal people."

The party froze stoic as I hobbled off into the dusk, wiping blood from my chin.

Outside, Secret Service stood stunned among the limos.

Aaron stood tall and saluted me.

Diana Herself rolled her eyes.

Pausing before passing thru the first thickness of trees, I turned back to the big picture window: watching me walk off, my ex and my sons stood expressionless.

CHAPTER 86 *Eleccion '88*

As VP, Pops deliberately chose a weak staff so there'd be no threat of even the *appearance* of competition with The Actor's staff.

But the psy-ops strategies of his past returned with the primaries.

His nemesis was Pat, a college professor who taught that God crafted the world in six days, and The Homelan, founded as a Christian nation, was threatened with destruction by secular ideologues.

As a Tube personality, Pat shouted that Israel's invasion of Lebanon marked the kickoff of Le Grand Finale *A-poc-a-lypse,* saying: "The whole thing is in place now, it can happen at any time . . . But by fall, undoubtedly something like this will happen which will fulfill Ezekiel."

He must've been *relieved* to be wrong so he could run for Prez six years later.

Pops positioned covert operatives within Pat's delegates and helped them win.

Then, once elected, they all switched their support to Pops.

A few months ago, Pops was eight points down in all the polls only hours before a crucial primary.

His nomination depended on that win.

So he told the state's Gov that if he delivered the state— Pops didn't care and didn't *want* to know how—that Gov would be chief of staff in Pops's administration.

And, of course, Pops is now about to be appointed Prez and this Gov is about to be appointed his chief of staff.

When asked whether he thought Pops's Opponent should release his medical records to the public, The Actor cracked with a grin, "Look, I'm not going to pick on an invalid."

Twenty minutes later he said that he'd "attempted to

make a joke in response to a question."

"I think I was kidding, but I don't think I should have said what I said," The Actor said.

The question was asked after reports of a series of personal struggles that Pops's Opponent had faced: His brother had a nervous breakdown and attempted suicide.

Aggressive, hostile, and unstable, he went so far as to pass out leaflets campaigning against his brother.

And in '73 this brother was hit by a car and lingered in a coma for four months before dying.

Their father had arrived in The Homelan at 16 with $25.

And 12 years later he'd become the first Greek immigrant to graduate from Harvard Medical School.

Pops's Opponent inherited this ambition.

His high school yearbook called him "Chief Big Brain-in-Face."

It was the end of his senior year before he went on his first date.

And the girl that he wanted to bring to senior prom went with his rival, so he checked coats instead.

Pops's Opponent beat DD from The KKK for The Other Party's nomination.

And then he edged out Biden when Biden got caught plagiarizing.

Pops's Opponent took the high road and fired his campaign's field director for spreading rumors re: Pops fucking with The Act of Love extra-maritally.

Le 24-Hour-News Channel *appeared* June 1, '80 with The Homelan's anthem.

It'd been announced in '79, ready to launch for the '80 *eleccion*.

60 Minutes and *20/20* had proven News could be profitized, but by convention time, it still wasn't taken seriously and was made to camp way in the back with the local news stations.

It took a couple years for competitors to enter the market, angling for ratings by heightening the contrast between their ideological filters.

And by the time of Pops's *eleccion*, the evolving format of *News* prioritized soundbites in a whole new way.

Pops had to be *seen* as a populist, so he strutted around with a well-known billionaire real estate conman and a shock-haired boxing promoter.

And when Pops said that he wouldn't be surprised if his opponent thought that a naval exercise is something you find in a Jane Fonda workout, the spectacle struck a nerve in a way that policy talk never could.

All three networks showed footage of Pops riding thru Boston Harbor, his opponent's home, pointing at all the pollution and saying, "My opponent's solution—delay, fight, anything but clean up. Well, I don't call that leadership, and I certainly don't even call it competence."

But none of the networks bothered to parse out the causes and effects of the mess.

More than ever before, the campaign became about symbols and drama, the choice between Willie Horton and pledging allegiance.

When Pops's Opponent's Wife was accused of burning a flag in The '60s, he responded by going on parade in a tank.

It'll be tough for Pops to eventually retire to the private sphere after his terms.

He'll continue to don those cufflinks and windbreaker.

He'll tour the world collecting honors and standing ovations.

He'll command a $100,000 speaking fee, and always be open to the possibility of stock options.

He'll finally be able to loosen up and let loose that nasty streak he's choked back for so long.

And, as former Prez, he'll have the right to weekly CIA briefings, so *imagine* the advantage his private equity firm will have buying low-valued defense contractors, securing "Government" contracts, then selling the firms.

Junior's *very first act* in office will be to put Pops's re-cords under lock and key *forever*: an executive order declar-ing that a former Prez can assert executive privilege over his papers against the will of a sitting Prez.

But *I too* had a Master Plan readied to launch, Authorized Reader!

My Report, this selfsame report you now hold; my vessel to correct the outlandishness, far-fetched, bile-inducing, foul-stenched, heapings of putrid *rankness* with which this so-called *Objective* biography *defiles* the very concept of *Truth*.

CHAPTER 87 The Vice Grip

Some secrets are easy to keep.

Take, for example, an ugly person with exquisite, *beautiful,* perfect genitals.

Other secrets, The Barbarians *refuse to see* what they're programmed to not see.

The *Truth* is too strange to be believed.

The Good Men of Diplomacy, Media, Military, Banking, Soda Pop, Communications, Transportation, Industrial Food, Sporting Goods, and Education all took a turn in that coffin.

This girl had a clit like a thumb in her parents' bedroom after school; this coach had a long purple shlong.

Personally, I've never found a hooded robe that didn't cinch, bunch, and itch, but we all persevered the same initiations.

No one *enjoyed* kneeling to lick the assholes of The Elders.

But only *The Chosen* got to drink the blood from a newborn baby's slashed throat.

And The Vice.

A dank subsidiary of my wit tempts me to quip that this is just one more item in the long list of traits The Oligarchs share with The Hillbillies.

One secret unifies The Family and its entire expanded network.

"The Vice" refers to only one thing.

This pleasure, the sweetness of its delicacy appreciable to only the most *discriminating* palettes, the most refined erudite, is of course *the most heinous* crime known to The Barbarians.

We bifurcate and partition, we redefine with intentional and weaponized touches.

Secrecy is the ideal.

Secrecy is the dream.

That is Freedom: no watchmen standing guard; no accountants double checking the books; no judges interpreting the law.

Secrecy is the means, and secrecy is the ends: it's the protection of the secret and the protected secret itself.

"Governments" remain in the hands of men that can be blackmailed.

Any haircut with a vacant gaze appointed to office knows who chose him and knows that it's *them* that he serves.

Meaning is the essential element of all initiations.

A secret to protect gives a sense of belonging, *meaning*.

The most *unthinkable* offense to The Barbarians' ethics makes for the biggest secret.

The Act of Love itself is the oldest of The Old Gods.

Warp that, and you control a person's sense of potentially being the Division A state football champion celebrating The Renaissance.

You control a person's sense of potentially being The Birth of Venus in shoulder pads calling a flea-flicker play after play, Myth, History, and the invention of Perspective driving down the field, even faking a punt.

You control a person's *being*: biocomputer and spirit.

Mind control works best when severe trauma is administered by the age of three.

The Vice fractures the mind of the victim, which attempts to shield itself from memories too painful to endure.

That's *deep* programming: partitioning sections of the muscly murk of subjectivity crowded within a singular skull.

Triggers then call forth a desired personality.

You slaughter a bunny first, bunnies become a trigger.

Controlling memory means controlling identity, the creation of the *perfect* spy: a double agent assassin who doesn't even *know* that he's that.

That was MKUltra's goal.

To work, reprogramming has to happen when the personality is still pliable, the ego still forming like a new egg's gelatinous shell, otherwise "de-patterning" becomes necessary.

De-patterning involves keeping someone drugged, half-asleep for extended periods of isolation, the intended messages on endless loop, and waking them up only for electroshock trauma.

This probably sounds familiar to The Barbarians as it's basically the same as *Life on Earth,* the endless gentle programming of pizza and cartoons, everyday brutality and systemized global resource wars on ze Tube.

Being victim to The Vice shames you in two ways.

First: why *me*?

What did they see in *me*?

You suspect you brought it on yourself, there's something instinctually dirty and primitively flawed unique to you.

This establishes the ongoing fetishization of secrecy.

And secondly: dragging other people into it.

You trust *no one* cuz you fear if you told anyone, they'd say you're a *pervert* accusing this highly respected man, this holy man and politician.

You intuit how to keep people at a distance.

The Vice is an attack *on* consciousness that becomes a disease *of* consciousness.

Memories *feel* like thoughts, but I think they're *feelings*.

You're my friend?

You're my friend?

CHAPTER 88 *The Moon Itself*

I get winded quick and I chafe easily.

My *present circumstances*—moving out thru the woods alone on foot—clearly reversed my bunker plan, but the isolating ends remained the same.

I sought only to scrap my impractical *subjectivity* bumping thru the undifferentiated surfaces of this watery and mysterious poisoned matrix.

My Diana granted me permission, obliterating the *totality* of my *Life on Earth,* commanding I *Start Life Over*.

I wasn't *mad* that she was never who I thought she was. No one could be.

And she never *claimed* to be anyone at all.

And she never claimed to *be* anyone at all.

Reaching the *open* beyond the trees, I came upon The Mustachioed EPA Cowboy working a small flamethrower along the edges of the prairie.

The expanse of the land was charred black.

I moved thru thick smoke, distant trees in low clouds and soft ash underfoot.

Did you know, Trusted Reader, that a controlled burn is a thing?

It releases needed seeds and kills off invasive species.

It's surgical and total.

The Mustachioed EPA Cowboy used the wind to his advantage like a masterful dancer, setting small fires so that they'd sprint tall and quick before extinguishing themselves.

Immersed in this same prairie that had so recently defined the boundaries of my confinement, watching it gladden and open in ecstatic flames, purge, prayer and sacrament all hit me instinctual and deep.

Smoke dampened the glare of the spike in the center of my field of vision.

Surrendering, disengaging, exculpating—spanning the

scorched and cauterized prairie—it felt more like Easter than *Eleccion Day*.

Moving back into trees thru fragrant, low-floating smoke, the dusk began to darken.

I approached the hazy border, where time stilts forward again.

Crowley, that postmodern occultist, claimed the primacy of the magickal practitioner's *experience* in granting rites their powers; rituals *objectively* allow you to enter a *subjective* state.

Intel operatives, like occultists, know the importance of having several names, often anagrams.

Their mission, total and sans restraint, is unfettered by morality.

The ambition is jellyfish pure: *Power*.

My five senses, however asymmetrical, and my memories—this sum of stitched particulars—conspire to create the *profound* illusion of subjectivity, its perseverance *primary* to how I understand whatever my *Present Circumstances*.

Controlling memory is controlling identity.

Controlling memory means the power to trigger different identities, the means to create the *perfect* spy: a double agent who doesn't even *know*.

No secret can explain or quell that *blind spot* at the center of each of us where we expect a *self* should stand, or duration's expanse when we suffer and its quickening thru joy.

The essential element of all initiations is *meaning*.

A secret to protect gives a sense of belonging and that itself is the *meaning*.

The attacks happen at the level most difficult to even prove the existence of: spirit.

The weapons of ideology get expressed thru symbols, symbols for nouns and symbols for verbs.

The Act of Love itself is the oldest of The Old Gods.

Warped and weaponized, it's also the oldest means of control.

The Vice teaches all involved to keep secrets, trust no one.

The Act of Love itself is the oldest of The Old Gods.

Forces ancient and amoral convulse and puncture.

It's a cognitive shattering.

The open prairie ahead of me required I meander same as the long shuffling halls behind me.

And still, my ultimate goal—amending that flagitious and yecchy so-called *Objective* or Subjective Biography—had *not yet* been achieved.

Of course, if My Report ever gets out, my life will be made *difficult* by The Family.

If I'm found hung lazily from a low towel rod, or I've shot myself in the back of my head with my hands tied, or it becomes common knowledge that I've supposedly lost my mind, recognize that as the confirmation of the *Truth* of My Report.

I am *no one's* favourite son, fated at birth to the grotesque distortions of my inbred genes.

The asymmetrical lurch of my *Present Circumstances* propelled me beyond thinning smoke, longer and further than I'd ever walked before, hypnotized by my panting and the burn of my body's limitations.

I maintained my pace until a paved road severed my path.

I'd reached the far end of the forest beyond the prairie.

The shock of the moon, low and huge ahead of me, halted me dead in my tracks.

Start Life Over needn't mean anything more than I am trying to remember who I am, who I was before they pro-grammed me.

That we live with paradox fixes it so that we do live.

With a bolt of corrective perspective, foreground and background reversed in my field of vision.

No silhouette in profile, no patriotic bikini.

No longer any longing.

No sense of suspense.

The Moon Itself.

My Moon.

FIN

Bibliography

Aburish, Said K.
The Rise, Corruption and Coming Fall of the House of Saud
1994, St. Martin's Griffin

Baker, Russ
Family of Secrets
2009, Bloomsbury Press

Bey, Hakim
*The Temporary Autonomous Zone, Ontological Anarchy,
    Poetic Terrorism*
1991, Autonomedia

Bowen, Russell
*The Immaculate Deception: The Bush Crime Family
    Exposed*
1991, America West Publishers

Epstein, Edward Jay
Legend: The Secret World of Lee Harvey Oswald
1978, Reader's Digest Press

Friedman, Alan
Spider's Web
1993, Bantam Books

Gura, Philip F.
American Transcendentalism
2007, Hill and Wang

Hedges, Chris
American Fascists
2007, Free Press

Icke, David
Tales from the Time Loop
2003, Bridge of Love Publications

Levenda, Peter
Sinister Forces
2005, Trine Day

Levy, Paul
The Madness of George W. Bush
2006, AuthorHouse

Mailer, Norman
Cannibals and Christians
1966, The Dial Press

Marrs, Jim
Rule by Secrecy
2001, Harper Perennial

Palast, Greg
Armed Madhouse
2006, Dutton

Sharlet, Jeff
C Street
2010, Back Bay Books

Talbot, David
The Devil's Chessboard
2015, Harper Perennial

Tapper, Jake
Down and Dirty: The Plot to Steal the Presidency
2001, Little, Brown and Company

Thomas, Gordon
Secrets and Lies
2007, Octavo Editions

Unger, Craig
House of Bush, House of Saud
2004, Gibson Square

Vidal, Gore
Imperial America
2004, Nation Books

Zinn, Howard
The Twentieth Century
1998, Harper Perennial

Acknowledgments

Super-ultimate eternal gratitude to Sammi Skolmoski, who with patience and precision carved a path thru the pile I'd amassed.

Totally indebted for life to my esteemed colleagues Zach Dodson, Karl Hofstetter, Jason Sommer, and my mom, Donna Kinsella.

Endless Love and Solidarity with my crew: Bobby and Theo and Melina, Jeremy, Todd, Neil, Lin and Matthew, Joe Proulx, Sheba, Rachel, Mike and Ryan and Mila and Archie, Liz Fjigu, Chris Strong, Bink, Bill, Ben, Jimmy, Christian and Beachy, Dee and Jimmy and Kenny and everyone at The Club.

Thank you to Jason, Jonathon Humphrey, and Joseph Demes for reading it at various stages and talking thru it with me. And Jack Dugan. And Janet Desaulniers and Hilary Plum for saying the exact right things at the exact right moments. And Jerry and Rosario for the hideout.

And Jen for providing the space in the end—both physically and psycho-spiritually—for me to finally work my way thru it.

About the Author

Tim Kinsella (born 1974) Libra / Chicago / Music

*f*eatherproof BOOKS

Publishing strange and beautiful fiction and nonfiction
and post-, trans-, and inter-genre tragicomedy.